NOW OR NEVER

ALSO BY VICTORIA DENAULT

The San Francisco Thunder Series
Score
Slammed
When It's Right
The Hometown Players Series
One More Shot
Making a Play
The Final Move
Winning It All
On the Line
Game On

NOW OR NEVER

A SAN FRANCISCO THUNDER NOVEL

VICTORIA DENAULT

FOREVER
YOURS

New York   Boston

Forever Yours
Hachette Book Group
1290 Avenue of the Americas, New York, NY 10104
forever-romance.com
twitter.com/foreverromance

First published as an ebook and as a print on demand: January 2019

Forever Yours is an imprint of Grand Central Publishing. The Forever Yours name and logo are trademarks of Hachette Book Group, Inc.

The publisher is not responsible for websites (or their content) that are not owned by the publisher.

The Hachette Speakers Bureau provides a wide range of authors for speaking events. To find out more, go to www.hachettespeakersbureau.com or call (866) 376-6591.

ISBNs: 978-1-5387-6315-5 (print on demand edition), 978-1-5387-6316-2 (ebook)

To anyone who has ever struggled with the monumental loss of a parent. You are not alone.

ACKNOWLEDGMENTS

First and foremost, I want to thank my agent, Kimberly Brower, and my editor, Leah Hultenschmidt. When my own dad passed away in the middle of writing this book, my life became an emotional roller coaster and you both went above and beyond to support me and juggle and manage things so I wasn't overwhelmed with work on top of everything else. Thank you so much for everything. I will forever be grateful to both of you for not only your professional expertise but your kindness and compassion. Working with you both feels like winning the lottery.

I want to thank my husband, my family and my friends who have supported me both professionally and personally while I finished this series. I couldn't have survived 2018, or written a word during it, without your support, love and encouragement.

Tatiana, Anna Maria and Lori, thank you for always being there for me when I come home. Even when it's for the saddest reasons, you find a way to make me smile and laugh. Mike H., thanks for always checking up and knowing exactly when to send a bacon meme or a poutine-related message.

To the superstar crew at Forever Romance, you guys are a true pleasure to work with and I appreciate all you do for my books. A million thanks to Mignon Mykel at Oh So Novel for your killer FB ad work, something I have yet to conquer on my own. To the Hearties authors who share ideas, laughs and support. You guys are my people, and I heart you. DeAnna Zankich, my writing sister from another mister, who is always there for a wine chat when I need it.

To bloggers and readers, thank you for embracing the Braddock family. This family started in my heart and mind as a lighthearted, goofy group but they grew into something deeper and stronger as their journey moved forward. They are more than hockey and so this series, even with a hockey series name, moved beyond the rink. Thank you for accepting that and sticking with them—and me—as their story continued. I hope you love Winnie's story.

NOW OR NEVER

Prologue

WINNIE

Age 16

My youngest sister is giggling and it makes me smile through the pain. "I wish someone had recorded it," Dixie says. "I would've seriously paid money to have been able to see you knock him out."

"Me too," I reply and grin sheepishly. "I was blind with rage, so it's a blur."

I'm not a violent person. I've never punched anyone in my life, nor did I think that I would ever punch someone, let alone do it here. After all, this was my happy place—our family cottage in Maine. I cherish our summers here and nothing really ever stresses or angers me when we're in this town. But tonight, Holden Hendricks's mean-spirited teasing and aggressive behavior just made me snap.

Sadie, my other sister, comes rushing in from the kitchen carrying a tea towel filled with ice. "Can you move your fingers?"

"Sort of," I say as I look down at my red, angry, swelling

knuckles. I try to stretch my fingers and then make a fist, but I wince.

"Nothing's broken," she whispers as she places the ice on my knuckles. "I don't think you would be able to move them at all if they were broken."

"I can't believe you punched Holden Hendricks," Dixie says in awe and I immediately shush her. We're only a few feet from our parents' bedroom and I'm sure I can hear my dad snoring peacefully through the partially closed door, but that doesn't mean Mom isn't awake, listening with her hawk-like hearing.

Sadie plops down on the floor in front of us, her blue eyes twinkling with humor, her wide mouth parted in a smile. "You should have seen it, Dix. He was being such a dick and then boom!"

"Tell me everything!" Dixie begs.

"He found out Cat's parents were in Boston this weekend and convinced her to have a get-together," I tell Dixie, who hadn't come out with us tonight. She's only thirteen and has an earlier curfew than Sadie and me. "Cat only agreed because she thought it would just be a handful of us. But then all these people she never met started showing up saying Holden had invited them, and the place was packed, upstairs and downstairs and Cat was freaking out. Her neighbor threatened to call the cops from the noise."

Dixie is glued to every word, like it's the best story she's ever heard. She tucks her wheat-blond hair behind her ears, leans forward and rubs her hands together. "Get to the punching."

Sadie and I both laugh and Sadie picks up the story. "Winnie was helping Cat, trying to get everyone to leave, and that pissed off Hendricks so he told Winnie she was a useless, ugly loser."

"He called me Cat's dumb, fugly sidekick," I correct Sadie.

Dixie's blue eyes get fiery. "And then you punched him?"

"No, then Jude got in his face and told him he needed to chill out and fuck off," Sadie says, and Dixie's eyes get even wider somehow. "And then Holden asked Jude if he wanted to go."

"Holden was going to fight our brother?" Dixie gasps and I nod.

"Yeah. Totally nuts. Jude is like the one decent person in town who doesn't hate Holden," I say and frown. "Anyway, Jude wasn't gonna fight him, but that seemed to make Holden even angrier and then he grabbed Jude by the shirt and—"

"And Winnie clocked him!" Sadie says gleefully and I can't help but smile again. "He went down like a sack of potatoes and there was blood. I think she broke his nose."

My heart stops for a second and I feel genuine remorse. When I first met Holden last summer, I thought he was cute. He played on Jude's summer league hockey team but unlike us, he was a local who lived here year round. He was almost a year younger than Jude but taller and broader. He was quiet, but polite when Jude invited him over for dinner one night. Then they decided to go to the movies with a bunch of other local friends, and Sadie and I tagged along. He became a different person without my parents around. He was loud and obnoxious and teased everyone in a mean, hard way, not a lighthearted one. Then the next time I ended up hanging out with him and a bunch of other people, he started a fistfight with someone. That's when I decided to avoid him, but in a tiny town like this, it proved impossible. And for some reason, Jude actually liked hanging out with him. Even though I punched him, and he really did deserve it, I hope I didn't break his nose.

"Don't! Stop looking all repentant and crap," Sadie says, and I swear sometimes she's eighteen years older than me, not eighteen months younger. She acts the most mature out of all four of us siblings and she's definitely the most sensible. She looks at Dixie. "Holden deserved it. He's deserved it all summer long. Her fist was simply karma's delivery vehicle."

I can't help but smile. I like the idea of being karma's instrument. Sadie leans forward, lifts the ice and looks at my hand again. "We need to figure out what we're going to tell Mom and Dad because it's still going to be swollen in the morning."

"I fell?"

"Dad won't buy it." Sadie shakes her head, long sleek blond hair tumbling around her shoulders. I self-consciously lift my hand to my own hair. The humidity this summer in Maine has been off the charts and so the waves that started in my dirty blond hair when I hit puberty have turned to a frizz I've yet to find a way to tame.

"How about you dropped something on it?" Dixie says.

Suddenly the front door slams and we all jump like terrified mice. Jude storms into the living room. His face is flushed and his eyes electric with anger. We have a sibling pact to be as quiet as possible when coming home so we don't wake up our parents. We also have a pact to keep each other's secrets and screwups from our parents at all costs, but clearly our pacts don't apply tonight—not for Jude. Sadie and Dixie scramble to their feet. I stay frozen in place. "You are a fucking jerk, you know that?" he yells at me.

"Fuck you!" I yell back.

"Shut up!" Sadie scream-whispers, which at this point is useless. There is no way our parents aren't awake by now.

"You broke his nose! And it took like an hour to stop bleeding," Jude says, fury making his voice vibrate.

"He insulted me, and he was trying to fight you!"

"Yeah, he tries to fight everyone at some point," Jude says with annoyance. "I was handling it."

"He was getting angrier and he cocked his fist and grabbed you!" I argue back.

"I get into fights all the time in hockey. I don't need you to defend me," Jude says and runs a hand through his hair in frustration. I notice the red streaks on it. Holden's blood. "Plus, he's my friend."

"Boys are so fucking dumb," Sadie mutters and rolls her eyes.

And then it happens.

"What the hell is going on here?" Dad's voice fills the pine-paneled room. We all jump and turn to look at him. None of us answers his question because we know he heard everything.

He turns to Jude. "Go to bed."

"But it's not even past my curfew yet."

"Tonight it is," Dad replies sharply. "Bed."

Jude glares at me one final time, then storms through the house and stomps up the stairs. Now Dad's focus is on his daughters. Me, specifically. "Is Jude right? Did you punch Holden?"

"Yes."

He looks more baffled than angry. I don't know if that's a good sign. It's not the reaction I anticipated. He turns to Dixie. "Go to bed, little D."

She scurries off. He turns his blue eyes on Sadie. "Did you see this happen?"

"Yes," Sadie replies. "And Holden definitely deserved it."

Dad raises a salt-and-pepper eyebrow. He sighs and runs his hand through his hair exactly like Jude did moments ago. I'm not sure who picked up the habit from whom. "Go to bed, Sadie."

"Dad, honestly, she wasn't the instigator. And Holden has said really mean stuff to her all summer long." Sadie should be a lawyer when she gets older. She loves to argue her points.

"Sadie, if I have to tell you again..."

"Night," she grumbles and disappears around the corner.

He walks over to me and squats down in front of me like Sadie had done earlier. He lifts the ice. The tea towel is soaking now and drips onto his black-and-gray-striped pajama bottoms just above his bent knee. "Follow me. I need to get a better look."

I listen to him and quietly go into the bathroom behind him. He flicks on the bright fluorescent light above and blinks as his eyes adjust. He gently takes my hand and examines it. I try to hold in my winces as he pokes and prods. Finally, he looks me in the eyes. "It's not broken. You'll have to ice it a lot for the next few days, but that's fine because you'll have nothing else to do since you're grounded."

I just nod. He leans against the sink and crosses his arms in front of his wide chest. "You and Sadie left here, laughing and smiling. You were going to Cat's for a girls' night. How did that end in you punching that Hendricks kid?"

"A bunch of people showed up at Cat's, and it turned into a kind of party," I explain. His expression says he's not buying it. I keep talking, explaining the whole thing with a little less detail than we gave Dixie. When I'm done, Dad sighs again.

"Winona Skye, I am disappointed in you," he says softly, and that makes my heart hurt me more than my knuckles do. "Violence is never acceptable. Unless you are in danger of being assaulted, then kick him in the nuts or whatever else you have to do."

I try not to smile at that, but he's been telling us girls that advice for a few years now and it's so awkward it makes me want to laugh. He clearly isn't in the mood for giggles. "But you never need to get violent to defend your brother. He's perfectly capable of defending himself. I know you know that."

"Dad, Holden Hendricks has been bullying me all summer long," I say. "He says the worst things to me. He picks on the way I look. He's just a completely horrible person and I guess I just finally snapped."

He seems to think that over for a minute. He frowns and then the gleam in his eye turns sympathetic. "Winnie, your own insecurities are why you let him get to you," he says and gives me a smile, but I'm instantly upset by his words. The fact that I'm not as confident as my siblings already feels like a fault and when he mentions it, I feel worse about it than normal. "You're a beautiful, bright, good kid. You don't give yourself enough credit. You let his words mean something. And you're also empathetic and kind, and you let him take that from you tonight."

"I'm sorry," I say and I'm suddenly on the verge of tears. I hate letting him down. He pulls me into a hug.

"To be honest, I might have done the same thing when I was your age if someone was picking on me that much," he says softly and he squeezes me. "But the thing is, which I only know now because I'm older, kids your age are usually mean or aggressive for a reason. It's rarely because they want to be that way. It's usually a reaction, a defense mechanism or coping skill, for something they can't handle themselves."

He lets me go. "Head to bed. I'm going to refill the ice tray so you'll have some in the morning. You'll need it."

"Thanks, Dad. Love you."

As I start up the stairs I hear him chuckle. "Love you too, slugger."

1

WINNIE

Someone is awake and walking around the cottage, but I don't bother to find out who. I just stay in my dad's rocking chair, holding my now cold cup of coffee, staring out at nothing. There's nothing about the screened-in porch that protects me from the chilly predawn Maine air but despite that I'm in only a T-shirt and thin pajama pants. The numbness the cold is creating in my limbs matches the numbness I've been feeling inside for the last five days. Since my father died.

"You can't sleep either, huh?" Sadie says as she steps into the doorway from the living room and immediately wraps her arms around herself. "Holy crap, it's freezing. You must be a Popsicle."

She disappears momentarily and comes back with two hand-knitted throw blankets from the living room. She hands one to me, but I don't move to take it so she kind of tosses it in the air and it lands across my lap. She sits down in the rocking chair next to mine and wraps herself in the other blanket. We don't speak for a few moments. We both just rock. I stare out through the screen at the empty street in front of the house and she stares at me.

"You can talk to me, you know?" Sadie finally says, her voice low but a little shaky. Sadie has been the strongest of all of us since our dad was diagnosed with ALS a little over four years ago. I think a lot of it has to do with the fact that she's a nurse. She deals with illness and death just about every day so she is able to compartmentalize her emotions. I'm twenty-nine, a year and a half older than her, and I've never learned to do that.

"Talking isn't going to help," I say in a scarily steady voice. "Nothing will help. It's over. He's gone."

She doesn't respond right away. Her features are ravaged with pain, but she swallows it down and pulls her left hand out of her blanket cocoon just long enough to wipe a tear as it starts to fall. Sadie sniffs and takes a deep, slow breath. Then she nods. "This is why we should talk about it. Remember all the wonderful times we had with him."

"I remember them," I assure her and take a sip of my cold coffee. The funeral yesterday was filled with good times. Fourteen people spoke, sharing funny and poignant memories of my dad. There were photos of all the great times—from his wedding to Mom to each of our births to his grandchild's birth to our final Christmas together—on display around the urn. I have no trouble remembering all the wonderful moments with my father, but they aren't bringing me the peace everyone seems to think they should.

"I still feel empty. Alone. Broken," I confess to my sister

and lift a hand, showing her my palm, before she can say anything. "And please don't tell me that I'm not alone. I know that I'm not, technically, but that doesn't change how I feel."

She sighs softly and nods. Now it's her turn to stare out into nothing, but she doesn't do it as long as I do. I would do it forever if I could. Sadie stands, pulling the blanket tighter around her. "I'm going to watch the sunrise on the beach. You should come."

I shake my head, no. I think she's going to argue with me, but then the floorboards in the living room creak loudly and I see her boyfriend, Griffin, appear in the doorway. He's bleary-eyed, dressed in only sweats and a T-shirt. Griffin is a coach for the San Francisco Thunder, the professional hockey team my brother plays for. He and Sadie have been dating only a year, but their bond is strong and she has never been happier.

"Hey," he says to both of us and then steps onto the porch. He reaches out to tenderly run a hand over the back of Sadie's head. "Couldn't sleep?"

"I'm going to the beach to watch the sunrise."

"I'll come too," Griffin replies simply. "Let me grab a jacket or something."

I hold out the blanket Sadie gave me for him to take. He hesitates, but accepts it. Sadie unlocks the porch door and starts down the stairs. Griffin hesitates again, his dark brown eyes on me. I give him a weak smile, which I can tell by the expression on his face he isn't buying it as a reassurance that I'm fine, but Griffin is a smart guy and he knows there's no way I can be okay right now, so he doesn't push me. He returns my smile and follows Sadie out the door.

The cottage is filled to the brim with family. On top of Sadie and Griffin we have my youngest sister, Dixie, and her fiancé, Eli; my brother, Jude, and his wife, Zoey, and their son, Declan; and my mom stuffed into this five-bedroom cottage. Oh and my boyfriend, Ty. So I know it won't be long before someone else is up and in my face. I love my family more than anything. I've willingly sacrificed a lot to be with them during the hard times, and I regret none of it. But...right now, for some reason I can't understand, I don't want to be anywhere near them. Or anyone. I feel a flicker of guilt at that thought, but I also know I can't control my feelings.

I stand up and put my coffee mug on the side table before heading inside. I can hear my mother in her room, which is the only bedroom on the main floor. She'll be out soon. I grab my purse off the kitchen table where I left it yesterday afternoon and walk back to the porch where I slip into some flip-flops that might be Dixie's and head out the door.

I wander around the small town, still quiet because basically no one else is awake, for over an hour, avoiding the beach and sticking to the streets so I don't run into Sadie and Griffin. My dad loved the beach, but he also loved other parts of Ocean Pines. The shuffleboard court where we used to have annual family tournaments. The ice cream parlor where we'd often get dessert. He'd always order mint chocolate chip on a sugar cone with rainbow sprinkles, or jimmies as they call them in New England. He used to play hide-and-seek in the small but thick pine forest at the edge of town when he was a kid.

This whole town—every inch of it—makes me feel close to him, like he's still here. That makes me feel better and worse because he's not. He's gone forever.

When I walk by the tiny grocery store, Cat Cannon, the owner and a childhood friend is flipping the sign from closed to open. She gives me a small wave, opening the door. "First batch of cinnamon buns are just being pulled from the oven."

"I'm not hungry, but thanks anyway, Cat."

She gives me a sympathetic, knowing smile and smooths her hands on her apron. "I know you're not. But fact is you have to eat something. Might as well be these works of art."

She opens the door wider and the sugary scent of the cinnamon buns her family is renowned for wafts out toward me. My brain may not want to eat, but my neglected stomach is controlling my feet. I start to walk toward her. Cat smiles as I walk into the store, which is about the size of a double-car garage. There are three rows of canned and boxed goods, a commercial refrigerator with cold essentials, and a deli and baked-goods counter where the best cinnamon buns in the state can be found, usually only briefly as they sell out as quick as they can be baked every morning.

Cat passes me and makes her way behind the counter. I've known her since I was six. We spent every summer hanging out at the beach or running around town. I even worked at this store with her, making subs and lobster rolls and ringing in orders for a few years. We both went off to college, but Cat gladly took over the store for her parents after she graduated. I swear she only did it so her mother would finally give her the coveted cinnamon bun recipe.

She pulls one warm bun from the tray as I step up to the counter. "Do you want one for Ty too?"

I shake my head before she's finished the sentence, which makes her expression dim. "Actually, give me six. If I bring one for Ty but not Jude or Dixie or everyone else, they'll disown me."

Cat smiles and reaches for a box under the counter. She opens it and starts placing the buns inside. "Are you heading back to San Francisco soon? The whole town is basically packing up right now, as usual, so I thought you would be too."

"I'm heading back to Toronto actually."

"Why?" she asks with a curious expression across her freckled face.

"Because I live there," I reply, confused by her confusion. "I was only in San Fran to be with my dad. Now...I'm going back to my life."

It doesn't feel right when I say that and Cat must agree with me since she just looks more confused. She places the last bun in the box. "Oh. Is Sadie heading back to Canada too?"

I shake my head and watch as she closes the box and begins to tie it closed with string. "No. She's staying in San Francisco. She's going to live with my mom for a little while longer while Mom adjusts to...the change. And then I'm betting she'll move in with her boyfriend. I'll be flying solo in Canada."

Cat hands me the box and I take it with one hand and start digging cash out of my purse with the other. She moves over to the register and freezes for a second. "Wait. What about your boyfriend? He still lives there, right?"

Right. Ty.

"Yeah. Right," I reply and nod, letting out a weird sort of laugh, like even I think I'm silly for forgetting my longtime boyfriend. "I meant solo as in no family."

"You guys have been together for what? Like seven or eight years, haven't you?"

"Ten going on eleven," I reply.

"He's basically family then," Cat surmises and I nod in agreement because that's how it *should* feel.

I place the box on the counter and head over to the coffee stand and pour myself a large cup using an ample amount of their complimentary hazelnut-flavored creamer. When I get back to the register, the amount she's rung up is far less than it should be.

"Locals' discount," Cat tells me with a smile. She's wearing her trademark red lipstick, which looks stunning against her pale skin and nearly white-blond hair.

"I'm not a local," I remind her. "I'm one of the dreaded summer people."

Cat laughs. "You feel like a local to me. Your whole family does. You guys love this place as much as we do. I always thought that your mom and dad would retire here one day...I mean before."

She looks awkward suddenly, like she thinks she said something wrong, but she didn't. I reach across the counter and give her hand a squeeze. "I'm glad that his love of this town was so evident. Dad did want to retire here. I want to too one day."

She smiles. "You should just move here now. Don't wait

for retirement. It's quiet in the winter. Actually, it's kind of a ghost town, but I'm here and we could get into all kinds of fun. Like when we were kids."

"Oh, if only I could," I say softly, handing her the paltry four dollars she will allow me to pay for the buns and coffee. I really am not looking forward to going back to Toronto. But the idea of going back to San Francisco is even less appealing. Dad got sick in Toronto and he died in San Francisco. Staying here…that actually sounds like something I would enjoy as much as I can enjoy anything, which is barely at all.

"You leave today?" Cat asks, and I nod so she walks around the counter and gives me a hug. "Safe travels."

"Thanks." I hug her back before picking up my coffee and buns and leaving. The sun is up and there's a soft, salty ocean breeze. I inhale deeply. It's the only thing left that still gives me the slightest sense of peace.

I get back to the house in less than two minutes and can tell, as I climb the stairs, everyone is awake now. I can hear them all talking and walking around. I step onto the porch and see Ty first.

"Hey, babe. Where did you go?" he asks.

"Buns." He smiles, and I hand him the box, which he carries through the house to the dining room in the back.

I follow. Dixie and Eli are drinking coffee at the dining room table. My mom is in the kitchen in her bathrobe, but comes wandering in as Ty puts the buns down on the table. She smiles at me. It's tired. "Oh Winnie, how sweet of you. Let me get the plates."

"It's okay, Enid," Zoey says from her position on the

floor in the sunroom playing with Declan. "I'll get them. You just sit."

"Who needs plates anyway?" Jude asks and gets up from the couch in the sunroom, walks to the table and immediately confiscates a bun.

Moments later we're all gathered around the table, eating buns and talking. So much talking. The problem is that they're talking to try and feel normal again. To force everyone forward. Past this. Past him.

"So have you set a date yet?" my mom asks Dixie and Eli.

Dixie nods. "We decided a few weeks ago that we'd get married next year. July first."

"Canada Day?" Sadie says with a smile. "Good choice. And it gives you almost a year to plan."

"And we want to do it here," Eli adds. My mom's weary face actually lights up.

"Oh, that would be so fantastic!" she exclaims and she cradles her coffee mug. "Your father always wanted you girls to get married here. Maybe I can even get those renovations done that we always talked about so it's even more perfect for the big day."

"I should go pack," I announce abruptly and stand up. "My flight leaves in a few hours."

Ty stands with me. Great. I give him a smile. "Stay here and enjoy the buns."

He hesitates, but nods. I ignore the concerned expressions staring back at me from everyone and head upstairs. I can't sit there and listen to everyone making plans for the rest of their lives. I get it, we need to move on, but Dad's been gone less than a week. Why can't we just stop and wallow? I need to wallow. I make it upstairs and into my bedroom and I shut the door and fall face-first onto my unmade bed. Tears prick my eyes and I let them fall. They all might be ready to move on, but I'm not and I may never be.

2

WINNIE

Four hours later I say good-bye to my entire family and we go our separate ways just past security, to head to our respective gates at Boston Logan International Airport. As my family walks one way, Ty and I head the other, to go through Customs and make it to our gate for our flight to Toronto. The line is huge, which is typical. I pull my passport out of my purse as we wait. Ty reaches up and wraps an arm around my shoulder. I try not to wiggle free as he rubs my arm and gives me a squeeze.

"Things are going to feel better when you're back home and working again and life is back to normal," Ty tries to assure me. "Did you return the school's call?"

"No," I reply. "I'll do it tomorrow."

"Oh. Okay," he says in a tone that says it's not okay, but he's not about to start a fight. I wish he would for some reason. "Well, the principal there loves you, so I'm sure they'll be thrilled to get you back."

"It's just a spot on their substitute teaching list." I step forward as the line moves up. Luckily, this makes Ty let go of me. "No one willingly wants to be a sub. I'm sure the spot won't be snatched up in the next twenty-four hours."

He nods and then his phone beeps, and I watch him pull it from his pocket. He turns away from me just the slightest bit, but I notice it. "Who is that?"

"No one," he mutters. The hairs on the back of my neck stand up as my stomach knots.

I hate myself for what I'm about to say, but more importantly I hate him for making me feel like I have to say it. "Then show me who is texting you."

He sighs. Loudly. I cross my arms and he turns to face me, frustration twisting his features. "It's my boss, Courtney."

He turns the phone toward me and I see her name. I haven't met this woman because he switched accounting firms while I was living in San Francisco. She could be his boss, or she could be someone else. "Courtney what?"

"Oh for fuck's sake, Winnie. When are we going to stop doing this?" His tone is hard and dripping in irritation. "I thought maybe once you got home, after everything with your dad was done, you'd be back to your normal self, but clearly, that's not happening."

After everything with my dad was done?

"Sorry I'm not perky and carefree five days after I watched my dad die," I bark back at him, and out of my peripheral vision I see a woman in line snap her head up. "Maybe if you hadn't made the last two years of watching him die a slow, painful death even worse by fucking someone else I'd bounce back faster."

Three more people in line turn to stare. Ty's pale complexion turns crimson and I don't know if it's with rage or humiliation, but the worst part is I don't care. I reach for the handle on my suitcase and as the line moves forward, I move back.

"Excuse me," I say to the woman behind us and then repeat it to the next twelve people in line as I make my way out of the line. I can hear Ty following me, apologizing to the people as he passes too.

I make it halfway through the terminal before he gets me to stop. "Winnie! Where the hell are you going?"

"Back to the cottage," I tell him. I don't even realize that's where I'm going until the words jump out of my mouth. "I'm staying."

"You're joking right?" I turn to find Ty even more red-faced as he angrily runs a hand through his blond hair. "Winnie, we can't keep making this work long distance."

"I don't want to make it work," I blurt out, and it feels so good to say it out loud. Finally. Liberating and freeing, which then makes my heart fill with so much guilt that it feels like it's sinking into my shoes. "You cheated on me."

"Fucking hell, Winnie." He's a shade of red now I don't think I've ever seen before. "I have spent the last two years of my goddamn life trying to make it up to you, and now you're done? Now you won't forgive me? You just wasted the last two years of my life."

"I'm sorry," I say as my eyes fill with tears. I wipe them away before they fall and glance around for a car rental kiosk. I need to get the hell out of here now. "Go back to Toronto. Fuck Courtney, or go back to that girl you cheated on me with.

I'm sorry I held you back from doing that sooner. Just go. You're free."

I see a sign for Concord buses. I know they go to Maine so I start walking that way. He is still following. Suddenly his hand is on my biceps and he's turning me around. Our eyes meet. His face has gone from red to white now. Ashen actually. "Winnie, please. Don't. I was sorry then and I'm sorry now. Just come home. You can't throw us away."

"I can't be who you want me to be," I reply in a flat monotone.

"You can't be you?" he challenges, and the anger and frustration in his voice is replaced with confusion and sadness. "Winnie, you will get through this. We can get through this. Your dad, my mistake, all of it."

I shake my head. "I don't want to."

And without another word I turn and walk away. He calls my name once, but I ignore him and when I dare look back, just before I turn the corner to the bus kiosk, he's gone. I feel relief. A little guilt but mostly relief. This is the right thing. He may not know it right now, but I know it. It's the only thing I feel like I do know at this point.

I buy my bus ticket back to Maine with shaking hands, but the attendant either doesn't notice or doesn't care. That is exactly what I want right now—what I need—to be around people who don't give a shit. Or be around no one at all. I just need time to wallow. I don't care how pathetic or lame that sounds; it's how I feel.

The bus is leaving in fifteen minutes, so I hurry outside and shove my suitcase in the hold under the bus and hand the driver my ticket. As I make my way toward an empty seat, I keep my head down, which is why I almost bump into the guy standing in the middle of the aisle. At the last second I see his feet and come to an abrupt stop. I glance up and find a wall of broad shoulders and wide chest wrapped in a flannel shirt with the sleeves rolled up and the edges of some kind of tattoo peeking out of the left sleeve just below the elbow. My eyes climb higher where I find a thick beard, light brown kissed by copper, piercing silver-blue eyes and a slightly crooked nose I would recognize anywhere. Because I'm the one who broke it.

Why the fuck is Holden Hendricks on this bus?

He stares back at me and his tongue wets his plump lips as his brow furrows ever so slightly. It still angers me that someone with such a dark heart is so physically attractive. Completely unfair.

"Sorry," he says and moves into a row so I can pass. I start to walk by when he follows me with his eyes and says, "Hey! You look familiar. Have we met?"

Seriously? I mean we haven't seen each other in fourteen years, but still. I recognized him immediately even though he's a few inches taller and has a beard and a whole bunch of things he didn't have when he was sixteen, like an imposing frame and biceps as big as my head. I keep looking straight ahead, down the aisle in front of me and not at him. "Nope."

I keep walking, settling in the window seat in the second to last row. I glance up and see he's tucked himself into a row of seats, but he's standing and facing backward, looking right at me. I fight the urge to stick my tongue out at him like I did the first time he was mean to me...when I was ten.

Our relationship only sunk lower after that, hence the broken nose. I move my eyes deliberately away from him and focus on digging my phone out of my purse.

Ty has left four text messages, each angrier than the next.

> **Ty:** Winnie we can't work this out if you don't come home. Eleven years of our life is worth some effort and you know it. Meet me at the gate.

> **Ty:** Winnie, why are you doing this? If you were going to break up with me you should have done it years ago, when I made the mistake. And it was a mistake!

> **Ty:** You are being selfish and stupid. Grow up Winnie and get your ass to the gate now.

> **Ty:** If you don't get on this plane and come back to Toronto with me, it is over. For good. And I will hate you for doing it this way.

I look at the time on my phone. Our plane leaves in ten minutes. He's probably already on board. I sent a quick text back.

> **Winnie:** I'm sorry for everything.

I've never meant four words more in my life. He cheated. He is responsible for that, but I was the one too weak or too stupid—or maybe both—to end it when I found out. Instead, I promised to forgive him, and then I never did. I couldn't. That's my fault.

I could go back to Toronto. I could move in with him, like I planned, at least for the first few months. I could start teaching again at my old school, first as a substitute and then hopefully back to full-time. I could pick up my old life almost exactly where it left off. But I can't forgive him. I know that now. Maybe I always knew it. I don't know. But since my dad died, my tolerance for pretending, for forcing myself to endure situations and feelings that I don't want to endure is gone. I just can't lie to myself anymore. Life's too short.

Ty and I are over.

I'm all alone.

I glance up again. The bus driver is dropping into his seat and yet Holden is still staring at me. I glare at him, then turn to look out the window.

I spend the entire ride with my iTunes cranked in my ears and my eyes glued to the scenery out the window. The closer I get to the cottage, the better I feel. This is irresponsible, irrational and selfish, but it's right.

When we pull into the depot, the sun is low in the sky and dusk is setting in. I wait until everyone else is off the bus, count to fifty and then grab my purse and make my way off. I want to make sure Holden has had enough time to get his bag, if he has one, and get the hell out of here. The bus driver has unloaded everything and my suitcase is on the curb. An older lady is walking toward the parking lot with her own bag and everyone else seems to have left. Good. I pull up the handle on my bag and begin to walk away.

There are a couple cabs idling by the curb, but it's just a fifteen-minute walk down Main Street and I need to stretch my legs. The summer season is officially over, so the usually crowded sidewalks are empty...except for Holden freaking

Hendricks. He's about half a block in front of me, walking in the same direction. Why is he walking? What is he even doing in Maine? I thought he moved away or ran away or was in jail or something. There were a lot of rumors when he disappeared at sixteen, but I didn't know which one to believe. If I had to bet, it would be on the jail rumor because he was always in trouble.

I make sure my pace is slower than his, so I stay half a block back and watch him carefully. He looks relaxed and not quite as…aggressive as he used to be. I know it's weird to think that someone looks aggressive, but when he was a kid everything about him oozed bad energy. From the way he walked to the tone in his voice—sharp, tight, ominous—he was just not a good guy. I mean, I never felt like he would hurt me physically, but he used to tease me mercilessly. Of course he teased just about everyone, but I am…*was* sensitive and took it to heart.

I'm almost at my street. In a few seconds I can turn left and leave him to wherever the hell he's going and never seen him again. There's a truck heading west toward us and it slows and finally pulls over, into oncoming traffic, to stop in front of Holden. He jerks up abruptly at the sight of the vehicle blocking his way, shoulders back, chin out, fists clenched. Yeah, there's the aggressive guy I knew and hated.

A head pops out the window. I'd know that greasy face anywhere. It's Stephen Kidd. He's a local guy and was one of Holden's best buddies back in the day. I guess he still is. Unlike Holden though, Kidd as they call him, is someone I *was* scared of back in the day.

Kidd waves at Holden. "Hey, buddy! What the fuck happened to your truck? I thought it was new?"

"It is," I hear Holden respond. "Long story."

Kidd makes a face, like he wants to hear this long story, but he doesn't ask Holden anything more. He just says. "Get in. I'll drive ya home."

Holden doesn't move right away. His hesitation piques my interest and causes me to slow almost to a stop. Kidd and Holden were like brothers when we were teenagers. Holden's reaction now makes me think something might have happened to change that. But then Holden shrugs and starts around the side of the truck.

That's when Kidd notices me. His dark beady eyes lock with mine and I look away and start walking again, quickly. I want to get out of his line of sight because the look on his face was one of recognition, and I don't want him telling Holden who I am and then the two of them attempting a conversation with me. But I'm not that lucky.

Out of the corner of my eye I see Kidd crane his skinny neck farther out the open window. "Hey! You're a Braddock chick aren't you?"

I think about ignoring him and just walking faster but the idiot will probably follow me with the truck. So I stop momentarily and look up again. Now Holden, who has climbed into the passenger seat, is leaning forward to look at me too. I stare back at him for a second and I can practically see his brain working, trying to grasp the reality that he does in fact know me. I turn my gaze back to Kidd. "Yep."

I start to walk again. But Kidd yells out. "Which one are you again? You all always looked like triplets to me."

I glance up again, my feet still moving, my suitcase wheels

squeaking as they frantically turn. I zoom right in on Holden's silvery gaze. "Larry."

I turn on the first cross street. Not my street, but I don't give a shit. I just want away from the two town goons. I can hear Kidd let out a hoot of laughter and Holden tell him to shut the fuck up, but I don't turn around and a second later I hear his tires screech as Kidd drives off. I'm so fucking glad they aren't going to pretend we're long-lost friends.

Holden decided, when I was thirteen and awkwardly tall for my age, battling bad acne and very frizzy hair I hadn't learned to tame yet, that my sisters and I were the Three Stooges. Dixie was Curly, Sadie was Moe and I was Larry. He referred to us by those names anytime we ran into him in town. I didn't even really know who the Three Stooges were, but I asked my dad and from the way he explained them, I knew it wasn't a compliment.

God, I think as I finally reach our family cottage, maybe this wasn't such a good idea if those two are going to be hanging around town. Ocean Pines is small and like Cat already mentioned there aren't a lot of people here in the off-season. Moving back to Toronto and forcing myself to make it work with Ty might be easier than running into those two jackasses every time I leave the cottage. Then again, I'm probably not leaving the cottage much anyway. I unlock the door and flip on the lights on the porch. I look right out at the dunes at the end of the block that border the seven-mile beach. The sun is almost completely gone, but it's painted the clouds a lovely pink color. I open the door into the main part of the house, and leaving my suitcase and purse on the porch, I head into the house and straight for the wine rack. I grab a bottle of merlot, turn around and head outside again.

I walk to the beach, drop down in the dunes and open the wine. Drinking straight from the bottle, I watch the waves crash against the shore, take a deep breath of cool salty air, and wonder what the hell I am going to do now.

3

HOLDEN

I wake up to the manager of the campground pounding on my door. Hard. I flip over and open my eyes, slowly, painfully. I blink until I can read the alarm clock on my night table. It's only seven in the morning. Jesus. What the hell is his problem?

"Hendricks! Time to move this hunk of junk!"

"It's fucking early, Jaime!" I bark back, lifting my head to direct my angry yell toward the door but not bothering to get out of bed. "Checkout time is noon!"

"Not on the last day of the season, Hendricks! It's eight a.m."

Is he fucking kidding me? Who the hell does anything at eight in the freaking morning? I groan but give in and throw back the covers, then grab my pants off the floor and tug them on, swearing the entire time.

I walk through the ancient Airstream trailer to the front door and swing it open. He frowns at the sight of me in nothing but my jeans, like I'm somehow offending his sixty-year-old senses. Fact is, I could be dressed in tux and tails and this guy would still look down his nose at me because he just doesn't like me. Because he remembers when I was a kid and my dad used to run this place. Back then he was just the maintenance guy.

"You have to go," he says firmly.

I give him a smile. "Sure thing, Mr. Moutis."

Calling him "mister" always takes his disdain down a notch. It's the sign of respect I should have shown him when I was running around this place as a kid. But back then I called him Marsh-Breath Moutis. To his face. Because I was an asshole.

He looks at his watch and back at me. "Twenty minutes."

I nod. "Yes, sir. Just gotta call someone to tow me out."

"Where's your truck?"

"I lent it to someone who needed it more than I do."

His watery eyes sweep from one end of my Airstream to the other and lands back on me. "Doesn't look that way to me."

He shakes his head disapprovingly and stalks off, back toward his office, which is also a trailer. I watch him go, squinting against the offensive way-too-early morning light and sigh. Fuck. This feels like yet another sign that you can't come home again...and maybe I was an idiot for trying. Maybe I really burned all my bridges here and there is no way to rebuild them.

I sigh and head back into my trailer to find a shirt. As I dress, wash my face and tidy up as quickly as possible, I rack my brain to figure out who I can ask to tow my trailer besides Kidd, but I come up empty. I've been living in Ocean Pines for three months and have miraculously managed to avoid him, and all my other previous partners in crime. And I mean partners in crime. I don't blame these guys for the fact that I ended up in juvenile detention for two years. That was all on me. But they certainly didn't help me make good choices.

Since I've been avoiding the people from my past and working my ass off all summer long, I haven't met new people. I'm stuck. I grab my phone off the tiny counter by the sink and dial the number Kidd insisted I take when he drove me home yesterday. He picks up on the fifth ring and sounds like a bear being woken from hibernation.

"Who the fuck is this?" he growls.

"Hey, Kidd. I am so sorry to wake you up," I tell him. "It's Holden. I have a bit of an emergency."

"Oh. Hey, Hendricks," he yawns. "Dude it's like predawn or something."

"Yeah," I don't correct him. "But you said you were looking for work and I have an emergency job. Just a one-time thing, but if you help me I'll give ya fifty bucks."

I'm really hoping that's enough to lure him out of bed because I don't have much more to give him. All the money I've saved this summer living in this dump and working construction I invested in my new business. And it's paying off because I booked my first big job—which starts tomorrow—but this, having to rely on Kidd, is a price I have to pay.

"Anything before noon requires a seventy-five buck fee, doesn't it?" Kidd replies.

"Sure. Seventy-five," I agree through gritted teeth because I have zero options. "And it'll take you only about twenty minutes and then you can go back to bed."

"Okay. What do you need?"

"I need you to haul my trailer," I explain, leaning against the counter. "Just like a mile or so. The park is closing for the season. I lent my truck to my sister who was stuck in Boston and took the bus back so I can't haul it myself."

"Okay," he says easily. "Where to?"

"I'm staying in the driveway of a job I'm doing over the next few months," I explain. "The Braddock cottage."

"Seriously?" Kidd questions and lets out a raspy chuckle. "You're staying at Larry's place? She hired you? She sure as hell didn't look like someone who would hire you yesterday. She looked like someone who would kill you. Bare-handed. And with a smile on her face."

"Yeah, she didn't hire me," I explain and scratch my beard. "Jude did. I guess she's not happy with it. Anyway, I doubt she's going to be in the place very long. Jude said the house would be empty all off-season so she's probably leaving any day now."

"Okay, whatever," Kidd replies. "I'm getting up now and I'll be there in like an hour."

"Make it twenty minutes and I'll pay you a hundred bucks," I counter.

"See you in twenty."

I end the call with Kidd. I want to call Jude and double-check that it's still okay to park my trailer, and my life, in his driveway while I do the job, but it's just after four in the morning in San Francisco so I can't. So instead, I put my phone down and head into the bathroom for a quick shower before I secure the trailer contents for the move.

Kidd shows up forty minutes later, which is not as late as I expected him to be, and gives Mr. Moutis an exaggerated friendly wave as he pulls in. I try not to crack a grin at that. He swings his truck around so he's in front of the trailer near the hitch. I pull in the awning as he gets out of his truck and walks over to me. "This is really where you're going to live from now on?"

"It's where I've been living," I say. "And where I'll continue to live for the next few months. I'll probably move back into a house or apartment or something by Christmas."

"You better," Kidd advises. "This thing is not going to keep you warm in a nor'easter."

Right. The infamous New England snowstorms. I nod and secure the awning to the side of the trailer. "I wasn't planning on staying in it through the winter."

"I'm on the verge of getting kicked out of my place," Kidd explains to me. "My girlfriend has turned into a total tight-ass since we had a kid."

I turn to him in surprise. "You have a kid?"

He nods, but he's frowning as he walks over to the truck again. "Yeah."

"Congrats," I say, but it sounds hollow because clearly he's not happy about it.

"Thanks," he pauses before climbing in the truck again. "He's a cool little dude. We named him Buck. But like, now my girlfriend does nothing but bitch about how I need to make more money."

"Well you're about to make seventy-five bucks," I say as he climbs in the truck. "That's something."

"You said a hundred," Kidd corrects.

"If you got here in twenty but you got here in forty," I remind him and he swears but doesn't argue. He starts the truck and sticks his head out the open window as he backs up, watching me as I guide him toward the hitch with hand signals.

"What about you?" Kidd calls back to me. "Kids? Wife?"

I point at the trailer. "Yeah. I've got a family of five in there."

"Still as sarcastic as ever," Kidd jokes.

A minute later, he's in the perfect position and I hook up the trailer, then walk around and get in the passenger seat. He starts to drive forward I stick my head out the window and wave at Mr. Moutis who is scowling, glad to see me gone. I've known him for twenty of my thirty years on this planet and he's hated me for every single moment of them. "Thanks for a great season, sir."

He twists his face up like he just passed gas or something and turns and heads into his office. Kidd laughs. "He still hates you."

"He's not the only one," I mutter.

"Well the boys don't hate you," Kidd explains. "Although they're a little pissed that you've been in town this whole summer and haven't hung out with us once."

"You told the guys I'm back?"

He nods, his greasy brown hair falling into his eyes so he pushes it back. "Yeah. Went out for beers with a couple of them last night. Kyle, Donovan and Ken's brother Pete. Ken is in jail."

"Ken's in jail?" I repeat, shocked. Ken and his brother Pete were some of my closest friends when I was a teenager.

"Yeah," Kidd shrugs. "He was borrowing money from his work. And product."

"Where did he work?"

"Same place I do. Super Shop and Slop," Kidd replies and scowls. "Fucking place pays shit and I've been part-time for a year even though they promised me full-time."

Super Shop and Slop was the nickname we used to give the grocery store that was actually called Super Shop and Save. We used to shoplift from their alcohol section all the time. The owner caught Kidd shoplifting a few times but never called the cops. Still, I'm surprised he'd hire him at all after that. I guess maybe Kidd has changed at least a little. Clearly, Ken hasn't.

"So now that you know what I've been up to, what about you? Where the hell have you been?" Kidd asks as we roll along with the minimal morning traffic. "You just disappeared all those years ago. Like, you weren't in jail this whole time, were you?"

"No," I reply and roll down the window to breath the ocean air. "Did my two years in juvie in Augusta. My dad was there to meet me the day I got out. He handed me some cash and told me he'd met a lady and they were in a good place and he didn't need me messing that up so he wasn't letting me move home."

"That's fucking brutal. I mean I hate my old man and he hates me, but he's never kicked me out," Kidd says and I watch his face twist in sympathy.

I shrug. "I was eighteen. It was legal. And honestly, it felt like a relief. So I called my aunt. My mom's sister. She said I could crash with her in Boston if I paid some rent. I started bouncing in bars and taking community college courses. Then I got into construction. I drifted around New Hampshire and Mass for a while and ended up back here on a job. I remembered how much I liked Maine and Ocean Pines, so I decided to move back."

"I thought about going into construction, but those hours are insane, especially in the summer," Kidd replies as he turns toward the beach. "I mean what the hell is the point of living here if you can't spend your summer days chillin' on the beach with some brews?"

He grins at me and I force a smile and a nod then look out the window at the passing pine trees. I want to remind him that you aren't allowed to drink on the beach, but he already knows that he just doesn't care.

He breaks at a stop sign and slowly starts to make a left-hand turn. He's being really cautious and I'm appreciative. "You should come join us for beers tonight."

"You'll be at the Brunswick, as always?" I ask and he nods. Good, now I know where not to go.

"It's this one on the right, isn't it?" Kidd asks and points to the cedar-shingled two-story with the large front porch and the chipped blue trim.

"That's the one."

He pulls past it and then carefully starts to reverse, slowly positioning the Airstream on their small parking pad. He does a fabulous job and I sigh in relief that this went so smoothly. He turns off the engine and as we both hop out of his truck to unhitch the trailer, he turns to me. "So what are you doing here again, besides squatting?"

"Jude wants some renos done to the inside and outside of the house," I explain as I lower the trailer. "Updates to the kitchen and bathroom, new wiring, some new plumbing, appliances, a couple walls removed and paint and trim."

"He's letting you do it?"

I nod and wonder if I'll regret telling him what I'm about to tell him. "I've started my own renovations company. He's my first big job, but I've reno'd some kitchens and a couple baths in some other local homes on the side this summer, on top of working for Carter."

His eyes flare and he gives me a lopsided grin. "No wonder you don't have a lick of a tan after one of our hottest summers on record. Dude, sucks to be you."

Oh God, Kidd, you're hopeless.

"Yeah, well, I'm hoping by next summer the business will be established and I can get some time off," I say with a shrug. "And have enough cash to help out Bradie."

"She still smokin' hot?" Kidd asks, his grin turning douchey.

"She's still my sister," I reply with a warning stare. He chuckles.

"You were always such a protective dick about her," Kidd chuffs. "Easy, killer. I'm not after her. I have enough female problems."

Truth is I wasn't protective enough over her and that's why she barely talks to me now, but I am not about to get into that with Kidd. I appreciate all he's done for me in the last two days, but I'm not about to make him a friend and confidant again. I reach in my back pocket for my wallet and pull out a stack of twenties. "Here ya go."

"A hundred?" he says counting them and I nod. He hands me back one. "Nah. You're right, I was late."

I'm actually shocked by that, in a good way, and then Kidd adds, "And if you need any plumbing help on this job, I still know a thing or two from working with my miserable old man from when I was a kid."

"I'll keep you in mind," I reply vaguely.

I take back the twenty, and as I stick it back in my wallet I hear the screen door slam. I glance up and Winona Braddock is standing on the stoop at the top of the stairs. Her hair is everywhere, she's got mascara making rings under her eyes, and she's in little shorts and a stained T-shirt. Somehow, though, she's hot as hell, even with the snarl on her face.

"What are you doing?"

"I'm out of here," Kidd announces and makes a beeline for his truck.

I turn to look up at Winnie again. "Don't leave your trailer here!"

"It's my trailer, not his," I call back and she turns her eyes on me instead of Kidd.

"Well why are you dumping it here?" she demands, arms crossed tightly over her chest.

"Have you talked to your brother lately?" I ask, and she frowns.

"He was just here yesterday, so yeah, I've talked to him," she barks back. "But he never said anything about you dumping this tinfoil box here."

I glance over my shoulder at my home. I guess there are worse things she could have called it. And besides, I remind myself, she has a right to not like me, like most everyone else. I turn back to her. "He didn't mention that he said I could stay here while I do the renos?"

A flicker of confusion replaces the spark of anger in her hazel eyes. "What renos?"

"Jude is renovating the cottage, mostly basic stuff but it'll take about six weeks," I tell her. "He gave me some old blueprints your dad had drawn up and I gave them to a local guy to double-check they're all still good and applied for a permit with—"

"I'm canceling it," she interrupts, causing my words to stop and my heart to drop. "No renos. Not right now. You can move your camper somewhere else. Thanks."

She turns and heads back into the house, slamming the screen door and then the oak door that leads into the house off the porch. I sigh and run a hand through my hair aggressively before sagging against the outside of the trailer. I pull my phone out of my back pocket. It may be early to call Jude but I have to now. I don't have a choice.

I start to dial his number as I call out. "I'll call your brother. He'll explain everything."

4

HOLDEN

The phone rings once before the oak door flies open again and Winnie reappears on the porch. Her cheeks are flushed, with what I can only assume is anger, but the look in her eyes is something else. Panic?

"Hang up," she demands as it rings a second time in my ear. She steps up to the screen. "Please hang up."

I hang up. She sighs so loudly in relief I can hear her down where I am. What the hell is up with this girl? I'm confused, even kind of annoyed, but also concerned. I take a step closer, toward the porch as she buries her face in her hands to muffle some sort of strangle cry sound she's making.

"Winnie?" I say tentatively. "You want to stop being a hot mess and tell me what's going on? Then you can just be hot, without the mess part."

She looks startled by my remark, but it manages to wipe the scowl off her face.

"My brother is saving the family once again," she announces, dropping her hands from her face. "Dixie wants to get married here next summer so he's fixing the place up. They're my dad's plans and Jude is taking it upon himself to see that they get done, finally. Of course he is, because Jude thinks it'll help. Jude is a fucking fixer."

"Okay…" I assess her words. It sounds like she might be mad at Jude. Or her dad? Or life in general. Definitely that last one. For the first time since I moved back, I kind of wish I was a little bit more in the loop of this little town so I would know for sure. This town may be small but it's big on gossip. "But you don't want me here?"

"Of course I don't!" she declares like I'm crazy to even ask. She runs her hands through her hair, but it does nothing to tame the mess it's in. "You were a complete bag of ass toward me my entire life."

"That's true," I agree, and she freezes and blinks. "I didn't know you'd be here. If Jude had told me that, I wouldn't have asked to set my trailer here. I might not have even taken the job."

"Because why would you want to hang around Larry from the Three Stooges, right?" she snaps.

"No. Because I know I was an ass to you and I wouldn't want to make you uncomfortable in your own home," I reply and once again she looks shocked. "I'm an adult now, Winnie. I'm not that much of an asshole anymore. I just want to do this job, and living on site makes it much easier."

I can tell she doesn't believe me, not fully. Probably because she doesn't trust me and that's fair. I've been back in her world for about fifteen minutes and her memories—wounds, really—have been reopened. But my memories of her are coming back full force too, and I didn't tease her because I hated her. I liked pushing her buttons. Teenage Winnie was beautiful but timid, and annoying her or insulting her brought out a fire in her...I liked it. Until she broke my nose. But something has to give here. Either she lets me stay and do this job, or I call Jude and tell him what's going on and why I can't. I am not just going to bail on him. And my only hope is he talks her into leaving or letting me stay, because I *need* this job.

"Look, I don't want to upset you, but if you keep insisting I leave, I have to call your brother because he's the one that hired me and quite frankly," I pause, "he's the only one who can fire me. I don't have anywhere else to go. I made plans based on this job."

Her expression softens. When she sighs this time it's definitely more resignation than anger. "Fine. You can stay and do whatever it is you're going to do as long as you can work around me. Because I'm staying here. I have to because...this is where I want to be."

Okay, that makes very little sense but whatever. "I can try to work around you, but it's going to be loud and dusty."

"Great." She replies with nothing but sarcasm. She turns to head back into the house but pauses and glances at me over her shoulder. "If you tell Jude I'm here, I will make your life a living hell. And I'll enjoy it. Like I said, he's a fixer and I don't want him rushing over here and trying to fix me."

She heads back inside and slams the oak door again.

What the hell have I accidentally walked into? Jesus, this is not the Winnie Braddock I knew as a kid. This woman...well she's beautiful but she's clearly broken. Like in a million pieces and I have no idea why.

My phone rings. I look at it in my hand and see Jude's name on the screen. I hold my breath and hit accept. "Hey, buddy! I just got to your place."

"Is everything all right?"

Umm...not really. Your sister is here and she's kind of spinning out of control.

"Yeah. Why?"

"Because you called me," he replies, his voice confused and sleepy. "Like a couple minutes ago."

"I did?" I lie like I've always lied, perfectly. "Shit. I must have pocket dialed you or something. Sorry about that! I hope I didn't wake you."

"I have a toddler. I haven't slept since he was born. No worries," Jude jokes easily. "Don't worry about it."

"You have a kid, huh?" I say. Jude didn't mention personal stuff when he called me yesterday. He just said he saw my flyer by the grocery store and recognized my name. He said he wanted a guy he could trust working on the place. That made me feel great. But then again Jude always trusted me, even when I was untrustworthy.

"Yeah, he's the best," Jude replies. "And I married the most incredible woman. Zoey Quinlin. You remember her?"

Zoey Quinlin? The hot redheaded pastor's daughter Jude and just about every other guy had a crush on. "Seriously? Yeah, I remember her. She was a great girl."

"So are you starting work today or tomorrow?" Jude asks again.

"Probably tomorrow," I explain. "I just set the trailer up

and I'm going to do a walk through later today. Will likely start in the kitchen."

"Cool." Jude sounds nervous. "Keep me posted, okay? The place is ancient and you're bound to run into unexpected problems."

"I've been working on renovations for years now. I've seen it all," I tell him as I walk around to the door of my trailer and unlock it. "Besides, your family takes really good care of this place. I'm sure it'll go smoothly. Does the rest of the family know about this or are you surprising them?"

"It's not exactly a surprise, but I haven't really mentioned the details of what I'm doing to my family," Jude explains, which is why Winnie was thrown for a loop. "And I haven't mentioned that I've hired someone to start on it."

So that's why Winnie doesn't know. But why doesn't she want him to know she's here? "So what are your sisters up to these days anyway?"

"Dixie and Sadie both live here in San Fran. Dixie is dating our goalie and works for the ALS Foundation. They just got engaged, God help him." He chuckles. "Sadie is a nurse. She's dating one of our coaches."

"Is Winnie dating one of your trainers or something?" I say jokingly.

"Thank the hockey gods, no," Jude replies and lets out a heavy breath on the other end of the phone. "She's had the same boyfriend for like a decade. A Toronto guy. She lived here for a while, but just moved back there."

Huh. I feel a little let down that she has a boyfriend, which is weird.

"So how is your family? Bradie? Your dad?" Jude says bringing my attention back to the conversation.

"My dad is remarried and lives in Florida," I explain. "We haven't really been in touch since I got out of juvie. Bradie is here in Maine and has a kid. I'm trying to get back into her life. Honestly, we were never really close, but I want to change that. I've been trying to fix all the stuff I fucked up when I was a kid. People hold grudges. I'm actually surprised you would offer me this job. Grateful, but surprised."

"Dude, I'm not judging you for acting like a punk when we were kids," he says easily and it makes me feel a wave of relief. Someone gets it. "Losing a parent destroys you no matter what age. And you were ten when your mom died and had zero support. I'm not holding that against you."

I appreciate him saying that. It really is a devastating thing to lose your mom at ten like I did. The whole world ends before it even began.

"If people didn't give me second chances I wouldn't be married to Zoey, and I wouldn't have my incredible son."

"Thanks, man. I won't let you down," I promise.

"I'm counting on it. Okay, well I'm going to go back to sleep while Zoey makes Declan breakfast," Jude explains and he lets out a sheepish chuckle. "Don't forget to keep me posted. I'm fucking nervous as hell about this."

"I promise it'll be fine," I assure him. "I'll treat it like it's my own place."

"I know you will. That's why I picked you for the job," Jude replies. "Later, Holden."

He ends the call and I stick my phone in my back pocket

and head into my trailer to make sure everything survived the trip. Nothing is out of place. I dig my Ray-Bans out of the junk drawer in my kitchen and shove them on and decide to head out for a walk, maybe grab some coffee. Then in a few hours, instead of using the key Jude gave me, I'll knock politely on the door and tell Winnie I need to do a walk-through. Hopefully she's in a better mood...or better yet, not even home.

I walk slowly down the side streets of this little Podunk town and let the sun warm my arms and the ocean air clear my lungs. I used to fucking hate this place after my mom died. It felt like a prison, which is why when I got out of actual jail—well, juvenile detention—I moved away. I didn't even care where I went; I just didn't want to be here. But now there is nowhere I'd rather be, even though moving back here means having to prove myself and earn back people's trust.

I open the door to Cannon's Corner Grocery and the little bell jingles happily. Unfortunately, the happy smile on Cat Cannon's face dissolves when she sees me. She gave me the same reaction the last two times I've come in. "What do you want?"

"World peace. A cure for cancer and a way to make you forgive me," I reply bluntly as I take off my shades. "But I'll probably have to settle for a coffee and a cinnamon bun."

"I should ban you," Cat says, her bright red lips set in a tight line as she crosses her arms. "But it's the off-season and I can't afford to turn away people. Even thieving assholes."

"Thank God for that," I mutter and head to the coffee station. I pour some hazelnut roast and add hazelnut creamer.

Enough to cause a cavity but fuck it, it's been a rough morning. I grab a strawberry milk out of the cooler and head to the counter where she's already got my cinnamon bun waiting in a small bag. "You didn't spit on it, did you?"

"I didn't think of it," she replies honestly and then gives me a humorless smirk. "But I will next time. Four bucks even. Hurry up and pay so I can kick you out."

I pull a five from my wallet and hand it to her. She shoves it in the register and practically throws the dollar at me as I pick up my cinnamon bun. She watches me with angry blue eyes. "Why did you come back?"

"Because I realized people can't know how sorry I am if I'm not here to tell them," I explain. "And they won't know I've changed if I don't show them."

"Wow. How selfish," Cat barks back and I really wasn't expecting that answer. "Maybe we don't care if you've changed. Ever think of that? Maybe we just want to forget you ever existed."

"Fuck, that's harsh." Her expression wavers, for just the slightest second, but then it goes back to angry.

"You convinced me to throw a party when my parents were out of town and then you stole from my house. I was grounded for half my junior year," she says, still as angry as if it were yesterday. "You took my grandmother's pearls, the only thing she left me, and pawned them."

"I know," I tell her. And sigh. "I also hurt your feelings. On purpose. I was a jerk."

"And I don't care if you're a fucking angel now. I don't like you," Cat counters. "I'll never like you. So I suggest you make the trek down to Hogan's Market next time you need coffee or sustenance or anything. I wouldn't piss on you if you were on fire."

"Fair enough," I say even though it doesn't feel fair. I know I earned her anger. I am a little disheartened by how much damage I did at such a young age and how no one is letting it go. Literally no one. I knew coming home wouldn't be easy, but I didn't think it would be this hard. I head to the door but pause before leaving. "For the record, I would put you out if you were on fire."

"You'd piss on me?" She cocks a blond eyebrow.

Oh fuck, that's not... "No I'd use water or a fire extinguisher. I just... forget it. Take care, Cat. I'll try to stay out of your way this winter."

I leave before I can make it worse or she can come up with another way to express her fury. I head up to the beach, sit on a bench and devour the bun and strawberry milk as my coffee cools. This was a treat my mom used to get me. I still love it. The tide is high and the waves are few and far between. There are very few people around. It's such a dynamic shift from last week when the tourists were still here and the beach was packed. The first week of September and the second are like pre- and post-apocalypse when it comes to the amount of people in this town.

I knew it was going to be a lonely winter, but I'm beginning to realize it's going to be a hostile one. I wasn't banking on that. I toss the bag from my bun and the bottle from my milk in the trash can and pick up my coffee as I take off my shoes and make my way back to the Braddock house along the sand. I guess if it gets really lonely I could call Kidd. Maybe I can hang out with those guys again without being brought into whatever bullshit they're involved in...Maybe they've changed? Even a little...Or I can just force Winnie Braddock to see me in a new light.

I laugh to myself at the improbability of that.

5

WINNIE

He's gone when I head out for groceries and, more importantly, wine. But he's back when I come home an hour later, with aching feet, sore arms and sweating like a stuck pig. I realized a few things on my walk to Super Shop and Save. First, I'm going to need a car if I'm staying. Second, I'm not going to be able to get rid of him. Which means I'm going to have to tell my family what I'm doing. I just hope I can wait long enough to figure it out myself.

I have no idea why I came back here. It's not going to help. Nothing is going to help, but I figured at least here, I would be alone. And everything—I mean every single thing—about this place reminds me of my dad. When I woke up this morning, to the sound of Kidd's truck hauling Holden's trailer, for a brief second I forgot what happened. I thought I was here with the family—all of them, including Dad. But then I remembered. And then I had to deal with Holden.

I'm furious at my brother, which isn't fair, but I can't

seem to shake the anger. He's doing a good thing, renovating this place, but I just want to be alone here. I want peace and quiet. But Jude wants to honor Dad by creating the cottage he always dreamed of. I feel tears welling up in my eyes and try desperately to ignore them as I approach the cottage. Holden's sprawled out in a lawn chair under the awning he's opened on the side of his Airstream.

He's shirtless, and I can't help but stare. Holden Hendricks, who started out as a good-looking boy, turned into one hell of a specimen of a man. When he was a kid, he was athletic and fairly muscular from playing hockey. But now...well, now his muscles have muscles. He's broad shouldered, with smattering of hair across his well-developed pecs and both his ample biceps are covered in tattoos. The tat on his left arm that I saw peeking out from his shirt on the bus the other night is an octopus, and his right biceps has a bunch of intricate images twisted together—a ship's wheel, an anchor, a nautical compass and words I can't catch without staring much longer than I should.

"See something you like?" he asks and it startles me back to reality. This man may look pretty on the outside but he's not on the inside. I will never forget that.

"Definitely not," I reply and turn to climb the stairs to the cottage.

"I need to do a walk-through," I hear him say behind me and turn to find him at the bottom of the stairs I'm halfway up. His abs look like they're cut from marble. And his well-worn jeans are so low on his hips I can see the waistband of his underwear.

"Why?"

"So I can get a feel for where to start tomorrow," he explains.

"You're starting tomorrow?" I repeat, stunned and annoyed. "Why so soon?"

"Because it's my job," he reminds me. "I promised Jude it would be ready in six to eight weeks, and I have other gigs lined up afterward."

"And you just have to start tomorrow or you can't make it?" I question and try not to sound as annoyed as I am. Again, Holden might be a dick, but he is just doing his job. It's not just the fact he's here that annoys me, it's the fact that anyone is here—in my space. I came back here to be alone and grieve without an audience. Now I not only have an audience, it's a childhood nemesis who used to make me feel like a loser on my best days...and I'm nowhere near my best days right now. "I was hoping to have a week before you started."

"I was hoping there wouldn't be a squatter on the property, but we don't always get what we want," Holden replies with a small shrug of those incredible shoulders. "You get today. Rest up. I work early and I work late."

"Well, I'm not even getting today if you need to bother me with a fucking walk-through," I snap.

He raises his eyebrows. "You have an inordinate amount of anger. Your boyfriend not giving it to you regularly?"

"Excuse me?!"

"You heard me. You need to get laid to get rid of all that anger."

"Sex doesn't fix things."

"Well, sweetheart, you should really try something because

being that infuriated all the time isn't going to do you any
favors." He gives me a wide, snarky smile. "Trust me I know.
And if you're trying to give me a taste of my own medicine,
it worked. You are on my last nerve right now."

"You haven't changed at all."

"I have, but damn you seem hell-bent on bringing out the
old me," he says and heaves a frustrated sigh. "Winnie…
we're getting off on the wrong foot."

"We've been on the wrong foot for years. There's no right
foot for us." I swing open the door to the screened-in porch. I
can hear him climbing the stairs and as much as I want to stop
him I won't. I put the key in the lock for the oak door and
glance at him over my shoulder. "Please be done by the time
I finish unpacking my groceries."

I swing open the front door and he steps in behind me, then
walks past me, his head turns to glance into the grocery bag
I'm carrying. "Not sure I can get everything done in the time
it takes to unpack some junk food and wine."

"Yeah you're a dick," I retort and stomp off to the kitchen
before he can reply. I start to unpack my groceries, which
include blueberries, yogurt, bread and four frozen dinners on
top of the two bags of Humpty Dumpty potato chips and three
bottles of pinot grigio that jackass noticed when he snuck a
peak. I can hear him walking around. I walk into the dining
room to put the wine bottles in the wine rack under the
window and can't stop myself from glancing his way. He's
crouched down in the bathroom measuring the width of the
room with a tape measure he must have had in his pocket.
Then he types the measurements into his phone.

He looks up and notices the Plexiglas box on the rickety shelf above the toilet and his eyes grow two sizes bigger. He looks at me and back at the trophy. "Is that a fucking Stanley Cup ring?"

"Yeah. Jude's first," I explain. "He gave it to my dad. Dad used to keep it here. It was a prized possession in his favorite place."

"In the shitter?" Holden is both stunned and horrified as he rises to his feet and leans forward to admire it.

"He kept it on his dresser, where he could see it first thing in the morning and last thing at night," I say and I almost smile as I explain the rest. "But Sadie, Dixie and I always move it to the bathroom. At first, Jude actually thought Dad kept it there, but then he realized it was our way of keeping him humble. Reminding him rings and trophies mean shit to us. He still has to be a good person."

Holden chuckles and I'm surprised by how good it feels to make him laugh. "You girls sure know how to keep a guy in place...and dishonor a symbol of the hardest trophy to win in sports."

"Whatever." I shrug. He shakes his head in disbelief, takes one last long look at the ring and lowers himself back down to take more measurements.

After a couple of minutes, he glances back and catches me watching him. The shithead grins, all cocky like I haven't seen on his face since he was a teen, and then he has the balls to wink. He fucking winks at me. "You can deny it all you want, you like what you see."

"I'm just admiring my handiwork," I flat-out lie. "I'm

assuming I'm the one who made your nose a little crooked when I clocked you."

He slowly stands up. I can't stop my eyes from slipping to his stomach to watch his abs as they flex and ripple with his movements. I know it's impossible, but I swear his six-pack is more of a twelve-pack. "Eyes up, Larry," he chides with amusement. I roll my eyes and then glare, but his smirk doesn't leave. "It's cute you think you're the only one I've ever made angry enough to attack me."

"Oh I'm sure I'm not," I reply coolly.

His eyes stay on me as he reaches up and runs his index finger slowly over the bridge of his nose. Honestly, the crook in it is barely noticeable. "You and your left hook broke my nose the first time. But it's been busted by a couple hockey pucks and a few fists since. I am happy to report it has stayed in one piece for about a decade."

"Are you almost done?" I ask, changing the subject because I just want him gone. This conversation is pointless and exhausting and his hot body is impossible not to stare at, which is annoying.

"Nope. Because you keep ogling me and reminiscing fondly about the time you punched me," he replies and my jaw drops. He ignores me and heads into the kitchen.

Of all the people in the entire world, my brother had to pick him. I sigh and walk over to the bar cart, grab the wine opener and head back into the kitchen. It's a small L-shaped room, which makes it almost impossible to not bump into Holden. I manage to squeak by him as he measures the counters by the sink, but after I grab the chilled bottle of wine from the fridge

I have to wait for him to move from the counter so I can uncork it. I sigh impatiently. He smiles passive aggressively and I swear he moves way more slowly than he has to. "Thirsty?"

"I just walked to and from the grocery store, so yeah, I've earned a beverage," I reply and wonder why the hell I feel like I have to defend myself to him. "And it's been a rough...couple of years."

That seems to take his snark level down a notch and his smirk disappears. "Yeah, I can only imagine how hard it is being from a loving family, with a rich brother who probably helps you out when you need it and a long-term boyfriend who puts up with your attitude. Completely rough. Drink up."

I tense. I can feel my anger rush through my entire body. I feel it in my earlobes, for God's sake. I turn to him with venom dripping from my voice. "Don't even begin to think you have any clue about me or that you have any right to judge. How do you even know anything about my life?"

"Your brother was more than happy to update me while I was talking to him, trying to keep the stupid secret that you're here," Holden says calmly, not ruffled in the slightest at my fury.

"My brother doesn't know everything," I say and pause. "Thank you for not telling him I'm here."

"You're welcome," he says simply.

The moment feels like a bit of a truce so I use it to retreat onto the porch with my wine, the opener and a glass. I'm half-way through my first glass, rocking slowly in my dad's old chair, when he appears in the doorway. He barely glances at me before he opens the screen door and starts down the stairs. Good, I think, but at the same time, I feel a little disappointed. Maybe it's because I feel like a good fight right now and well, he was giving me one.

He walks straight to his trailer and instead of hanging out in front, on his shitty lawn chair, he heads inside and closes the door. I hear my phone ring from where I left it on the dining room table. It's probably Ty. Again. He's called about twelve times today, but he has yet to leave a message. I should talk to him. I know that, but instead I head into the kitchen to grab a bag of salt-and-vinegar potato chips. I haven't eaten all day and my stomach is growling. I refill my glass while I'm in there too.

With an open family-size bag of chips in one hand and my wine in the other, I wander back toward the porch but pause at the open door to my parents' room. I stare at the oak sleigh bed and old white chenille quilt that they've had since... well, as far back as I can remember. I walk into the room and my nostrils are instantly hit with familiar scents. The room is an elixir of pine from the floors and walls, roses from my mom's perfume and musk from my dad's aftershave. An almost empty bottle of it sits on his tallboy dresser next to the small closet. I walk over, put down my chips and wine and gently pick it up. I pop the top off and sniff. The scent fills my heart, but it also makes me ache and tears instantly start falling down my cheeks.

"Oh God, Dad, I miss you so much."

6

WINNIE

It's been two days. Two long days. This guy gets up at the crack of ass and marches in here to start work every damn morning and it's killing me. I haven't been able to sleep much at night. Somehow I can only fall asleep around four or five in the morning so I need him to not wake me up at nine. But that's what he's done for the last two days. And it's only going to get worse. He's spent the last two days clearing the rooms of belongings and pulling down the wallpaper in the bathroom, but eventually he's going to start knocking down walls and my sleep, and any sense of quiet, will be gone. I feel like him being here, ruining my chance at peaceful mourning, is the universe kicking me while I'm down. That and the sleep deprivation is making me feel like a cornered animal all the time.

He steps onto the porch at almost six in the evening and glances over at me. His silvery eyes land on my wineglass. "Wine o'clock again, huh?"

I ignore the comment. "Done for the day?"

"Yep. Fair warning. Tomorrow is the last day before demo. Then it'll start getting loud and dusty in here." He opens the door and leaves without giving me a chance to respond. He probably assumes I'll complain, and he's right.

I sigh and watch him go. When he closes the door of his trailer, I stand up and head inside. I have to eat something. I'm not doing enough of that. Cooking has always been a passion, since I was a little kid. But now it feels like a chore. I head into the kitchen, there are boxes piled up everywhere so my path is a long, meandering one. I open the fridge and stare inside. I could make a grilled cheese. I could whip up a salad. I sigh, sip my wine and give up, grabbing a jar of spicy mustard out of the fridge and reaching for the bag of pretzels on top of it.

I head back to the porch, sit down, dip a pretzel into the mustard and pop it into my mouth. I can hear Holden banging around inside his trailer. He's playing music—Foo Fighters—and he must have made dinner because the scent of something tomato-y and garlicky wafts through the screens. I glare at my pretzel. "Why can't you be pasta primavera?"

A car drives slowly up the street and I wonder if he's expecting company? Having someone over to share that delicious-smelling dinner? A woman? My brain jumps there immediately. I have to be honest with myself, Holden Hendricks is a great-looking man. It would make sense that he has a girlfriend. I mean, some girls like the bad boys. They feel like they can love them into behaving better. I've never been that woman.

But when the car door opens, it's Ty who steps out. The pretzel in my hand drops to the floor. I stand up. He doesn't know I'm here, I haven't bothered to turn on the lights and the porch is shrouded in darkness. And for a brief, crazy moment, I ponder ducking down and hiding until he goes away. But he came all the way here from Toronto, I doubt he'll go away.

He starts toward the porch, but his head is turned toward the trailer. I put down my wineglass. "What are you doing here?"

That finally gets his head to swing toward me. He finds me, or probably just a dark shadowed outline of me, on the porch and starts to climb the stairs. "I came to get you back."

I wish those words made me feel good and loved and gave me hope, but they don't. "Ty, I don't want to work through this."

He opens the screen door. "I can't believe that."

"You're going to have to," I reply and glance at his car. "You came all the way back from Toronto?"

He nods. "I can't just walk away. I'm not going to let you."

Oh God. Why is this happening? He's standing in front of me, looking anguished. Guilt floods me. "I'm sorry, Ty. I handled it poorly. I know that. But I still know that it's the right decision. We can't be together anymore."

"I begged for your forgiveness. I quit my job so I wouldn't even work with her anymore. I let you move to San Francisco without me. I put up with all your tears and mood swings and—"

"Let me move? Put up with me?" All the guilt I was feeling turns to dust and is replaced with the strongest sense of validation I think I've ever felt in my life. "When did you become that guy? The one who thinks being in a relationship means you control another person's actions? That you have the right to give me permission like you're my parent, not my partner?"

"That's not what I meant!" he yells, but it's exactly what he said. "When did you become the girl who walks away from a decade-long relationship in a fucking airport line?"

"When my dad died. When my life became too hard. When I decided I couldn't lie to myself anymore," I yell back. "I can't trust you. I want to. I tried to. I can't."

"I told you, she didn't mean anything. I was lonely. You were spending all your time at your parents'. We were barely seeing each other." He runs a hand through his light blond hair, causing a big chunk of it to stand up awkwardly. "And then you told me you wanted to go to San Francisco and that we could do long distance. You didn't ask. You told me!"

"I don't have to ask your permission or get your approval on how I deal with my dying father," I reply heatedly. "You should have been supportive. You should have been understanding."

"You should have fucked me," Ty blurts out and I freeze. "We hadn't had sex in a month."

"So four weeks is your limit?" I ask and every fiber of my being is drowning in sarcasm. "I'm sorry I didn't see that section in the relationship handbook. I thought that if you'd been with someone for years and you claimed to love them and want to spend your life with them, the grace period for wanting to fuck like a porn star when you just found out your dad was dying a slow horrible death would be longer. My bad. I'll read the fine print next time. With someone else."

I start toward the interior of the cottage. "Go home, Ty. Or go to a hotel. I'm done."

I feel his fingers wrap around my arm—tightly. Too tightly. I wince as I spin to face him. He has a look in his eyes that's a dangerous mix of desperation and frustration and it makes my blood run cold. "You don't get to end this with a sarcastic rant. You said you'd forgive me and you'd give me a chance."

"Let go of my arm," I say firmly, eerily calm.

He ignores me. "I've had lots of chances to be with someone else since you ran off to California. I could have fucked tons of girls, but I didn't. I swear to fucking God I didn't. Even though you've been a horrible bitch to me almost the entire time."

"Let go of me," I repeat. "And get the fuck out of here."

"No."

"I think you mean yes." The voice comes out of the darkness behind Ty. It's hard, rough, menacing and I've heard it before—repeatedly—when I was a teenager. "Because when a woman wants you to leave, you leave. And you also take your hands off her when she tells you to. Or else guys like me do it for you, and trust me, buddy, you don't want that."

Ty's fingers slowly loosen and he turns around. I hear the screen door open and I fumble for the switch on the wall, flooding the porch with a creamy yellow light from a bug-deterring bulb in the wall sconce.

Holden is standing just inside the door, his shoulders back, his fists clenched by his side and his bearded jaw tense. The look in his eyes is hard, unforgiving, dangerous. Ty is not a small guy. He's six feet and broad, but Holden looks like a bear in front of him protecting his cubs—protecting me.

"Who the fuck are you?" Ty asks. He looks tough and he sounds harsh, but I know him and I know he's shocked and probably intimidated by this hulking stranger.

"I'm her neighbor," Holden replies and takes one simple but aggressive step forward. "And I heard her tell you to leave. So I am here to find out if you need help with that since, you know, you're still here."

"I'm having a private conversation with my girlfriend," Ty tells him.

"Ex-girlfriend," I mumble and absently rub my arm. I'm dazed, I think. He's never laid his hands on me—ever. I look at Ty. "I'm sorry you came all this way. I'm sorry it has to be so…messy. But you need to leave. I think we both need to cool off."

Ty looks furious and, at the same time, devastated. "Ten fucking years, Winnie, and you can't let me stay in a guest room?"

"House is under renos," Holden says easily. "Winnie shouldn't even be staying in it. All the extra rooms are filled with crap or covered in dust."

Total lie. The entire upstairs, all four bedrooms, are just fine. But I am not about to correct him. Ty turns to him again. "Wow. You know a lot about your neighbors. Are you a fucking stalker or something?"

Holden chuffs. "I'm the contractor. It's my renovation project."

"Contractor and neighbor?"

Holden gives him the coldest, darkest smirk I've ever seen. It says *Fuck you, douchebag* better than words ever could. "I'm a lot of things. Most importantly, I'm the guy who isn't going to leave until you do. And you are leaving. Willingly or not."

"Jesus, enough with the threats, asshole," Ty snaps and turns back to me. "I'm going to find a motel, but I will be back. I deserve more than this from you, Win."

He turns and Holden gracefully steps aside as Ty storms out of the house. A few seconds later he's in his rental speeding down the street. I stare at his taillights until they're gone, and I let out a breath I didn't know I was holding.

"Did he hurt you?" Holden asks and reaches up and stills my hand. I didn't realize I was still rubbing my arm where Ty had gripped it.

"No. Not really," I say softly. "I think I'm just in shock. He's never done that before."

Holden stares at me intently. I can see some kind of war being waged behind those spectacular eyes that are more sky blue than silver in the yellow light shining down on us. He sighs and rubs his beard pensively as he breaks the eye contact, looking out toward his trailer. "Look, I know I'm the last person you want to get advice from and, trust me, I'm usually the last one to give it. But any guy who would do that, at any point in a relationship, isn't a good guy."

"I know."

He looks at me again. I can tell there's more he wants to say, but all he responds with is a nod. "Good."

Before I can thank him for stepping in and for not pounding

Ty into oblivion, which would have only made everything worse, he swings open the screen door and disappears down the stairs, across the lawn and into his trailer.

I barely sleep all night and the next morning just before seven, I text Ty to see if he's awake. He is. He's at a motel a half mile away in Old Orchard Beach. I ask him to meet me at a small diner near there and then I shower quickly, get dressed, throw my wet hair in a bun and head out the door. Holden's trailer is still dark. The one time I wish he was up early, he's not. Of course. I really want to see him and thank him. I sigh and walk toward Old Orchard Beach.

As I open the door to the diner, I see Ty in a booth at the back. He seems far less angry and much more resigned. And exhausted. He looks absolutely spent. I know, as our eyes meet, that he's accepted this. Finally.

We spend about an hour holding coffees we don't drink, talking out everything. The good, the bad and the ugly. He's still upset. I'm still sorry. But we both know it's over. A few hours later when we're ready to leave, it's started raining lightly. More of a mist really, but Ty offers to drive me home and I really don't want to walk.

When he pulls to stop in front of the cottage I start to unclip my seatbelt, but he stops me, placing a gentle hand over mine. I look up at him. "I'm sorry. For yesterday. For everything."

"I know. I believe you," I tell him. "I'm sorry too."

"I hope things work out for you," he says quietly.

"I hope they do for you too," I reply and then, as he lets go of my hand and I release my seatbelt, I reach across the seat and hug him lightly. "Bye, Ty."

"If you change your mind...," he says, but he doesn't finish the sentence and I don't reply. I simply get out of the car. I hear him pulling away as I climb the porch stairs. As soon as I open the screen door, I'm shocked to see Holden standing there, staring at me with a scowl on his face.

"Hey," I say.

"You're with him again?" Holden asks, clearly not happy with it. "After last night?"

"I was just—"

He storms by me. "Forget it. I don't care. You had self-esteem issues when you were a kid and clearly you still do if you think that type of guy is the best you can get. But whatever. Not my business."

He marches out the door and stomps down the steps. I walk up to the screen and call through it. "You're right. It's not your business! So do your job and leave me alone."

He slams his trailer door. I turn, march into the house and slam the front door. Who the hell does he think he is? Yes, I had self-esteem issues when I was a kid. Who doesn't? I was too tall, too skinny, with bad skin and bad hair. Big deal. Who is he to judge me? Maybe if he hadn't picked on all my weaknesses, I wouldn't have had so many self-esteem issues. Fuck that jerk. I could march over there and explain to him I was simply saying good-bye to the only real boyfriend I've ever had and that civilized people do that, but he doesn't deserve to know the truth. He probably wouldn't understand it anyway.

I glance through the window toward the trailer.

Neanderthal. I hope this renovation goes smoothly so I can rid myself of this asshole as soon as possible.

7

HOLDEN

I've almost survived thirty-six hours without fighting with Winnie. It's honestly the closest I've come to a miracle in my life. After I watched her hug that asshole who had his hands on her, and told her how stupid I thought she was for taking him back, she has been avoiding me. I've barely even seen her. She's kept herself hidden upstairs while I've been in the house, and when she leaves, she walks past me, and the trailer, like we don't even exist. But today, we're gonna have to confront each other again. It's demo day. Walls are coming down. She won't be able to ignore that.

I woke up this morning early, and exhausted. I couldn't sleep most of the night because earlier, as I puttered around the trailer, made dinner and tried to watch some Netflix on my laptop, but I could hear her. Again. Like every other night, she was crying. I could tell she was drunk because when girls drunk-cry it's way louder than their normal cry. Guys too for that matter, although I've only witnessed my father drunk-cry, for weeks after my mom died, and he didn't know I heard him. I didn't dare talk about it. Anyway she didn't cry long, at least not that I could hear, but it stuck with me.

I lay awake much longer than I should have thinking about whether she was okay, knowing she wasn't. What had this girl so distraught? I thought, from what I'd seen, she'd worked things out with that boyfriend. But if so, why did he leave? Why hadn't I seen him again and why was she still here? Was it something else that had her so wounded? If it wasn't just the boyfriend and it was something else, that just proved this guy is a world-class piece of shit. Because if a girl I loved was this broken up over something, I would be there to help her through it, at all costs. He had left her here.

As I opened up the storage hatch in the side of my trailer and started to take out my tools, I called my own sister not just to get my mind off Winnie, who I have yet to see this morning, but because I needed to know when I might get my truck back. She answered on the first ring.

"I was going to call you after work," she explains without so much as a hello. She sounds defensive so I try to defuse the situation immediately.

"How did Duke's hockey tournament end?" I ask. "Thanks again for letting me stay and watch a game."

She had been at my nephew's hockey tournament in Boston when her car died on the way to the arena from the hotel. She had it towed to a garage and called me in a panic that night when she found out it would take a few days to get the part it needed. I know it killed her to have to call me. When I came back to Maine, I reached out to her right away. But just like she said the last time I saw her, when I was sixteen and she was almost eighteen, and she still wanted nothing to do with me. I made a point of running into her a lot this summer because this town was so damn small I knew what places she would frequent. She begrudgingly introduced me to my ten-year-old nephew, Duke, but not as his uncle. She just called me Holden, which stung but it was better than nothing. She stayed aloof and distant—until the call.

So without hesitation, I drove straight down there and insisted she take my truck until her car was fixed. Duke's team was in the middle of a game when she met me in the arena parking lot, and she invited me to stay and watch it. They won and Duke even scored. It felt like we made progress that weekend—like maybe we were inching our way back to a family relationship again. But now, she sounds distant and aloof.

"They lost in the finals," she explains curtly and I can hear a lot of noise in the background of wherever she is. "Anyway my car is fixed. I just have to pick it up in Boston. We were going to take a bus there after work tonight. I think if I hustle and Duke isn't late coming home from school, I can get us on the seven o'clock one. You're in Ocean Pines, which isn't far from the bus station, so I can drop off your car on my way there and walk from your place."

"You can just drive it to the bus station and I'll pick it up there," I offer. "If that'll be easier."

"I don't want to put you out any more than I already have," Bradie replies.

"It's not putting me out and, if you want…" I pause,

worried volunteering to do her another favor will piss her off. Everything about me kind of does. "I can swing by tonight and just drive you guys to Boston."

"I can't ask you do that," she snaps.

"You're not asking. I'm offering," I correct her gently. "I'm working a new job, but I can wrap it up around five and head right over. It'll be quicker than taking the bus and cheaper. I know the new alternator you had to get isn't cheap."

All I can hear is her breathing. It's almost labored. Like the debate going on in her head is actually physically taxing. I try to put her at ease. "I'm not asking anything in return, Bradie. I'll just drop you off and go."

"I'm still not telling him who you are," Bradie replies, her tone serious but also a little heavy with guilt. "His dad disappeared on him. He never had any grandparents and I just don't want him to get his hopes up on you. Okay?"

"I know. I have a lot of trust to earn back," I reply. "I'll just be your friend Holden who is doing you a favor. That's it."

"Okay," Bradie relents and I can't help but smile. "Thanks. I appreciate it."

"I'll be there at like five thirty," I tell her. "I'm going to walk there so it'll take a minute. You're still on Union right?"

"Yep," she says, sounding embarrassed. "The dilapidated white one on the left."

"Your brother is a contractor," I tell her. "You should see if he can do something about that."

"Yeah, well right now I just need my car back," she mutters. "See you tonight."

She hangs up. I shove my phone in my pocket and glance up

at the Braddock cottage. Everything is quiet and dark. Winnie clearly isn't up yet. I decide I'll walk down to Hogan's, since Cat doesn't want me at her store, and grab a coffee. If Winnie isn't up by the time I get back, I'll have to wake her ass up. I have work to do.

I think about the Braddocks as I walk east to Hogan's. I used to watch the Braddock kids with wonder. Jude and his sisters liked to pretend they hated each other, but everyone knew they didn't. The three girls would go to all his summer games. Even on the hottest beach day, they'd be in that crappy indoor rink cheering him on…admittedly, it did sometimes sound like heckling. But I remember him getting into a fight once, some kid went after him and dropped his gloves first, and those three were at the glass threatening his life and calling him names that even made me blush.

My sister and I were nothing like that, even before my mom died. We didn't fight all that much, but we certainly didn't support each other. We were just two very different people coexisting in the same house. And then after our mother died, we handled it two completely opposite ways—Bradie with-drew and I lashed out. My dad and I fought every time we were near each other. She would always ignore us and lock herself in her room. She never took my side or defended me, which is what I desperately wanted. So, I started picking the lock and I would take or break her stuff. I hated her for not taking my side, not reacting, not helping me through my grief, but I realize now that I wasn't helping her either. The day I got busted and went to juvie she told me that she never wanted to see me or hear from me ever again. She was angry I was tearing the family apart even more, which at the time I told her was bullshit because she never acted like she wanted me around in the first place. Anyway, she got her wish for over a decade until this summer.

Hogan's is empty, so I get my coffee and am back at the house in less than half an hour. I drink half of it on a bench on the beach, watching the tide come in, but then it's nine o'clock and I have to start work, especially now that I have to quit at a certain time to get Bradie and Duke. I head back to the cottage, up the front stairs and knock on the door to the porch. No response. So I walk across the porch, and knock on the heavier, oak door. Still nothing, so I open it with the keys Jude gave me. The whole first floor is empty and quiet.

"Winnie!" I call out, but she doesn't answer. "I'm starting work now!"

Still nothing. Maybe she went out while I was off getting coffee? Oh well, fact is I'm here to do a job and I'm going to do it. I head back out to my trailer to grab my tools so I can get started demoing the bathroom. Fifteen minutes later, as I'm breaking up the tile, I hear stomping and she appears in the doorway looking rougher than a homeless alley cat. Her ash-blond hair is sticking out every which way, and she's got makeup smeared around her eyes, which are puffy and red, giving her a distraught raccoon look. "What the fuck, Holden!"

I stop hammering the tile and look up at her. "I'm sorry, did I wake you?"

"Yes!" She blinks and crosses her arms. She's wearing a gray sweater three sizes too big for her. "Why do you have to start so early?"

"I hate to break it to you, princess, but this is starting late." I hammer another tile, as if to prove a point and it makes her flinch like she's been physically assaulted by the sound. "I'm planning on starting at seven every morning going forward."

I hammer a couple more tiles and pieces fly up. She places her hands, covered by the cuffs of the sweater, over her ears. "You're trying to kill me."

I laugh at her overdramatic act.

"And where am I supposed to shower? This is the only bathroom!"

"Yeah, I guess that's why Jude wanted me to do this when the house was supposed to be empty," I remind her and she narrows her eyes on me, like she's trying to wither me with her stare. "You can use the bathroom in my trailer while I'm working in here. I'll pull out the toilet last and turn the water back on so you can use this place at night."

"Use your trailer?" she repeats, clearly horrified. "For showering?"

"Yeah. The bathroom is pretty decent actually," I say trying not to sound too defensive. I mean, yeah it's a trailer, but I've made it as nice as possible and I'm not a slob. I keep it neat and clean.

"You think I'm going to shower in your bathroom?" she repeats, still annoyed and somehow offended.

"What's your problem?" I demand. "Use it or don't. I don't care. You can always go stay with your boyfriend, wherever the hell he is. That option would suit me best, actually, if you were just gone completely. Now if you'll excuse me."

She's so defensive and angry all the time I feel like I should be sympathetic, because I was like that once too. But instead it makes me want to challenge her more and push her buttons. It's a very old, very bad habit I thought I kicked. The fact that she keeps making me realize I haven't just annoys me more.

I hammer another tile, much harder than required just to make as much noise as possible. She makes this strangled, gurgle of frustration in the back of her throat and storms off. She stomps her way all the way up the stairs.

For the next twenty minutes she's banging around the house. Her frustration is starting to thicken the air in the whole house. I find myself grinding my teeth and scowling, but at least it seems to make me work harder and faster. I've finished breaking up all the tile so I head outside for the big rubber trash can I bought for hauling out debris. It's around back from the trailer and as I walk by the window in the bathroom I hear the shower running. Good, Princess is taking me up on my offer. I grab the bucket and head back inside.

As I'm hauling out the first load of broken tile, Winnie is walking around the side of the cottage pushing a very ancient looking bike. I have a vague memory of her traipsing around town on it as a kid. She doesn't say a word to me, just shoots me a quick, penetrating glare, hops on the bike and rides away very unsteadily.

Whatever. At least she's gone for now.

Winnie doesn't come back for hours and I'm able to get all the demo done and then I take a quick break for lunch, scarfing a turkey sandwich in front of my sink in the trailer before spending the afternoon clearing out the rest of the debris. As the day went on the temperature rose. It was an abnormally warm September day and since Winnie was gone, I pulled off my shirt and used it to mop my face as I worked. I leave the toilet intact for now and I'm debating whether I should try to haul out that ancient metal shower stall before cleaning up to go meet my sister when I hear the bang of the screen door.

I freeze in the doorway to the bathroom and slowly turn my head toward the porch. Winnie appears and whimpers softly as she steps into the house. I'm instantly concerned. "You okay?"

"Fine," she says, but it's through gritted teeth. I turn away from the bathroom so I can face her completely. My eyes sweep over her as she visibly limps and I immediately notice a tear in her jeans, at the knee, that wasn't there before.

I point to it. "What happened?"

"Nothing," she replies tersely but as she reaches out to balance herself on the nearby table, I notice her palm is full of angry red scrapes. I walk toward her. Her eyes snap up and meet mine. She looks like a wounded animal. "I fell off the bike. It's nothing."

As I get closer, I can see the extent of her injuries and I know immediately it's not nothing. Both her palms are badly scraped up and there are bits of gravel and dirt still in them. I can't see her skin, where the knee of her jeans has torn away because it's nothing but a bloody pulp. I wince and when our eyes meet again, hers are watering.

"I just need to clean it up," she insists.

"You need to see a doctor about that knee," I argue. "I think it might need stitches."

She shakes her head furiously. "No. It's just a scrape."

"Winnie…" She just keeps shaking her head and she's got her bottom lip pulled between her teeth and her eyes are glassy and she looks like she's about to come undone under the weight of the lie she's trying to make me believe. I don't know if it's her raw emotions or my own panic that she's really hurt herself here but for some reason I reach out and gently cup the side of her face. "You're right. It's a scratch. But let me help you clean it up, okay?"

She doesn't want to say yes. I can feel the tension in her neck as she stops herself from shaking her head, no. She bites her lip a little harder, swallows and says, "Sure."

I help her to the dining room table and get her to sit down in one of the chairs and then I grab some scissors from the kitchen. I start to cut the torn bottom half of her pant leg off. She doesn't complain, just watches. The jeans are destroyed anyway and I think she knows that. As soon as I have a better look at the wound, I know for a fact she's entirely wrong. This thing is way worse than a scrape. I'm squatting in front of her knee, my hands gently holding her calf. There are streaks of blood running down it. I look up, and our gazes connect. "I've got a first-aid kit in my trailer."

I stand up and reach out for her hands. She looks startled and kind of leans back, away from me. "It's easier if you come with me," I lie. "Come on. I'll help you."

She looks like she knows I'm up to something, but she puts her hands in mine anyway and lets me help her to her feet. But when I quickly step forward and scoop her up so I'm carrying her, she gasps and squirms like an earth worm on a sidewalk. "What the hell do you think you're doing?"

"You can barely walk," I remind her and start toward the door. "Now, stop squirming or I'll drop you."

She stops moving but not talking, unfortunately. "You do *not* have to carry me. I am not an invalid. It's a scratch. I don't want your help if you're going to be all Neanderthal about it."

"You should really stop insulting me as I'm doing you a favor," I warn and as soon as we're on the drive, I walk past my trailer and start down the street. That makes her start squirming again and I almost drop her, so I yank her even closer and turn my head to glare directly at her.

Our faces are so close together the tips of our noses are almost touching. Her eyes, although filled with anger and pain, are mesmerizing. I always knew they were hazel, but I thought that just meant a really light brown. This close I can see that there is hardly any brown in them. They are a mix of amber and green and a touch of gray. "You're incredibly beautiful, despite your personality, you know that?"

She blinks and rears her head back a little. "What the fuck."

"I'm just saying." I shrug as best I can with her in my arms. "If you'd just calm the fuck down and maybe cut me some slack you'd be irresistible."

"So I should what? Smile more?" she asks, seething. "I'm kind of going through something personal and I'm currently being taken against my will God knows where by a man I dislike immensely, so excuse me if I'm not perky enough for you. And another thing, I don't want to be irresistible to you or anyone else."

"Well then, goal crushed!" I announce with mock enthusiasm.

She flips me the bird a millimeter from my face and I pretend to bobble her, like I might drop her, so she squeaks and wraps her warms tightly around my neck. "Also you don't know me."

"Excuse me?" she asks.

"You're with a man you don't know," I explain. "Not one you don't like. I was a boy you didn't like. I'm a man now, and you don't know me, so you can't dislike me."

She stares at me as if to say *Get the fuck out*. And so I grin at her and wink. "Trust me, sweetheart, Holden Hendricks the teenager was a piece of work worthy of hate. But Holden Hendricks the adult is actually a pretty decent guy."

"Maybe you can be a decent guy," she says but she's still glaring at me. "You coming to make sure I was okay when Ty and I were fighting was a decent thing to do. And I was grateful. But you assuming that I forgave him and calling out my childhood self-esteem issues was a totally judgmental dick move."

"So he isn't your boyfriend?"

"What the hell are we doing?" she asks in a heated whisper, ignoring my question. "Tell me or I'll just start screaming."

"We're going to Dr. Whittaker's place."

"His house?"

"Yep." I turn left toward the center of town. "He lifted the cottage and had a small separate office built under it last year so he could still work part-time. Said he wasn't ready for retirement."

"Didn't you knock his kid Robbie's teeth out in a fight at the beach when you were fourteen?" Winnie questions.

"Wow you have a better memory than an elephant," I snark back.

"Did you just call me an elephant?" she snaps.

"No," I retort. "Dr. Whittaker doesn't even remember that by the way. I know because I apologized to him when I worked on his renos."

"He forgave you?" She seems so baffled, like it's an impossibility.

"After I reminded him what I did, yes," I smile at her. "You can actually blame him while he stitches you up because he's the reason I'm back in town permanently. When I did the job here for him, Carter Construction was looking for people and I was short on jobs so I came out. When Dr. Whittaker forgave me, I decided to see if I could make amends with everyone and I came back."

"You can't," she says after a moment of silence.

"We'll see," I reply as I climb the stairs of the Whittaker house. The shingle on his office door says "closed," as expected. He only works three days a week and only until three. I had to see him once this summer when I stupidly put a nail through my finger.

I gently place Winnie on her own feet once we hit his large wraparound porch. She immediately pulls away from me, but she can't put her full weight on her bad knee so she has to reach out and grab my shoulder again. I circle her waist with my right arm to hold her steady and ring Dr. Whittaker's bell.

He answers right away. I haven't seen him in a couple months, but he hasn't changed. He's still got a slight belly, curly salt-and-pepper hair, kind brown eyes and a warm smile. "Holden! How are you?"

"I'm good, Doc, but my friend Winnie fell off her bike," I explain as we shake hands and I motion toward Winnie, who is clutching the back of one of the rocking chairs on his porch.

Dr. Whittaker recognizes her immediately. "Winnie Braddock!" he exclaims, and his brown eyes shift to her exposed knee. "Oh dear! Let's go down to my office so I can get a proper look at that."

He steps onto the porch, but reaches back in and grabs something from a hook by the door—a white lab coat. He closes his front door, slips the lab coat on over his checkered blue shirt, and starts for the stairs. I lift Winnie back up before she can object and the look on her face says that she wants to, wholeheartedly. By the time I get us down the stairs, Dr. Whittaker has already opened the door to his small office. As he turns on the lights, I stride right in and drop her butt onto the exam table. She looks angrier than a nest of hornets, but she manages a "thank you."

Dr. Whittaker puts on his glasses and some weird headgear thing with a light on it I swear he must have gotten at an antique sale and bends down over her knee. "Yeah. You're gonna need some butterfly tape or maybe even a stitch or two. But first, we have to clean it up. There's still gravel in this. When did you have your last tetanus shot, Winnie?"

"I have no idea," she answers back.

"Okay, well you're getting one today," the doctor says and I watch her groan and drop back on the table. I glance at my phone and realize it's almost six thirty. I was supposed to be at Bradie's house long before now.

"*Shit.*" They both turn and stare at me. "I'm so sorry. I have to make a phone call. I'll be right back."

I step out of the office and, once on the sidewalk outside I dial Bradie's number. She doesn't answer so I dial again. She still doesn't answer. I dial again.

When she finally answers, she doesn't let me get a word in. "I get it. You're not coming. I'm already on my way to the bus station with Duke. Your car is in front of my place. Keys are in the wheel well. Pick it up when you want but that's it. I don't want to see you."

She hangs up just as I'm about to say I'm sorry.

"Fuck!" I hiss and fight the urge to punch the tree I'm leaning on. I totally fucked that up. I didn't even get a chance to tell her why, not that it matters. I had one chance to fix things, or at least start to, with my sister and I blew it.

I decide to text her anyway, even though I don't think she'll even read it. I send three texts in a row explaining Winnie was hurt and I was helping her out. She's here alone, no family, and I didn't want to leave her. And I beg Bradie's forgiveness.

I don't get a response, just as I expected. The door to the office opens a second later and Winnie hobbles out followed by Dr. Whittaker. Her knee is now wrapped in white gauze. "Thank you so much," she tells him. "I'm so sorry to bother you after hours and I insist you bill my insurance, Dr. Whittaker."

"I'll do that, if I get around to it," he replies and winks before turning to me. "She's going to be just fine. No stitches, just some butterfly tape."

I nod and shake his hand. "Thanks again."

"That's what I'm here for." Dr. Whittaker starts up his stairs to his house but stops for a moment. "Winnie, be sure to keep it clean and no baths or swimming for seven days."

She nods and turns hobbling down the street back to her house. I fall in step beside her. "You're welcome."

"I didn't want to see a doctor," she replies tersely.

"You needed to see one. If you didn't get the doc to patch it up, you'd have a big nasty scar," I tell her.

"Oh no. What would I ever do with a scar on my knee," she says, rolling her eyes. "Who would want me without perfect knees?"

"With that sparkling personality, you need all the help you can get," I reply.

She's stopped walking now, stunned by my comment. "Fuck you."

"Yeah fuck me," I bark back. "I'm such an asshole for trying to make sure you don't die from your own stupidity. Dumbass me should have ignored you and all your blood just like I'm trying to ignore the bitter sadness on your face every minute of the day and the sobbing you do at night that gets so loud, it's like you're a wounded animal. I should have just walked out of the house when I saw you hobble in all bloody and broken. I should have just gone about my day. But I didn't. And now I've got a sister who hates me, still…or again, not sure which, and I can't even get a thanks from you. So yeah. Fuck me!"

I storm off and leave her standing in the middle of the sidewalk. I don't head home, I head toward my sister's house and I curse Winnie Braddock with every step.

8

WINNIE

Two hours later, I feel like shit—emotionally and physically. The physical part is from the knee, but the emotional part is from the way I treated Holden. I was way harsher than he deserved. I know that. I knew it when I was doing it, yet I still did it. He's not home when I get home, so I can't fix the situation, not that I know exactly how to do that, but I was hoping to start with an apology.

I don't know where he went, but I expect he'll be home eventually so I grab a bottle of wine and sit on the porch and wait. My phone rings and for a fleeting moment I find myself wishing it was him, which is crazy because he doesn't have my number. It turns out it's Dixie. I answer it, even though I don't want to. I've been avoiding calls from my entire family since I didn't get on that plane to Toronto, but I know if I do it for much longer they'll call Ty and then my alone time will turn into family time because they'll all show up here and try to fix me.

"Hey, Dix," I say. "What's up?"

"Nothing," she replies. "Just driving home from work and I wanted to check in. How's Toronto?"

"Good," I lie without even thinking about it. I don't want her to know I'm here. Not yet. "Same as always."

"Does it still feel like home?" she asks, but she answers the question before I can. "I'm sure it does because of Ty. So how is living together going? Is it a permanent thing or are you going to look for your own place?"

"I want my own place," I repeat a little too firmly. "I just spent the last two years living with half my family. I *deserve* my own space."

"Okay, relax," Dixie replies. "I just...I don't know. I can't imagine not living with Eli."

"Ty is *not* Eli," I reply and try to make a joke to keep it light. "And besides wait until you're over ten years in. Knowing you, you'll be build a she shed in the backyard to get away from him. Unless you two dummies are still in that shoebox you call an apartment. Then it'll be a murder-suicide thing."

"Ha. Ha," she replies. "Actually, we're looking at bigger places now. We want a second bedroom I can use as a home office and a guest room. In case you and Ty ever come back here."

"Look at you growing up," I say with a smile.

"Yeah, well it was bound to happen." Dixie laughs but it stops as quickly as it started and her voice gets heavy. "I miss you, by the way. It's hard enough not having Dad here, but not having you here either makes it harder."

Her confession makes my heart ache so painfully my eyes

water. "That's why I couldn't move back to San Francisco. I couldn't be there without him. I couldn't be around all of you and not have him there."

"Oh Win, it's got to be harder on your own," Dixie says softly. "We're helping each other through it here, and we'd help you through it."

"You wouldn't be able to," I whisper back and fight the overwhelming need to cry. "Alone is better for me."

"Alone with Ty," Dixie corrects and I let out an audible sigh. "You are with Ty...right?"

"Are you concerned about me or about Ty?" I snap.

"Whoa. What the fuck, Win?" Dixie says, offended. "We shouldn't be fighting. Why are we fighting?"

"I'm sorry," I reply. "I just...I'm sorry."

"It's okay," she replies and pauses. "Is this about the letters Dad left us?"

My heart pinches painfully like it suddenly doesn't fit in my chest. She hit the nail directly on the head. My dad left each of us letters, which my mother gave us the morning after he passed. None of us knew he was going to do that, so it was a shock and it was also bittersweet. We had one last chance to have some of his humor and wisdom, but he was candid and open even more so than he'd ever been in life, at least in my letter. I didn't ask what he'd written to my siblings. I didn't want to know and I didn't want to share my letter with them. This was my little piece of him to hold on to alone forever. And now that she's brought it up, I can't take a deep breath and I can't respond to her even if I wanted to, which I don't. Dixie being Dixie just talks for me. "I know Dad said a lot of really amazing things in mine, but he also said a lot of things that were so insightful they were almost painful."

"Yeah," I whisper, managing to get my voice back just a little. "He gave me a lot to think about."

"Me too," she replies softly. "Winnie, if things don't feel right in Toronto with Ty . . . come back. Anytime. Please. You are not alone."

"I'm good where I'm at," I reply vaguely so I'm not technically lying to her. "I mean it's hard. It's the hardest time of my life. But I'm where I need to be to get through it."

"Okay," Dixie sniffs and I realize she might be crying. "We all miss you, Win."

"I miss you guys too," I confess and it's the truth. I just know that I need my space right now. "I'll call you soon. Love to everyone."

"Love you too. Hi to Ty. Bye."

"Bye," I reply and hang up.

I instantly regret not telling her I broke up with Ty and came back to the cottage. But I know that I would regret it more if I did tell her. She would tell everyone. Mom would be worried. Sadie would be calling me all the time. Jude would take this as some kind of project—fix broken Winnie—like he used to do when we were kids and I was self-conscious and painfully awkward and he would always try to make me feel better. Jude's easy confidence always made me feel like it made my awkwardness more evident and I think he felt guilty about that. I love them all—desperately—but I need to find my own way through this. Through my dad's death and my failed relationship and my feelings about the rest of my life.

I take a sip of wine and stare out at Holden's dark trailer. Guilt fills me again. I was an ass to him when he was just trying to help me. I have been an ass to him since I saw him, not that he didn't deserve it. Ugh. I take another sip of wine and tip my head back. My stomach growls. I decide to order some pizza and as I'm on the phone with Bill's Pizza I spontaneously order two large pies. One with my typical cheese blend and one with pepperoni, pineapple and mushrooms—the pizza Holden always ordered when he was a kid. I remember it because I thought it was a weird combination and because, to me, pineapple on pizza is a blight against humanity. I don't know why I remember that about him, but I do.

It's the off-season, so Bill's isn't too busy and the order shows up, delivered on the back of a scooter as usual, by the same guy who has been delivering pizzas since he was sixteen. Then he was a pimply faced, gangly thing. Now he's a heavy-set, bearded guy, but he still has the same thick New England accent.

"Sadie, right?" he says as I open the screen door.

"Winnie," I reply and I hand him the cash in my hand.

"Oops. Sorry," he says. "I think this is the first time I've seen one of you without the others."

I try to give him a smile as I take the pizza boxes from him and wait for my change. "Tell your brother good luck this season. San Francisco Thunder is my favorite team."

"Yeah, I'll tell him." I smile again. I never tell him. If Jude knew how many times someone gives me a message about how talented, cool, hot he is, his ego would be bigger than he is.

The pizza guy leaves and as his scooter starts away from the house, I notice Holden walking toward it. Well, weaving is probably a better description. Huh. Holden is drunk. This both disturbs me and fascinates me in equal parts, but it shouldn't. It should only make me fearful because I remember drunk teenage Holden and he was mean. I remember it clear as day. We didn't drink a lot as kids, mostly because everyone knew we were underage and we had to walk two towns over to find a place that would take our fake ID, but on the occasions we managed to get alcohol, Holden would end the night punching someone or something. Mostly it was people—he'd pick a fight with anyone. And if no one took the bait he'd punch trees, kick parked cars, knock mailboxes off their posts. He was just plain scary.

I watch him as he stumbles, tripping over a slight lip in the sidewalk, curses and continues on to his trailer. It's dark outside and he's on a crash course for the lawn chair he left in the driveway so I reach over and flip on the outside lights. He stops and looks up, but he doesn't say anything. He just stands there staring. He isn't frowning or snarling, which is a good sign, so I open the screen door and hobble out and down the stairs, still holding the pizza boxes.

I stop before him and hold the boxes a little higher. "I bought you a pizza as a peace offering."

His silvery eyes drop to the boxes and then slowly rise back to find mine. They're glassy, probably swimming in tequila like the rest of him. I can smell it, along with the natural scent I've noticed is grown-up Holden. I can't describe the smell only the feeling it gives me: a happy flutter deep inside my gut. The same feeling I get when I hear waves crashing or smell a salty ocean mist.

"Peace?" he repeats skeptically but not maliciously. He raises one of his eyebrows. "I'm not at war, Winona."

Why does he call me by my full name? No one has, since birth. I was actually shocked to find out at five years old that my full name wasn't actually just Winnie. I rearrange the boxes in my hand so the one with his pizza is on top and open it. "I'm sorry for being a bitch when you were just trying to help me with my knee. And I'm sorry that helping me messed up something for you. This pizza is my way of trying to express that."

He looks down at the contents of the box and gives me a big drunken grin. "Pineapple, mushroom, pepperoni?" I nod and his grin somehow gets even bigger as he reaches for a slice. "Shit, I forgot how much I fucking loved this."

He takes a huge bite, closing his eyes while he chews. I just stand there, leg throbbing, staring at him. Why am I so…mesmerized. It's just a drunk childhood bully eating pizza. Yet I'm captivated and…well, a little enamored. He's not mean drunk Holden like he was way back when. He's actually kind of goofy. And cute.

I jerk slightly at that thought. I just called him cute. He notices the movement and our eyes meet again. "What?"

"Nothing." I shake my head. "So where'd you go tonight?"

"I went for a walk. Ended up buying some booze and drinking it down by the beach." He takes another big bite and cocks his head toward his trailer. "Wanna come inside and grab a beer?"

I nod again. Why am I nodding? This was not part of the plan. The plan was to hand him the pizza and go back to my cottage and finish my bottle of wine and cry some more. But I'm doing that every night, and it's a habit I should be trying to break. He walks over to his trailer and opens the door, holding it for me to enter.

"Drunk adult Holden is not what I expected," I blurt out as I walk up the steps and into his trailer. I'm as surprised as I was the first time I came in here to take a shower. It's so clean and well kept and smells like pine and lemon. I was expecting some dank, run-down thing that smelled like stale beer and mildew. He slips past me, placing a hand on my hip like it's not big deal. It isn't. It just feels like one.

"Have a seat, gimpy," he says casually and points to the built-in couch at the end of the countertop. I shuffle that way and sit. As he opens his fridge, he says, "You expected me to be the same ranting, rage-filled drunk I was as a kid, right? Sorry to disappoint. I can go outside and punch something if it will put you at ease. Wanna head to the beach and watch me tip a lifeguard stand?"

A laugh bubbles up from my chest and escapes, making a light cackling sound. I haven't laughed in literally months. It feels as awkward as it sounds. He hands me a Sam Adams and reaches for another piece of pizza. I open the other box, grabbing a slice and taking a bite.

"I'm not that guy anymore, Larry," he replies and I snap my head up to see a feisty grin on his face and he winks at me. I smile. "Careful now, you almost look like you're happy."

"I'm not," I reply firmly. "But I'm working on it."

"Wanna finally tell me why that is? Or do you want to just keep crying and bitching like Emo Barbie until I figure it out?" he says with a teasing smile.

I slowly swallow down a bite of pizza, take a deep breath and say it. "My dad died."

It's like someone hit a pause button. He stops chewing, stops breathing, stops moving. The only thing that changes is his expression. The cheeky, self-assured drunken glimmer in his eye and smile on his face disappear and are replaced with pure and simple sympathy.

"Winnie, I am so—"

"Please don't offer condolences," I say as tears prick the back of my eyes. "I don't want to cry again tonight. I'm not handling it well at all. Obviously. I'm in a very dark place, but that didn't give me the right to be a bitch to you when you were helping me out."

He pauses to take another bite and wash it down with some beer. "You have every right to be in a dark place. I was in a dark place for a very long time after my mom died when I was ten."

That information is completely new to me. I knew his mom wasn't around when he was younger. He never talked about her or where she was but he would constantly mention his dad's girlfriends and how much he hated them. I thought maybe his mom had just left the family.

"Is that why you were such a dick as a kid?" I ask boldly because I'm tipsy myself and this whole day has turned me upside down emotionally. I'm not sure where my —our—boundaries are and I'm wondering if we have any. "Because your mom died?"

He nods. "Mostly. I mean there were a lot of factors, but that was the trigger. She was no Randy Braddock, but she was the best thing I had."

I feel winded by that statement. By the fact that he lost someone who clearly meant everything to him and by the declaration that he, a relative stranger, knew my dad was something special. "What happened, if you don't mind me asking?"

"One March we had one last blowout storm, as we do here in New England," he says, winking at me. "My dad ran the trailer park in the summer but in the winter he ran a snow-removal company and he was out all night clearing driveways and roads for his contracts, but he didn't bother to clear ours yet. So my mom went out there, at like five in the morning to shovel the driveway. I don't know why she didn't wake me to do it. I always shoveled. But she didn't. And she slipped on some black ice, fell and hit the back of her head on the steps. And she died. Just like that."

"Oh my God," I whisper. He nods.

"Yeah. It was so stupid and so fucking random." The bitter quality in his voice that he had in the past is back, as if it never left. He takes a long, deep breath before speaking again, his eyes on the floor of the trailer. "I handled it as badly as anyone possibly could have. But you know all about that."

I blink and he looks right at me. "I could handle it a hell of a lot worse, trust me."

"That statement wasn't a challenge," he replies quietly with a small smile. "It's not a hold-my-beer moment. I'm just saying, it's clear you're struggling. And I'm not judging that.

I just would hate for you to make mistakes, because you're so blinded by grief, that you live to regret."

"I'm not doing that," I reply. "I'm doing the opposite."

He stops eating, pizza crust inches from his full, pretty mouth. His eyes look more silvery and wolfish in the fluorescent trailer lights than they normally do. And it's making me warm in places that shouldn't be—not over Holden Hendricks. I hate him.

"Does your boyfriend think that?"

"We broke up," I reply tersely, take another bite of pizza and chew on it like I'm teaching it a lesson. "That hug you saw was a good-bye hug. That's why he's back in Toronto and I'm still here."

He has this way of staring at me that hasn't changed in decades. He did it when we were kids too. It's like my face is some kind of foreign novel he's trying to translate. It's annoying as all hell and makes me want to blush. When I was a kid I wouldn't be able to fight the blush that came from his attention and then he would smirk, like he thought I was a joke, and laugh at me. Holden doesn't do that now, but I also keep my cheeks from turning into flaming red balls. "So you lost your dad and your boyfriend at the same time?"

"Not really. I lost Ty years ago," I tell him and take a big swig of my beer. "Well, he lost me."

"Why?" Holden asks.

"Because he fucked someone else." I am shocked I just came out and said it. I've never told anyone what Ty did. No one. I was humiliated and blamed myself. But I always thought when I did tell someone it would be Dixie or Sadie and it would be with less cussing. "And I spent a year trying to forgive him, but I couldn't. I decided I didn't want to and that makes me a giant bitch, because I think he was really truly sorry."

"That doesn't make you a bitch, Winona," Holden replies firmly. "There's some things that don't deserve forgiveness and that's one of them, in my opinion."

The conversation lulls. He finishes his beer and grabs another one. I keep sipping mine. I watch him move around the small trailer. He looks like he's physically too big to be in here, yet he moves fluidly and gracefully.

"Did you ever cheat on someone?" I ask softly, almost expecting him to ignore me.

"Nope," he replies easily. "I was too busy fighting, stealing and vandalizing."

He grins and it makes me laugh again and he laughs too. When our laughter dies it leaves a new, sexually charged energy in the room. This somehow now feels like a date, and I don't like that I like it. I finish my beer and get up off the couch. I hobble toward his recycling bin and drop the empty bottle in it. He's leaning his butt against the counter between the recycling bin and the door.

"I'm going to go," I say.

We stare at each other. I can't fight my blush under his attention this time. He notices and his lips slowly pull up into a smile. Shit. He's going to laugh at me just like he used to. I try to brush by him quickly, but he's quicker and blocks the door with his broad frame. I take a step back and my butt is against the built-in dinette table. He leans forward, placing his hands on either side of me on the table. If this were younger

Holden I would be a bit scared by the closeness, but with grown-up Holden, it feels exhilarating to have him this close, not scary. It feels *good.*

"You know why I called you Larry when you were a kid?" he murmurs in a deep rough voice that makes my belly flip like I'm on a roller coaster.

"Because you were an asshole." Our faces are inches apart, nose-to-nose. He's so close his ruggedly handsome face is almost blurry.

He chuckles and nods. "But also because he was my favorite. And you were my favorite."

I used to spend hours—nights—stewing over that nickname and why he would give it to me and of all the possible answers, I never came up with something so simply sweet.

"I was your favorite Braddock sister?" I ask in awe because it sure as hell didn't feel that way.

"You were my favorite everything."

I don't take my eyes off him. I'm waiting for him to laugh, like this is a joke. Because it is. He hated me. He hated everything. I don't know if it's the trauma of losing my dad or being face-to-face with my childhood nemesis or just the alcohol I've consumed, or maybe all three, but my childhood insecurities are back with a vengeance. I feel awkward and uncomfortable—unworthy of his attention, like I'm still an oily-faced, fuzzy-haired, painfully thin girl he's playing a joke on. I try to take a step away from him, but I can't because of the damn table and his thick strong arms on either side of me. So instead, I say, "If you're teasing me, remember, I can always break your nose again."

"I don't doubt it," he says. His expression is raw and real. He is serious. "But I'm just telling you the truth. I was a mean little brat back in the day, but I saw you, Winnie. I saw your kindness and your intelligence. I still see it. Difference is back then it made me feel worse about myself. Now I can just admire it."

He steps back, giving me all the space I need to escape. "Thank you for the pizza peace offering. Have a good night, Winona."

He waits for me to leave. I wait for me to leave, but my feet aren't moving. I don't want to go. What I want to do is touch him. I reach out and caress his cheek with my palm. His beard is rough, but his skin is warm. I pull him to me and I kiss him.

It's the most surreal moment of my life. A week ago, I had forgotten he existed. Two days ago, just seeing his face again filled me with anger and now my lips are on his and it feels...right. He's kissing me back, and it's raw and rough and taking my breath away. His hands grab my hips and his tongue slips into my mouth. He lifts me up onto the table and I immediately wrap my legs around his waist and start falling backward because there's nothing but table behind me. I pull him down with me and he goes willingly. I want him with a primal urgency I've never known before. This is more than a kiss; it's a surrender. I want to give him everything.

There's a loud, jarring knock on the trailer door, and I freeze and Holden jumps back, leaving me sprawled across the tabletop. He takes a ragged breath, runs a hand through his hair and his whole demeanor switches. He looks suddenly surly. "What?"

"Dude, open up! I got your phone!"

Holden's hands fly around his body, checking all his pockets frantically and then he sighs. "Fuck," he whispers and then walks the short distance to the door and opens it just a crack. But Kidd's not having it and smacks the palm of his hand against it and pushes it wide open and steps inside.

He holds up Holden's phone as I scramble off the table to my feet. "Hey! You forgot this at the bar when you were hustling that dude at pool. How much did you make off him anyway? Like, fifty?"

"Thanks," Holden grumbles.

He lied to me. He said he was alone, but he was with Kidd hustling someone out of their money. Just like old Holden. Kidd's beady eyes skitter over to me and widen before narrowing in a way that can only be described as unsettling. He licks his lips. "Didn't realize you were leaving us for Larry."

Asshole. His stare is making me self-conscious and I suddenly do not want to be here—especially not in my dad's old sweater and worn out cutoffs. I realize with the length of the sweater it might look, to his drunken eye, like I don't have any bottoms on at all. I need to be anywhere but here. I limp past him toward the door.

"You two got a little rough or what?" he asks no one in particular as he points to my knee.

"Shut the fuck up," I snap.

"You're a little darker than you used to be, Larry. I like it," Kidd remarks. I ignore him and fling open the door.

"Call her Larry again and I will deck you, Kidd," Holden says and reaches for my arm as I start down the steps totally awkwardly thanks to my throbbing, swollen knee.

I look up at him and yank my arm free, which makes me stumble and almost fall. He jumps down and grabs for me again. Damn it. "We made a mistake."

"I didn't."

"I did," I say and pull away from him. "You lied to me and you're still hanging out with him. We both know he's bad news."

"No, I wasn't," he says with conviction.

"That would be believable if he didn't have your phone," I reply and pull my arm free. "Later, Holden."

I march up the stairs and onto the porch, grabbing the wine bottle I left there before heading into the house and locking the door behind me. He hasn't changed...at least not much. Not enough.

9

HOLDEN

Two days go by and we walk around pretending we don't know each other, which is bullshit and awkward as hell because we are the only two people in this house. But I let it happen because I feel like a bit of an asshole. I lied to her. I was drunk, but I knew I was doing it. I just didn't want her to know the truth and I figured she'd never find out. She wouldn't have hung out with me if she knew where I'd been. We wouldn't have had that intense connection or that fucking hot-as-hell kiss. Everything about hanging out with Winnie that night was like nothing I've ever experienced, if I'm being honest with myself. The alcohol made us honest and that made the kiss heated and vulnerable all at the same time.

If Kidd hadn't shown up, I had every intention of turning that kiss into much more. But he did and the expression on her face went from beautifully vulnerable to horrifically exposed. I don't want to be the guy she knew who hung out with Kidd and so I don't hold it against her for not wanting to kiss that guy.

I shouldn't have gone out and gotten shit-faced after I fought with her. I was just so fucking frustrated and I felt like I couldn't do a goddamn thing right. I needed to let off all the steam boiling inside of me. So after I picked up my truck at Bradie's, I went to the Brunswick. I totally forgot that Kidd said he hangs out there all the time. And of course he was there with all the other guys I knew when I was young and stupid and making poor choices like it was my job. I ignored the gut feeling to turn around and leave. I bought them a round of tequila shots instead. And then they bought me a round and then Kidd somehow convinced me to play some pool and then these local punks thought they could beat me so of course I had them bet on it. It was my old self, not the totally bad self, but the one who walks a slippery slope and didn't mind slipping off it. And I got drunk, which never has never led to great decisions. So when Kidd and the guys started talking about the old times and how cool we were and how we should hang out more often, I realize I was full-on wasted because it started to sound like a good idea. So I told them I needed to take a piss and slipped out the back door. I was in such a stupor and such a rush I didn't realize I didn't have my phone. At least I was smart enough to leave the truck in the parking lot and not drive.

When I got home and saw her standing there, and realized she not only turned on the lights so I didn't kill myself on lawn furniture, but she also ordered me a pizza—*my favorite childhood pizza*—I felt like the universe was rewarding me for making a good decision. Finally. She looked fucking glorious in those little shorts and an oversized sweater that I realize now must belong to her dad. That kiss, it felt like a reward. Like I was finally worthy of a good girl.

But it turns out, like with everything in my life, the universe wasn't rewarding me. It was setting me up for more punishment. Because Kidd had to fucking bring me my phone—and then ogle her like a piece of meat in a butcher shop window. I told him off and threatened to punch the attitude out of him, but she'd already disappeared into the house. And I doubt Winnie is the type of girl who's impressed by violence.

Now it's two days later at eight in the morning and I'm standing in the driveway, sipping my coffee and trying to figure out how I can get us back to that moment where we connected—mentally and physically. I don't like being at odds with her. It's easy to fight with her, it's comfortable, which is something I haven't felt since being back in this town. But bonding with her felt *good*. I liked it because I like her and easy or not I don't want to go back to being enemies. I want to feel her touch me again. I want to kiss her again. I think that's an impossible task and I just need to settle for getting us back to acknowledging each other's existence. I finish my coffee, place the mug on the small patio table by the trailer door, grab my tool belt off the lawn chair and head up to the porch.

I knock, knowing that she won't answer because she never does, and then stick my key in the door. On the porch, there are two wine bottles on the table by the rocking chairs. One is empty the other only half full. There's still wine in a glass next to it. Same scene as yesterday and the day before. I step into the house and walk back to the kitchen. I ripped out all the counters and cabinets yesterday. Some of my coworkers from my last job have agreed to freelance for me and are coming over today to help me get rid of the appliances and take down the wall that separates the kitchen from the dining room.

I pause and listen. If she's here, she's still asleep. I walk over to the fridge and open it. Exact same contents as yesterday when I snuck a peek, which means she didn't eat last night. I heard her crying again. I feel for her but I know, now that I realize she's mourning her father, that she has to have her tears. For now.

"Winnie?" I call out and I'm not surprised when she doesn't respond.

I walk through the house to the staircase and call out again. "Winnie! I have some crew coming over to help me with demo."

Nothing.

I sigh in frustration and walk to the front of the house again. I don't want to go up there and walk in on her, so I have to hope she's gone. I pass the first-floor bedroom and something catches my eye through the half open door—a long, toned, bare calf. I step closer. She isn't moving and judging by the position of her leg, she's facedown on the bed. I knock on the door, which causes it to swing open more but doesn't make Winnie stir at all. She's out cold.

I take a step into the room. Just as I guessed, she's splayed out across the queen bed, face mashed in a pillow. She's wearing tiny pajama shorts and a T-shirt with what appears to be concert dates on the back but it's hard to tell because it's all crumpled up, leaving most of her lower back exposed. Her skin looks so supple and perfect and the bright pink dots on her pajama shorts are forcing me to look her ass and admire the full round shape of it.

She lets out the softest little groan and her left leg, which was bent, straightens slowly. I clear my throat. "Winnie. There's a bunch of guys coming to do more demo. You probably wanna go upstairs or get out of here. It's gonna be loud."

"You're loud right now," she says, but it's muffled by the pillow.

I smile. I'm actually talking in a softer voice than normal. I clear my throat and raise my voice a little. "Hungover just a little, huh?"

"Why are you yelling?" she groans and starts to roll over but somehow fails and falls back into the pillow.

I look around the room. This is clearly her parents' bedroom and I don't think she slept here so much as passed out here. She's still wearing one slipper and there's an empty chip bag on the floor and some paper. I grab the crap off the floor. "Winnie, you have to get up. I'll go make some coffee for you. And you'll probably want to grab a shower before everyone gets here. I'm going to have to turn off the water."

She starts to roll over again. Her stomach is exposed stomach and I find myself running my tongue slowly across my lips. I feel my jeans start to get tighter and I know if I stay in the small room with her, which is taken up mostly by a bed, things will only get worse. So, I turn and leave the room, carrying her garbage to the kitchen. I'm flipping open the lid on the trash can when I hear her yell out my name in a voice choked with panic.

"Holden!"

It sounds like there is a herd of elephants coming at me and suddenly she's banging into me and grabbing the crap in my hands. The look on her face is pure hysteria. The chip bag and Kleenex flutters to the floor and she's standing there clutching the paper in her hands. "You almost threw it out!"

"Threw what out?" I ask because I can't tell what she's holding.

"Don't touch anything, okay?" she says her voice shaky but also furious. And I glance down at the paper in her hands, which are shaking. I can only make out four words in neatly printed penmanship—*My sweet Winona Skye*. It's a letter from someone. I'm guessing her dad or her ex.

"Not a thing," she says hotly. "If you want to throw anything out, ask me first. I can't believe you almost threw it out!"

She turns and storms from the room. I follow behind, confused as fuck. "Threw what out? Jesus, Winnie, talk to me."

"Why?" she snaps back. "We've been doing just fine ignoring each other. Besides, I said everything you need to know. Do *not* throw anything out without asking me."

She's stomping up the stairs now and I can do nothing but stand at the bottom, rigid with frustration. This woman is making no sense and I don't have the time or energy for this ridiculousness. "You can make your own damn coffee!"

"I don't want coffee," she calls back and then she's stomping down the stairs, wrapped in a robe, holding a towel. She barges past me. "Now can you go wait somewhere else until I am done?"

"I'll be on the porch," I bark back.

Fifteen minutes later, my crew is pulling to the curb in

their trucks and as I lead them into the house, I can hear her thumping around upstairs. Good, she's out of the way.

We go about demoing for a good three hours and I don't even try to be quiet. I fully expect her to leave the house to get away from the noise and dust so I'm not surprised, as we take a quick break and the guys head outside for a smoke, when I see her come downstairs. I can't help but notice she's not limping anymore, which is good.

I'm standing next to where the wall used to be between the kitchen and dining room. She stops and surveys the pile of drywall on the ground. Her eyes move from the pile to me. "Is there some bylaw that handymen don't wear shirts in this state?"

I glance down at my bare chest. "Have you ever busted down drywall? You work up a sweat."

"I haven't," she says, walking past me and into the bath-room. She leaves the door ajar and I watch her open the medicine cabinet and pull out a bottle of Advil. "But you know Jude sweats a lot during hockey and he wears a special shirt. Dri-Fit or dry weave or something. You should look into that."

She palms two Advils.

I point to the drywall debris and try to ignore the fact that she has an aversion to seeing me shirtless and that it makes me a little disappointed. "You should really try breaking up some drywall. It's great for anger management and you seem like you could use some."

"I'm not angry." She argues and downs the pills without water and then puts the bottle back in the medicine cabinet.

"That's coming down later today too," I say, nodding toward the medicine cabinet and I'm greeted with a slightly softer look of panic that I got earlier.

"Do *not* throw this out," she says, pointing to the medicine cabinet. "My dad made it himself. He gave it to my mom when they first got married."

"Okay," I say. "I will make sure we keep it safe and sound. Now you want to tell me what was on that paper that I was going to throw out?"

"No." She steps out of the bathroom as the guys come back in from their smoke break.

I pick up a chunk of drywall and hold it out as if to show her. "I'm going to toss this in the construction bin Mike hauled here this morning. Is that okay?"

She scrunches up her eyebrows and looks at me like I'm nuts. "Yeah."

Mike bends to grab another piece but as he tries to walk toward the door, I stop him. My eyes find her again. "Is it okay if he throws that piece out?"

"Yes," she snaps. Her hazel eyes are dancing with irritation, and she puts her hands on her hips. "What are you doing?"

"You said I had to check with you before removing anything," I remind her.

She looks incredibly annoyed, which is great because that's exactly what I was going for. I glance over at Mike and Dave, who seem to have caught on to my game and are both trying to hide smiles. Winnie glares at me. "I give you permission to remove all the drywall you spent the morning tearing down. Happy now?"

"Delighted," I reply and give her a wink, which makes her hands ball up into fists at her side. I motion toward the heap of drywall again. "You sure you don't want to take a swing at that? Break up a few of the bigger pieces. I know you said you aren't angry but that look on your face—"

She's stomping back upstairs before I can finish my sentence. She's more than a little bit gorgeous when she's furious, which doesn't make me want to stop annoying her. Mike chuckles as he walks by me with an armload of debris. "She's a firecracker," he says. "You keep playing with that you're going to get burned."

"Yeah or have your dick blown off," Dave adds and grins. "Get it? Firecracker."

"Don't quit your day job, Dave," Mike mutters and I nod as I follow him out the front door to the bin he brought over here this morning.

As we're outside hauling our second load of debris, Winnie emerges from the screened porch and grabs her bike from the side of the house. I give her a look, like a judgmental father. She looks sheepish for a fraction of a second before she goes back to glaring at me. "I hope you're done by the time I get back."

"I've gotta be outta here by four, if that helps," Mike says.

"Only helps if you take him with you," Winnie replies, hops on the bike and pedals off. I try not to worry about her having another wipeout. It's not my business, but yet...it's in the back of my mind.

After she's disappeared around the corner, I turn to Mike. "Dude, I was hoping we'd work longer today."

"I have to go to practice," he explains, wiping his brow with his meaty forearm. "I'm an assistant coach for the Portland Pirates now."

I blink. The Portland Pirates is the hockey team my nephew Duke is on. "Since when?"

"Since the guy they had was caught drinking at the pre-season tournament last week," Mike explains. "He was totally drunk during one of the games. You know my kid plays for them and they're already short on coaches. They should have two assistants and they only had this douche."

"Wow. I didn't know." I scratch my beard and try to ignore the ache in my chest. If Bradie trusted me or even just liked me, she would have told me about that kind of thing. "What do you have to do to coach?"

"Take a test and have experience," Mike explains and then he looks a little uncomfortable as he adds, "And have no criminal record."

"I don't have a criminal record," I explain because my past has been widely exaggerated by the small town rumor mill. "I have a sealed juvenile record."

Mike looks shocked, which I'm annoyingly used to by now. We head back inside to grab another load of debris as Dave passes us carrying a load out. "Oh, I thought...sorry. So yeah, you could be a coach. You would be excellent at it. You've got a ton more experience than most of us. Hell, you were a heartbeat from the NHL."

I haven't had that fact thrown at me in a long time, but it still stings when I hear it. It's not Mike's fault though so I just nod and push it down to that place in my gut that's overflowing with regrets. I put my work gloves back on and grab some of the drywall. "I'd love to apply or whatever, if you really have an opening."

Mike pauses, pulls off his work gloves and takes his phone out of this back pocket. "I'm emailing you the head coach's info right now. Bruce Skelton. You might know him."

I do know him. He was about five years older than me but played with Jude and me in the summer league here when we were kids. I give Mike a thankful nod and go back to hauling out the mess. This is the perfect opportunity to spend more time with Duke, and hopefully force Bradie into seeing me in a better light. And honestly, I never thought of coaching hockey before but now that I am thinking of it, I am excited by the idea. My love for the game has never faltered, even when my chance to play professionally disappeared. I would love the opportunity to get out there and be involved with hockey again.

The rest of the day is grueling, but we get more accomplished than I expected. The kitchen is basically a shell and will be ready tomorrow for the electrician I'm bringing in to rewire everything. As Mike and Dave leave, I lock up the house and then open the email Mike sent me and call Bruce. He not only remembers me and sounds happy to hear from me, he's thrilled with the idea that I want to coach. I find myself wandering up the street to the beach as we talk. He says he'll send me the application and the test and if all goes well I can start next week.

I get off the phone feeling excited for the first time in a long time. I've spent months just busting my ass at work, planning, budgeting, worrying about getting this business off the ground. I haven't done a thing that was pure enjoyment. Coaching feels like a treat and I get to be around Duke. From what I can see so far, he's a great kid and I'm looking forward to really getting to know him.

My muscles ache and I'm drenched in sweat, but I feel good. Instead of showering, I decide, fuck it. I'm going for a swim. The beach is basically deserted. There's an old guy way at the other end with his dog and I can see the tops of two heads near the dunes really far at the other end. No one will notice that I'm just in underwear so fuck it. I bend down, pull my feet out of my work boots and socks and then start undoing my jeans. I wore black boxer briefs today so that helps. I leave everything in a heap and break into a run across the warm sand.

10

WINNIE

Holy shit, he is stripping," Cat exclaims suddenly, pulling my attention from the lobster roll I'm devouring. I look up and follow the tilt of her head. "Check out at that body. He's a work of art. Oh and speaking of art, tattoos! I love tattoos. Oh God, I hope he thinks this is a nude beach."

Cat has no idea who he is, but I do. I recognized him instantly, even from this distance. And I find myself wishing he thought it was a nude beach too, which is why I'm blushing. Cat gets to her knees on our blanket, but I grab her arm. "What? I think I should introduce myself. I can offer him my lobster roll...or anything else he wants."

"You know him," I tell her. "That's Holden Hendricks."

Cat's mouth drops open and her head spins around to look again, squinting as she examines him. He's running directly at the ocean and he doesn't slow down, even though I know the water must be frigid. It's always cold. His muscular arms extend above his head and he dives into an oncoming wave.

"What the fuck." Cat gasps. "Why does he get to be the hottest thing in this town? He's a dick! Why can't it be a nice, sweet boy who gets nearly naked on the beach and makes me want to give him my virtue and my lobster roll."

Internally I ask the universe the same question, but out loud I say, "Never give up your lobster roll, Cat. To anyone."

I take another bite of my own, but my eyes won't leave the surf and as Holden emerges, dripping wet and gleaming in the late afternoon sun, I have to admit, he's more decadent and satisfying than my meal. "I know my eyes are bad without my glasses, but how did you recognize him so quickly?"

I reach for my cream soda and take a sip. Holden dives into another wave. "He's renovating my cottage."

I can feel Cat's disbelieving stare even though I'm not looking at her. "Right now? While you live in it?"

"Yep," I say with a nod. "Jude hired him and I didn't know."

"Oh God, no wonder you've been coming by every day," Cat says and pauses to take another bite of her own lobster roll. "I'd be avoiding my house too if he was in it. But then again, I'd probably stick around to make sure he doesn't steal anything."

"I trust him," I reply without even thinking about it. I do. I know his reputation. I saw firsthand what Cat went through, but something in me wants to believe I can trust him.

"You think he's changed?" Cat sounds absolutely astonished at the thought.

Holden body surfs a wave almost to the shore, then pops up, shakes the water from his hair and runs his hands through it. I wonder what it would be like to kiss him again, his body slick with water. He'd be slippery and his mouth would taste like salt.

"Winnie!" Cat's sharp tone snaps my head toward her. She's got an incredulous look all over her face. "You're attracted to him."

"I...I mean..." Why am I going to lie about this? "How could I not be? Look at him."

Cat laughs at that but grows serious a second later. "So you think he's changed? He's not a thieving, borderline psychopath like he used to be?"

"Definitely not," I reply. "He's been kind of sweet to me. He helped me when I wiped out on my bike. And we had a really good...talk."

Cat's eyebrows jump at that. "Talk? You said that weird. Why?"

Because the talk was interrupted by our make-out session.

"Because it felt like I was really getting to know him and he wasn't who I thought he was, but then Kidd showed up," I explain as my eyes drift over to the ocean again. Holden is just standing there, his back to the shore, letting the waves crash around him. "Holden had been out drinking with him and swindling people at pool and so I wonder if I was wrong."

"If he's still buddies with Kidd then yeah, you're wrong," Cat says decisively as she crumples up the wrapper from her now demolished lobster roll. "That guy was, is and always will be trash. You know Kidd knocked up a girl I went to high school with but doesn't do shit for her or the kid. He's like an absentee dad but he lives with them. She can't get him to change a diaper let alone pay some rent."

Holden is walking out of the water now. I can't stop my gaze from drifting straight down to his soaking wet underwear. It's clinging tightly to his thighs and ass and the impressive bulge in the front. Desire ripples through me. I don't know if he can feel my eyes on him, but he turns his head and looks right at us. His step falters for a moment and then his whole, wet, chiseled body shifts and he starts walking toward us instead of to his discarded belongings.

Cat grabs her bottle of root beer in one hand and her flip-flops in the other. "I don't think he's changed," she announces. "And since he's not renovating my house, I don't have to talk to him. See you later. Remember, you promised to go out with me tonight."

Cat turns away and starts up the beach toward the boardwalk. I watch her go and fight the urge to change my mind on the whole going out thing. She really wants a girls' night and I really should try to do something other than drink and cry.

"Hey," he says and I turn back to find him about a foot from me. Just standing there in his wet underwear like some kind of *Baywatch* extra. "Was that Cat Cannon with you?"

I nod. "Yeah."

His eyes drop from mine and land on the small scrap of lobster roll still in my left hand. "Is that a lobster roll from her store?"

I nod again. He groans. It's wanton and the sound creates a warm sensation between my legs. "God, those things are the best in the state. I fucking love the way they butter then grill the bun and don't drown the lobster in mayo."

Without even thinking about it, I hold out the remaining chunk. Those silver-blue eyes widen. "It's all yours."

He steps closer, now his perfect body is so close that when he leans forward to take the roll, I'm lightly sprinkled with ocean water from his hair and shoulders. He plucks it from my hand and pops it in his mouth and I'm greeted with another one of those shameless groans. So. Hot.

"You know you can buy your own. You don't have to eat my scraps," I tell him as I start to get up. Sitting here on the blanket with him right in front of me means my eyes are in line with his package. And that view combined with that groan is too much for my girl bits to take.

He reaches out to help me to my feet, but I ignore his outstretched hand and manage on my own. A disappointed expression drifts across his face but it's gone in seconds and he shrugs. "Cat made it clear I'm not welcome at Cannon's Corner Grocery."

I'm torn between feeling sorry for him and completely understanding Cat's point of view. I reach down and grab the blanket Cat and I were sitting on. "I should get going."

"You headed back to the house?" he asks and runs a hand through his hair sending any remaining water droplets flying. My eyes follow one as it lands on his shoulder and starts a leisurely decent down his chest. "Water is back on in your place. Still have to use the trailer for showers for now, though, until the new one is installed."

My mouth starts to water and all I can do is nod. He smiles and I'm worried he's getting off on my getting off on his nearly nakedness. It makes me blush. "You know they make these things called swimsuits."

"I've heard that rumor," he replies with a smirk. "But the

boxer briefs work in a pinch. You look a little warm yourself so you should try it."

"You want me to swim in my underwear?" I raise a brow.

"I wouldn't complain if you did," he says. His voice is heavy and low like it was the other night in his trailer when we drunkenly kissed. However neither one of us is drunk...I don't think.

"I like my underwear dry," I declare and instantly regret it.

If this were a baseball game, I would have just served him the perfect pitch and of course he knocks it out of the park when he replies. "It's more fun when it's wet."

The smile on his face is pure mischief and damn...my underwear is definitely not dry. "You're a child," I tell him, but I'm biting back a smile and he can see it so I turn and start toward the boardwalk.

I can feel his eyes on me as I go and it's doing nothing to quell my overwhelming attraction to him. I know what I heard and saw the other night, after the make-out session when Kidd showed up. It should make me wary—and it does—when I think about it. But when I'm near him...when we're just hanging out like we were just now—all of that concern disappears. I want to be close to him, not keep my distance.

As I reach the end of the boardwalk and start to slip my feet back into my flip-flops, I glance over my shoulder and find him walking toward me. His jeans are back on but the button is undone and he's shirtless, carrying his shoes.

"You need to live a little," he says as I start walking and he falls in step beside me.

"I'm living."

"I'll rephrase. You need to start having fun," he says.

"You think swimming in the freezing cold ocean in my underwear would be fun?" I ask as we pass Cat's store and I stop to grab my bike and put the blanket in the basket.

"I enjoyed it," he says and glances at the door to the grocery store. I can't tell if he's nervous Cat will come out or he's trying to decide whether to risk his life for his own lobster roll and go inside.

"I'm going out tonight," I announce and that turns his attention, and his gaze, from the grocery store door. "Cat asked me to go out with her."

I can't tell if he looks impressed or concerned. He rubs his beard. "Where you guys heading?"

"No idea," I reply because I don't know. I didn't ask.

He nods and we walk the rest of the way back to the cottage in silence. When we hit the driveway, he pauses near his trailer as I keep walking to tuck the bike in against the side of the house. "So are we ever going to talk about that kiss?" he asks.

Oh God. I stop at the foot of the stairs to the porch, and shield my eyes against the sun so I can look at him. He is so damn handsome and the look on his face is pure vulnerability again. He is just as uncomfortable about this as I am. So why is he bringing it up? I decide to let us both off the hook. "You're acting like you've never made a drunken mistake before," I say and give him a small shrug before climbing the stairs. "If you're worried about what I'm thinking, don't be. I'm not blaming you for it. Have a good night."

I don't give him a chance to respond because honestly,

anything he could say will only make it more awkward. As I walk into the house, I look around and try to absorb all the changes. The whole ground floor looks bigger now with the wall down. I wonder if my dad would be excited to see it this way. He always planned on doing these renovations. My heart starts to ache again. God, I wish he were here. I take a shuddering breath and wipe the tears from my eyes and head upstairs to get ready to go out with Cat.

Four hours later, I'm sitting at a table by the plate-glass window at Riptide's, a bar at the end of the pier in the next town over. Cat has just told me a story about her last Tinder date. "How many ex-girlfriends' names were tattooed on him?' I ask, trying not to laugh as I sip my piña colada.

"Fourteen!" Cat squeals, still clearly horrified by the experience. "But he told me not to worry, he had room for my name if I played my cards right."

I almost choke on my drink. "Oh dear God."

"I know, right?" Cat shakes her head. "So if a cute guy named Tony swipes right on you while you're here, you've been warned."

"I'm not on any dating apps and I don't intend to be any time soon," I say. "But thanks for the tip!"

"How long are you staying? Have you decided?"

I shake my head. "I don't know. I'm thinking about staying until spring. I have enough savings to get by."

"Wow, really?" Cat looks stunned. "I'm telling you, it's very boring and very lonely in the winter."

"I know." I take a sip of my drink and push my hair back over my shoulder. "I'm actually looking forward to that.

I spent the last couple of years living with my sister and my parents again, with the rest of my family within walking distance. I need the alone time."

"Maybe, but I don't think you grasp how incredibly boring it will get," she replies and sighs. "It really is a summer town and that's the income that floats us through the winter. I can go two or three days and not have one person come into the shop."

"Maybe you shouldn't ban people then," I say half jokingly. "I bet Holden would be in there every day for lobster rolls if you let him."

"I'm not that desperate for cash," Cat says tersely and finishes her drink in one big gulp. "Where's Ginny?"

Just like with everyone in this town, Cat is on a first-name basis with the staff here. She waves at Ginny who comes right over with a big smile on her face. "Another?" Ginny asks. After Cat nods, she looks over to me. "How about you, sugar?"

I look at my almost empty glass. "What the hell."

"Gin, before you go, explain to Winnie here why we hate Holden Hendricks," Cat says.

Ginny, who was about to walk back to the bar to get our order, pauses and puts a hand on her hip. "I don't hate him," she announces and for a brief, fleeting moment I relax. I really just don't want to hear bad things about him, which is crazy because I shouldn't care, but that kiss made me care. "I just don't trust him as far as I can throw him, and there's no way I can throw him. That boy is the size of a small pickup truck."

"See?" Cat says with a triumph smile on her cherry red lips. "It's not just me."

"Oh, he's banned from here," Ginny explains. "Been that way since he was sixteen and came in here with fake ID and started a brawl that brought the cops and got the owner fined because he didn't catch the fake ID. Plus his sister, Bradie, used to work here and we're all still good friends with her including the owner. I saw her just last week and she says he hasn't changed. He pretends he's different, but in the end he pulls the same old garbage, like offering to help her out and bailing on her."

I have no reason not to take Ginny's words as the truth but...for some reason I don't. I feel like there's more to the story than she knows. Why would the guy who went out of his way to help me when I was hurt blow off his own sister when she needed him? He wouldn't. Would he? Unless...were those the plans that got messed up because he helped me when I wiped out on my bike?

Ginny looks at me. "Didn't you punch him in the face when you were younger? Or was that one of your sisters?"

I give her a sheepish smile. "Yeah that was me."

Cat giggles. "Oh my God, I had forgotten about that! Why did you do that again?"

"Because he tried to fight my brother," I reply. "It was dumb. Jude didn't need me to defend him. Holden was drunk and really angry and just picking on Jude for no reason and honestly, he used to pick on me all the time when we were teenagers so I think I just needed an excuse."

"You're my hero," Ginny says and winks. "I'll be back with the drinks in a jiffy and consider them on the house."

I watch her head back to the bar and turn back to Cat. She gives me a sympathetic smile. "Look, I know that you're going through a lot right now. Of course you're feeling raw and kind of alone, but please think twice before you lean on that boy for anything—emotional or physical. I mean, I get it. He is pretty, but that's the outside. On the inside he ain't pretty."

I avert my eyes, staring out at the churning water beyond the windows and I nod. Not because I agree with her but because I just don't want to talk about it—him—anymore. My stomach churns, and I feel so conflicted. I can see Cat and Ginny's points. However, I also feel like I know him in a way they don't. I'm also worried I'm letting that kiss color my opinion.

Cat and I stay at Riptide's for another couple of hours and then she tells me she has to get home or she won't be able to get up and make the cinnamon buns tomorrow. Not wanting to deprive the locals of the delicacy, I don't argue, even though I'm not at all tired and not looking forward to going home and being alone. Being out and doing something has been good for me.

The walk home isn't long, but the temperature has plunged in the last few hours and fall weather is definitely here. It's downright chilly and I didn't bring a sweater. Cat notices me shiver and gives me a sympathetic smile. "If you think this is bad, wait until November."

"It's just that it was so warm this afternoon," I complain and she nods.

"Yep, you know what they say, if you don't like the

weather in Maine, wait a minute." She grins at her own joke. "Your place is heated, right? I know not all cottages are."

"Yeah, my dad had it winterized when I was a kid because he had always planned on retiring here," I say and that all too familiar wave of grief crests inside me.

"I can't believe you don't want to go back to San Francisco," Cat says and looks at me like I'm a puzzle she can't solve. "You'd have better weather and more nightlife and your family. Hell, just talking about it makes me want to move there."

I laugh but it's hollow, just like I feel. "San Francisco is nice—don't get me wrong—but it never felt like home," I say, which is something I haven't told anyone. "And Toronto isn't home anymore because there's nothing left there for me. This place was always the one constant in my life and I love it here."

"I do too," Cat replies and gives me a quick side hug. "I'd never leave the business or the state, but...California just seems like such a dream."

"It's not a dream when you're there to watch your dad die," I blurt out.

She gives me another side hug and I look away, willing the sadness to stay at bay. I had been doing so well tonight. As I blink back tears, I notice two men standing on the edge of the sidewalk, near a hedge just up ahead. They're huddled together, heads down, as if having some kind of secret conversation. My step falters. "Is that Holden?"

Cat's head snaps forward and her eyes narrow at the very same time the two men step apart and look at us. She doesn't need to answer because it's clear as day—that is Holden Hendricks. I'm startled because I didn't expect to see him out at almost midnight but Cat's expression is more than startled, it's disturbed. "Yeah and that guy he's with is the town drug dealer."

"What?" I gasp, like an idiot.

"Hey!" Holden says and starts toward us. He glances back at the guy he was talking to. "Take care, Kevin."

Kevin nods and walks away without looking back. Holden stops on the sidewalk directly in front of us. "You guys have a good night?"

"Until now, yes," Cat snaps at him and it makes him frown. She doesn't seem to care as she looks over at me. "Come on, let's go."

I try not to look him in the eyes as she tugs me down the sidewalk. I shouldn't feel bad, but for some reason I do. We walk another two blocks and Cat looks over her shoulder and frowns as she stops and turns around. "Why are you following us?"

"I'm not. I'm heading home," Holden replies, frustration tainting his voice.

"Can you walk some other way?" Cat asks.

"No," he says flatly and his shoulders visibly tense. "Look, I get it. I fucked up with you—with everyone—when I was a kid and you're never forgiving me. Fine. But let me fucking live my life."

He brushes by us on the sidewalk and storms ahead. His aggressive reaction startles me, but I get it. He's frustrated. I find myself feeling bad for him. I want Cat to give him a chance...I want to give him one too...I just don't know if I can. We walk about a half a block behind him until we reach Cat's street and she stops and gives me a hug. "You going to be all right?"

"Of course," I say with a chuckle that I almost choke on. "Holden is harmless."

She looks like I just told her Hannibal Lecter likes to snuggle. I ignore it and wave good-bye as I continue walking. "Save me a cinnamon roll in the morning."

I can hear her sigh as she turns down her street. Holden is just a shadow up ahead—shoulders hunched, head down. I find myself picking up my pace until I'm almost stepping on the back of his heels. He knows I'm there but he doesn't acknowledge me and it makes me feel worse. "I'm sorry about Cat."

"Don't be," he growls back. "It's fine."

"Yeah, I guess," I mutter. "I mean she is still bitter about her grandmother's pearls and I would be too if you took something sentimental from me."

"Like whatever the hell is on that paper you had with you the other day?"

I wasn't expecting the conversation to move to that, so it's like a bit of a gut punch. But when he finally glances over at me, as I step up beside him, I nod. "Yeah. Like that."

"Are you going to tell me what that was?" Holden asks.

"A letter from my dad," I say but my voice is scratchy and dry so I force myself to swallow. "He left each of us a letter to read after he died."

He doesn't say anything for a second as we walk and then

he nods slowly. "That's gotta be nice and yet painful at the same time."

"Exactly."

We turn onto our street. The air is getting cooler and cooler because we're getting closer to the ocean and I shiver. He notices and starts to pull off the jacket he's wearing. I shake my head, but he ignores me and drops it over my shoulders.

"God, you're confusing," I sigh.

"Excuse me?" I can tell by his tone that he's annoyed.

"It's just the way you are with me is the opposite of the way you are," I say in the worst attempt at an explanation ever. The confused and annoyed look on his face reflects that. So I try again. "I mean, you're nice to me and funny and even borderline charming."

"Borderline charming," he repeats and smirks. "I should put that on a T-shirt."

"But then you're still friends with assholes like Kidd and I find you on a dark street corner talking to a guy Cat claims is the local drug dealer," I say and lift my hair out from under the jacket he draped around me. "And I hope I don't have to say that I don't want any drugs anywhere near my property."

He stops dead in his tracks a few feet from my driveway. His jaw is clenched and his shoulders are rigid, but he has a wounded look on his face so I'm not surprised he turns and starts storming toward his trailer without another word. I find myself chasing after him. "Holden, look, I'm just saying you confuse me!"

He turns so quickly it shocks me and I step back. "No. You're saying you think I'm still a fucked-up kid. Or worse, that I wasn't just a fucked-up kid, I'm an inherently bad human being. And that's not at all the case."

"I don't...I'm sorry," I stumble over my words like a guilty-as-sin, completely inept criminal because that's what I feel like.

"You should be," he snaps and steps closer so we're toe-to-toe and then he reaches out. I assume he's reaching for his jacket but his arm circles my waist instead. He yanks me until our torsos bump. I shiver again, but I'm anything but cold. "The truth is, whether you know it or not, you're searching for excuses. Reasons why you can't like me. Because you do. You like me and you loved that kiss."

His arm around my waist tightens and my heart takes off in a gallop. I open my mouth to speak—but what am I going to say? *You're right.* Because he is, but I'm not willing to admit it, at least not in words. I'm pretty certain that, as I rock up on my toes and wrap my arms around his neck as I lay one on him that he's getting the message.

He takes over the kiss, parting my lips and claiming my mouth with his tongue and my body collapses against him in relief. I realize in this moment, that no matter who he is or isn't, he is exactly what I need. And that revelation is chilling because I'm still so lost. He might be my light at the end of the tunnel, but I don't know if he's as dangerous as an on-coming train. So when he pulls away abruptly, that too feels like a relief.

"What are we doing?" I ask desperately.

"I know what I'm doing, Winnie," Holden says firmly as he slowly takes a few steps backward, away from me. "I'm building a new, better my life with my business and falling for an amazing girl…but I don't know what you're doing and I'm pretty sure you don't know either and that's why I'm walking away right now. Good night."

He walks into his trailer and shuts the door, leaving me alone and flustered in his jacket with the taste of his kiss still on my lips.

11

HOLDEN

Duke smiles at me, and I swear to God it's the best thing in the whole damn world. It's so bright and so genuine that it completely overrides any whisper of guilt gnawing at me over the fact I didn't mention this to Bradie at all...yet. But in my defense, she's not talking to me anyway. I figure she'll find out now, since I'm waiting with him in the lobby of the arena after practice. Duke hitches his hockey bag higher on his shoulder. "So is this, like, permanent? Are you our coach now?"

I nod. "Looks like it. I mean, Coach really wants me on the team and I want to be here. How about you? You good with it?"

"Totally!" Duke exclaims with an even bigger grin than before. "Mom said you used to play, but she didn't say that you were good."

I chuckle at that. Of course she didn't. "I had my moments back in the day."

"Yeah right. Coach said you were almost in the NHL. That's awesome." Duke is awestruck and I don't feel the least bit worthy but it still makes me feel incredible.

"What would have been awesome is if he had stuck with it and made the NHL." Bradie's hard voice fills the air and I turn and see her standing behind me. Her slender arms are crossed and her lips are set in a hard flat line. She is pissed to see me. What else is new?

"It would have been much better," I agree with her. "Hey, Bradie. How are you?"

"What are you doing here?" she asks.

"I'm coaching hockey now," I explain with a shrug.

"Since when?" she asks.

"Since last week," I reply, trying not to feel sheepish for purposely avoiding running into her after practices. "A friend of mine told me they were short, so I volunteered."

Bradie is still annoyed. "So he knows? I didn't say you could tell him."

"Knows what?" Duke asks.

"Coach kept it vague. I asked him not to include my last name," I say and Duke is hanging on every word. "If I take the job, he'll have to give the parents my last name, though."

"What are you guys talking about?"

Bradie looks at her son and sighs. "Holden is my brother, which makes him your uncle."

Duke's eyes get bigger and ping-pong between Bradie and I and then he grins. "Can I call him Uncle Holden? I want the kids to know we're related."

Oh my God. My heart swells. Bradie looks at me. I nod. "Yeah sure, bud. Call me whatever you want."

"He's great, Mom!" Duke says. "He taught us this new stick-handling drill and it was awesome."

Man, I remember being his age and being so damn excited about everything. Those were the days. Bradie was never like that. She was always serious and skeptical. When Mom died, I once accused her of being relieved, like it finally gave her a valid reason to be miserable. Yeah, not my finest moment. But I was thirteen and lonely and wanted a sibling I could bond with since I didn't feel like I had anyone.

"You don't like it, clearly," I say to her and step closer, lowering my voice so hopefully Duke doesn't overhear. "I'll quit if it's really that big a deal to you."

She sighs. "Whatever. You can keep coaching. I'll probably have to pull him from the team one day soon anyway. He has to maintain a certain level of grades to be allowed to play and he isn't doing that."

Duke's face falls. "Mom!"

She turns on him with a stern but sympathetic look. "I'm not changing the rules, Duke. I was very clear from the beginning. B average or no extra sports crap. And your math teacher emailed me and said you're barely holding onto a C and you only have a couple of tests left to bring it up."

"I'm trying. I suck at math because math sucks," he declares his voice filled with frustration.

I want to help plead his case, but it's not my place and Bradie isn't stupid. School is more important than sports. I wish someone had made me see that when I was his age because I would have probably had the grades to get into college instead of having to take online business classes from some made-up college no one has heard of.

He makes a noise like a huff choking on a groan and storms

toward the doors to the parking lot, well, as much as a ten-year-old can storm. Bradie glares at me again. "I'm not being a bitch. He needs good grades."

I lift my hands. "Hey, I get it. But, like, is there a tutoring program he can take or something?"

She shakes her head. "The teacher has tried to keep him after class to give him help, but he has to be at practice. It's a double-edged sword. And I can't afford a private tutor."

"Yeah, I get that." I don't know what else to say. I'm not just doing this to see Duke, but it's a big factor. I really want to get to know the kid. I want to have family in my life again. "If I can think of anything, I'll let you know."

"You do that," Bradie says flatly and turns to leave. "Don't get too attached, Holden."

Too late, I think as I watch her leave. I head back to the rink and find Bruce in the stands going over something on his clipboard. He glances up at me, his face ruddy from skating around with the kids earlier. "Your weeklong trial period ends today. So, you staying?"

"You want me to?"

"Hell, yes! You were great with them and they were clearly inspired by your story and have been more engaged at practice since you got here," Bruce says. He introduced me to the kids by explaining how I was the best local player in town and how NHL scouts used to come see me. He, luckily, skipped the part where my career ended when I was arrested for theft and punched two police officers in the process. "I'd love you to stay permanently but I won't be shocked if you don't."

"Why wouldn't I?'

"Practice is four days a week and we play almost every weekend. You'll have trouble maintaining a social life," he says and chuckles. "Hell, my wife calls herself a hockey widow."

"Yeah, well lucky for you I don't have a wife or a social life," I smile. "See you tomorrow."

"Same time, same ice," Bruce replies and nods as I head back out of the rink.

The air outside is just as cold as in the area. Hell, it feels even colder because it's so damp, that kind of cold that seeps into your bones. I zip up my hoodie. Normally I'd have brought my jacket to wear as well, but Winnie still has it and I haven't seen her all day. The electrician and I started work on the house at nine and she was already gone. She didn't come back before I left for practice.

As I climb into my truck, my cell goes off and Jude's number flashes across the screen. Huh. He must be calling to check on the work. I hit accept. "Hey, Jude. How are you?"

"I'm good," he says. "How's Winnie?"

What. The. Fuck.

"Umm...what?"

"I know she's there," Jude replies. "At least I hope to hell she is because I called Ty and he said she never got on the flight to Toronto a couple weeks ago. So, is she at the house? Is she okay? I mean she must not be, but...I mean tell me how she's doing."

"I...well..." Fuck. I'm not supposed to tell her family. She explicitly said that. But...

"She told you not to tell me didn't she?" Jude asks and

before I can answer he swears under his breath. "Why the fuck is she shutting us out? Listen, Holden, you're not volunteering the information, so you're not violating her wishes. I'm demanding it from you. So tell me. How is she doing?"

I sigh and lean back against the headrest and close my eyes. "She's okay. I mean she's devastated, but she's trying to pull herself through it, you know? Slowly."

"Yeah...but why does she have to do it there? Alone. Fuck," Jude asks and I have no answers. "And she dumped Ty. Why the hell do that? I mean I could think of a thousand reasons, but she never wanted to hear them. She was with him ten years and then she suddenly decides to leave him the same week we lose our dad and then she runs off and doesn't tell anyone about it?"

"Dude, I know you're my boss and everything and I like you as a friend, but I am not getting into the details," I say and scrub my beard. "I don't know exactly what she's thinking and what she has told me is in confidence."

"Yeah, yeah I get it," Jude grumbles and I can tell he wishes he could be mad at me for it. "I'll find out for myself. I just don't want her suffering through this all alone."

She's got me, I want to tell him but I don't because I don't want him to know about whatever the hell is happening between us, at least not right now. I should probably figure it out myself before I started talking about it with her family.

"How's the house?" he asks as an afterthought.

"Coming along really well. No big problems." Renovating the cottage is the only aspect of my life that I feel I have a handle on right now. That reminds me, the electricity is still shut off and I can't turn it back on until tomorrow afternoon since we're not done rewiring the kitchen. I left Winnie a note about it and I'm sure she'll be pissed off.

"Okay, well do me a favor and call me immediately if that changes," he says. "With my sister or the house."

"I will..." I pause. "And do me a favor and make it clear I didn't rat her out."

"Worried she'll break your nose again?" Jude laughs and I force a laugh too.

"Something like that," I reply.

"I won't involve you in our family drama. But please don't tell her I know she's there," Jude says and I want to groan. I don't want to keep anything from her. "I worry she'll up and leave if she knows we know. I'd rather she's there with you, someone I trust, than off in some motel or something by herself."

"Yeah. Okay," I say because I don't want to lie to her but I, like Jude, want her to stay at the cottage.

After we say our good-byes and hang up, it takes me about twenty minutes to get back to the Braddock cottage. As soon as I pull in, she comes out of the house, wrapped in what looks like every blanket and jacket in the place. I try not to smirk.

"You forgot to turn the electricity back on before you left for wherever the hell you snuck off to," she says.

"I didn't sneak off. I had somewhere I needed to be," I say calmly. "And I can't turn the electricity back on. I left you a note on the dining room table."

She huffs and storms back into the house. I shake my head and walk to my trailer. I'm inside, staring at the meager contents of my kitchen cabinets trying to decide between mac and cheese or spaghetti when she bangs on the trailer door. "Come in!" I call out in the most annoying cheerful singsong voice I can muster.

She swings the door open still wrapped up in her cocoon of blankets. "I need electricity tonight! I'll freeze to death!"

"Did you read the note?" I ask. "It can't be turned back on until tomorrow afternoon at the earliest. There are live wires everywhere and nothing is grounded yet."

"I'll freeze to death!"

I can't help but laugh and I try to cover it but she is being such a drama queen. She must realize it too because her face twists up and I realize she's fighting a smile so I let my laughter out and a second later she joins me. "Okay, that sounds a bit overdramatic but seriously, I have California blood now and I need some kind of heat. Everything is electric. I'm going to be shivering all night."

"I gave you some options," I say casually as I lean against the counter by the stove. She looks at me long and hard.

"I can't stay here," she says finally. "I mean...you only have one bed."

I point to the couch. "That pulls out into a double. The mattress isn't the best so I'll give you the bed and I'll take it. It's one night."

"Not a good idea," she says but her voice is weak and when she glances over at the queen bed you can see through the open curtain at the end of the trailer, I can see the longing.

"It's toasty warm in here thanks to my generator," I say. "I also have hot water. Lots and lots of it if you want to take a shower."

"I'll figure it out," she says and takes a step out of the trailer. She hesitates before she closes the door. "Thanks anyway."

I stare at the door after she closes it for a good long minute. I want her to come back. Spending the night with her, even platonically, would be a good thing. But I know, just like she knows, it wouldn't stay platonic. And that would be a great thing. But she has to want it. She has to be the one to come to me. My cards are on the table. She's the one who isn't sure she wants to place a bet on us.

I grab a beer out of the fridge and throw myself down on the couch, flipping open my laptop and cuing up an episode of *House Hunters* on Netflix. I'm halfway through it, and my beer, when there's another knock on the door. "Enter!"

I crane my neck toward the door to see Winnie walk back in. Now she's also got the hood up on a sweatshirt she's got on under the blankets. I notice she's wearing my jacket too. I smile. She holds out her hands and there're two oblong objects in them wrapped in white paper.

"I brought you a lobster roll, in case you're hungry," she says. "Consider it payment for letting me hang out in here and warm up."

I grin and pull myself to a sitting position, moving the laptop to the table. "You don't have to pay me with anything. But I'll take it."

I grab one of the rolls and stand up, motioning for her to take a seat in the breakfast nook. She slips in, not an easy feat with all the blankets. I smile. She does too, sheepishly. "Drink?"

I hold up my mostly empty beer and she nods so I grab

two more out of the fridge. She takes hers and glances at the laptop screen. "Is that *House Hunters*?"

Damn. Busted. "Yep."

"Oh my God you watch that?" She looks positively blown away. "I love that show. I've never met a guy who willingly watches it. Usually they're forced to by their girlfriend."

"It's *House Hunters Renovation*," I explain. "I consider it research. Some of them come up with some cool ideas, but a lot of it is what not to do."

"I believe it," she says with a nod and starts to unwrap her roll. I've already torn the paper off mine and am ripping into it. "And seriously, they always pick the house they can't afford or the one that has nothing they said they wanted. Like, I need a three-bedroom house with a big yard and two bathrooms, but then they pick the loft condo that's over budget. People are dumb."

I swallow the chunk of lobster roll and groan in satisfaction. "Yeah, what always gets me is their jobs and budgets. It's like 'Hi, I'm a goat yoga assistant and my husband is a mime instructor and our budget is seven hundred thousand dollars.' Really? Shit, how much do you charge for those butterfly nets?"

She laughs, but she's sipping her beer and her hand automatically flies to her face as she struggles not to choke. When she finally swallows, she laughs. "I almost brought that through my nose. Thanks for that!"

"My pleasure." I wink at her and take another big bite, groaning again.

"You make the best noises," she whispers almost under

her breath, and I stop chewing and look at her. "Sorry. It's just…whatever. I didn't say a thing. Let's change the subject. Why did you pick construction?"

"It kind of picked me," I reply, but I really want to go back to talking about the noises. I'd love to tell her just how much I would like to find out what noises she makes when she's satisfied. "I needed a job and a friend needed guys who could do manual labor, so I took it. I did a lot of years just hammering nails and hauling drywall and lugging debris. But I liked it and the idea of fixing stuff, and making old places new again, was appealing so I took some online classes in business and project management and a weekend intensive in renovating and building codes."

"Well for something you fell into you're busting your ass at it and doing a good job," she says quietly, almost like she's embarrassed to give me the compliment.

I grin at her and lean closer. "Did you just say something positive about me?" I glance up at the roof and then out the window.

"What are you looking for?"

"Locusts falling from the sky or the horsemen of the apocalypse," I say and she laughs and gives me a playful shove.

"Stop with your snark and eat your lobster like a good boy," she says, but the smile on her face brings me that same inner warmth and happiness that Duke's did earlier. I've never felt so pleased with myself for making a woman smile. She looks like the Winnie I remember—relaxed and beautiful.

I hit play on the laptop and we watch the rest of the show while eating the lobster rolls and sipping our beers and all

I can think is how content I am with her just here—being her—and in my space. A space I haven't really let anyone into for a very long time.

Does she feel it too?

12

WINNIE

How does a man turn me on just by eating food? Holy crap, watching him devour that roll and throw back his beer is the most sensual thing I've seen in my life. My attraction to him is rising to undeniable levels and it's starting to make me panic. I can't do this right now—not with him. I'm still so upside down emotionally and in my life in general.

I get up, under the guise of getting us another beer, but really I just need to not be so close to him. If I stay on that bench seat, right next to him, I will lose the ability to control myself and end up kissing him again. And I won't stop at kissing. Jesus, how am I supposed to spend the night here with him a few feet away?

"Can I help myself?" I point to the fridge and holding up my empty beer bottle.

He gives me that seductive smirk he seems to have perfected in adulthood. "You can help yourself to whatever you want, Winona."

That spark of desire in my belly turns into a fire licking its way through my veins. I should probably drop all the blankets and jackets I'm swaddled in and go back to the house so I can cool off. Instead, I open the fridge and pray the cool air will keep my cheeks from turning red. I pull out the beers and when the door swings closed it ruffles some papers on the counter. My eyes glance over, to make sure nothing fell, and the words catch my eye. The first page, in Holden's neat handwriting, is a list of names. Right Renos. East Coast Renovations. Coastal Homes. New Old Homes.

I pick it up and walk over to hand him his beer. Holden sees the paper in my hand and looks uncomfortable. He stands up and reaches for it instead of the beer. "You don't need to see that."

"What is it?"

"I'm brainstorming," he mumbles and folds the paper and shoves it in the back pocket of his jeans. "Company names. I have to file the paperwork to officially register my business and I'm trying to figure out what to call it."

"Hendricks Homes," I say simply because it's a no-brainer if you ask me, but he just shrugs. "Seriously? It's the perfect name."

He finally takes the beer from me and twists off the cap. "Nah. I think I'm leaning toward Coastal Homes or Coastal Renos. What do you think?"

I twist the cap off my own beer and take a slow sip before answering. "I think that's shit."

Those wolflike eyes flare and he looks almost wounded. I decide to soften my approach. "What's wrong with your name? It's your business."

He takes a long, slow breath and his expression darkens.

"Because when people in this town hear Holden Hendricks they think *That's a trustworthy guy I want in my house*? That's what you think, right?"

He is being sarcastic and my face flushes but this time, hormones have nothing to do with it. I'm embarrassed for being called out. He gives me a bitter smirk and takes another sip of his beer. "I'm sorry."

"Saying you're sorry for something that you truly believe is bullshit. Don't do it," he says tersely and drops back down onto the bench by the table.

I place my beer on the counter with a thud, no longer thirsty. "If you wanted people to actually believe you'd changed you wouldn't be lying about hanging out with Kidd or that drug dealer dude."

His smirk hardens. "If you think I'm still a sketchy douchebag, then what the hell are you doing here?"

"I'm cold," I say even though right now, my blood is boiling. "You gave me no choice by cutting the power."

He lets out a hard laugh. "You've had choices this entire time, Winnie, and you know it. You could have told Jude to fire me. You could have left. You have the money to stay in a hotel or even rent a different place. You could have gone to Cat's tonight, but you didn't. You're here. With me. The big bad wolf."

He's taunting me and it might be in jest, but it reminds me of young cruel Holden too much. "Fine. I'm leaving," I say and start toward the door, but I spin back to face him. "And if you don't start working full days instead of sneaking off in the afternoons to do whatever, I will tell Jude to fire you."

"You do that, Larry," he snarks.

I have one foot out the door, but that snide comment freezes me in my tracks and I decide he's not getting the last word. I don't know what the hell I'm going to say to him, but it's not going to be pretty. I turn back around and he's stepped forward and is right behind me.

"I hate you," I blurt out in pure frustration.

"No, you don't," he says confidently. "You want to and that's why you're doing this. You want to hate my guts because you want to hate everything. You're in mourning. You've had your heart swallowed by grief—after it was broken by a *real* douchebag—and you want to wallow in it and being around me makes you happy. You like it. You like me. And you want me to like you, which I do. A lot."

Why am I no longer ready to punch him again? Why am I...feeling like I might cry? He takes my silence as an opening and steps even closer. His hand slowly and gently slips around my waist.

"You think you know everything," I say but my tone is soft, my voice breathless. Oh God he is so right. I didn't even realize it until he said it out loud, but he is right.

"I think I know you," he replies and dips his head ever so slightly. "And I think you want me to kiss you."

"I do," I admit despite the confusion and anxiety swirling inside me. Is this right? Am I crazy? Can I do this right now—after everything? He tilts his head and our lips connect, then our tongues collide and all my doubt is gone, my fear turns to desire. Right or wrong, I need this man. Now. So when he tries to pull away I curl my fingers in his hair to keep his mouth on mine, but I can't.

He pulls away just an inch and whispers, "I think you want me to fuck you."

"I do," I say, panting with want. "I do."

He reaches down, cups my ass, lifts me up and I wrap my legs around his waist. Then he presses my back against the closed trailer door. There's no denying the man is in perfect shape—all hard muscle from his abs to his arms and his sculpted thighs. I'm eager to see—and feel—every part of him. I push his shirt higher and higher as I explore the rippled flesh of his torso with my hands.

His lips suck their way down the side of my neck and he moves us off the wall, walking toward the bedroom. As he carries me, I break our kiss long enough to pull off his shirt and drop it on the floor. He moves his lips back to mine, his tongue sweeping forcefully into my mouth as he drops to his knees on the bed and carefully lays me on the mattress. His big, strong, rough hands start to peel off my layers. With every blanket and coat he removes, the flutter in my belly grows stronger. It's a mix of nerves and desire. I want him—I want this—but I've only ever slept with Ty. That fact weakens my confidence until, as he finally strips away all my clothes and looks at me in nothing but a thong and bra, and his hands ghost across the bare skin of my stomach he whispers. "You're more beautiful than I imagined."

Then, I have the confidence to move my own hands to his jeans and start to undo his belt. He helps me push his pants down and takes his underwear with them. Now he's even more naked than I am and far less concerned about it. His left hand wraps around his long shaft and his eyes fill with dark passion as he pumps himself once before dropping down on top of me and capturing my lips again. "Can I touch you?" he asks pulling back from the kiss just enough to get the words out. "Because I really need to slide my fingers in you and feel your heat."

"God yes," I moan shamelessly. I push my underwear down my hips to give him access. A second later his hand is between my legs and he gently slides two fingers into me at once while his thumb finds my clit and his lips find my ear. I can feel his dick against my thigh and I try to reach it, but only graze it with my fingertips. "It's okay, baby. Watching you get off on my touch is pleasure enough."

I gasp as he twists his fingers and pushes up, and pleasure pulses through me in short, intense bursts with every thrust. "Holy fuck, Holden. Please…" I grab the back of his head, my fingers cutting through his thick, soft hair, and come. It's short, it's hard, it's glorious.

His hips are moving against my leg and suddenly he stops and pulls back. "I need to get a condom."

"I want you to get a condom," I reply breathlessly trying not to focus on how my pussy is still quivering. He gets up and strides naked into the bathroom and comes back with a silver foil package in his hand. He tears it open and rolls it over himself as he climbs back onto the bed.

He lies down on top of me and reaches down to hook the back of my right leg and hitch it higher, as his tip aligns with my entrance. He pauses, kisses me so gently it takes my breath away in a completely different way and then pushes into me—hard and fast. The juxtaposition of the two things—the soft, slow kiss and the hard, quick way he enters me—awakens the desire that had been sated by that first orgasm. I'm instantly chasing another orgasm. But more importantly, I'm desperate to watch him have his first.

And when he does, several minutes later, it's a beautiful thing. His body tenses, his eyes snap closed and his head tilts back and he moans, a sound so deep and rough I swear I feel it in my clit and it sends me tumbling into my own orgasm.

I lie there listening to him catch his breath and try to come to terms with the fact that my childhood enemy is the best lover I've ever had.

13

WINNIE

The next morning I'm woken up by the feel of his beard grazing my neck. The rough sensation creates a flutter of desire in my belly instantly. I sleepily roll toward him and open my eyes but it's excessively dark. I realize we're cuddled deep under the blankets.

"Morning, Larry," he whispers against my shoulder and I laugh.

"Shut up, jerk," I say and let my left hand drift between us until I find his dick. He's hard as a rock. "You're in a vulnerable position here so I'd watch it if I were you."

He moves, rolling on top of me, his lips skimming my neck and then my cheek before finding my lips. My hand is still pinned between us around his shaft and I give it a slow, soft tug, which makes him groan in that way that makes my insides boil. It also gives my tongue just enough room to slip past his parted lips and claim his mouth. I want to repeat last night more than I want anything in the world. I part my legs so his hips slip between them and I tug on him again. "Is that an invitation?"

I smile and kiss him again. "Only if you don't call me Larry."

"How about if I call you beautiful, and so fucking sexy I woke up with the worst hard-on of my life," he says slipping his hips forward, bringing himself closer. I move my hand around to his ass as he reaches for a condom from the bedside table. He still has that tight round hockey ass. "How about if I call you perfection. Because you are."

I wrap my arms around his neck and tilt my pelvis toward his as he rolls the condom on. Then his tip grazes my entrance. "How about if you just—" He pushes into me in one steady long thrust. "Yeah...that."

The sex is as passionate and perfect as it was last night, the only difference is it doesn't feel as crazy, or as rushed because we're both confident now that this is what we need—each other. There's no hurry to see how this ends because we know the answer—it ends in pure, raw pleasure. We enjoy it, teasing, licking, touching, until we're panting, groaning, shuddering. I come just as hard as last night and with just as much abandon. This man has set me free—for these fleeting, euphoric minutes—I am free of pain and sadness and I feel good again. I cling to his shoulders, nuzzling my face against his scruffy beard and moan against his skin. "I need you."

"You have me," he grunts as he pushes hard into me. "You fucking own me."

His hips snap, his head tilts back and he grunts as he shudders his release and it's the most fucking amazing thing I've ever seen. This man who, from the moment I met him, has been nothing but toughness and darkness, has slowly started to show me more and right now, in the middle of his release he is nothing but pure vulnerability and I am just in awe.

He collapses on top of me and we stay that way for a while, wrapped up in each other, drifting in and out of sleep. The weight and warmth of his body on mine fills me with a peace I haven't felt in years. When the sun starts to poke through the blinds on the window behind the bed and he stirs, rolling over, I fight the urge to stop him. He rubs his eyes and picks up his phone from a tiny shelf next to him. "My electrician is going to be here to finish up the wiring in twenty minutes or so."

"Boo," I mutter and Holden laughs as he climbs out of bed. He stretches, butt naked, and yawns again. My eyes shamelessly sweep over him, drinking in every sculpted inch of him. Boy is a beast. And then he turns and walks toward the bathroom and his perfect, tight round ass is on display. "You want to shower first?" he asks as he stops in front of the tiny door. "I'd just carry you in there and do it together, but it's definitely not big enough."

"We can break in the new shower in the cottage that way," I suggest and he smiles.

"I like the way you think," he says. "And now I'm going to bust my ass to finish that bathroom as soon as possible."

"Good," I say and sit up, holding the blankets against me. "You shower first. I don't think my legs work right now anyway."

"I did my job then," he chuckles as he slips inside the tiny bathroom. He leaves the door open and I'm tempted to just sit here and watch him, but I force myself not to and crawl from the bed to hunt down my clothing.

As I dress, reality starts to set in and my brain starts to fall back into its old patterns of self-doubt. What did we just do? What does it mean? Was it one night? Am I ready for something? I just came out of a ten-year relationship that went nowhere. What the hell am I doing? What is he doing? What does he want? I wish my dad were here to talk to. I used to be able to tell him anything.

I'm in full-on mental free fall by the time I've got all my clothes back on, so I decide I need some air. I walk through the trailer. "I'm going outside for a minute," I call, not sure he can even hear me over the water, but I don't wait to find out if he did.

I swing open the trailer door, hop down the steps and as soon as my feet land on the driveway I am face-to-face with Sadie and Dixie.

I gasp in surprise. Dixie has her arms crossed. Sadie has hers on her hips and they're both staring at me with wide, shocked eyes, which I'm sure match my own.

"What the hell are you two doing here?" I ask.

"What are you doing here?" Sadie replies.

"What are you doing in there?" Dixie adds, uncrossing her arms long enough to point at Holden's Airstream.

"There's no heat in the house," I say.

Sadie's left eyebrow rises. "And so you created heat in the trailer?"

"What? No. I...what are you doing here?"

"Jude told us you were here," Sadie says and I freeze.

How the hell does Jude know where I am? The trailer door swings open behind me and a shirtless, towel-clad Holden is standing there.

I should be embarrassed because my sisters are looking at me like they know exactly what happened last night but instead I'm angry—at Holden. "Did you tell Jude I was here?"

"No," Holden says firmly. "He told me you were here and I didn't lie."

"What?"

"Ty told Jude you didn't get on the plane, Win," Sadie says and I'm still mad at Holden. Why couldn't he lie for me? He must know exactly what I'm thinking because his eyes soften.

"I had to tell the truth, Winnie." He wants me to forgive him, I can see it all over his face and I will. Eventually. Right now, I have to deal with this.

I turn away from him to face my sisters again. They're both still staring at him. "Long time, no see Holden," Dixie says with a small wave and a smaller smile. She didn't like him either. Hell, none of us did except Jude.

"Dixie. Sadie." He nods at them both. Sadie gives me a bigger smile, but I know it's more because he's naked and she thinks I had something to do with that. "I'm going to get dressed."

He shuts the trailer door and my sisters attack.

"Oh. My. God. Did you sleep in there last night?" Dixie demands. "With him."

"Did you *not* sleep last night in there, with him?" Sadie asks.

"I thought he was a dick? Are you fucking a dick?" Dixie says. "Why are you fucking a dick?"

"Technically we all fuck dicks," Sadie quips and Dixie rolls her eyes at the bad pun. Sadie looks over at me again. "But seriously, Win. Is this like some kind of...I don't know...like grief therapy or something? Are you really with him? Do you like him? How did this happen? When did you break up with Ty? Are you seriously just going to hide here forever?"

"Please just stop," I say and for some reason tears are building behind my eyes. "I don't want to discuss my life with you guys, which is why I was hiding out here. So I could be alone."

They both look wounded by that and I feel bad but it's the truth and I've spent way too much time in recent years avoiding the truth. Sadie's face falls. Dixie looks like she might cry. I feel that cold dark ball of guilt and sadness starts to fill my gut again.

"Winnie," Dixie says with a trembling voice. "We lost him too."

And the tears fall. From my eyes, from hers and from Sadie's. We're three sobbing messes. Sadie grabs us both and pulls us into a hug. I hear Holden's trailer door open and then close. I think he probably saw us and scooted back inside to give us privacy, but then I hear him clear his throat. We pull apart and I wipe at my eyes. Holden is hunched over with his hands stuffed in the pockets of his jeans. "You ladies are welcome to talk it out in my trailer. I have to get in there and work."

I shake my head. "Let's go to the beach."

They both nod and as we head down the driveway, I try not to look directly at Holden. I'm a big enough mess as it is, but he squeezes my shoulder as I pass by, and I have to look up. He hands me the blankets I was wrapped in last night. "It's chilly. Take these."

I let him pile them in my arms. "Thank you."

At the beach it's low tide, so we walk all the way down the where the sand starts to dip and we drop down, side by side, to stare at the surf. Dixie and Sadie drape a blanket over their shoulders and I wrap myself in the other one. It's not as cold as it was the last couple of days and I think it might be warm and beautiful today. We don't say anything for a long while and just watch the waves crashing on the shore. The finally Sadie speaks. "Is it really over between you and Ty?"

I take a long, slow breath. "Yes."

"Why now?" she says.

I close my eyes and tip my head up to the sun. "The month before we all moved to San Francisco, I found out he was fucking one of the other accountants in his office."

"Winnie, oh my God," Sadie gasps.

"That fucking piece of human garbage," Dixie says furiously.

"I'm the asshole that was too weak to leave him," I say and open my eyes to look at their faces. Dixie's expression is pure anger and she looks like Jude right before he punches someone on the ice. Sadie looks concerned, which reminds me of my mom when we used to do stupid stuff as kids. "I should have just ended it back when I found out, but I didn't because he was sorry and said he loved me and I decided to try to forgive him."

"I could never forgive that," Dixie says.

"I couldn't either and I think I knew it," I reply and run my fingers through my hair, trying to tug out the tangles out from the night before. "But I still didn't end it."

Sadie sighs, tracing lines in the sand beside her left knee. "Well at least I finally understand why you two were fighting so much. You could have told us. We would have been there for you just like we're trying to be here for you now."

"We were all already dealing with so much," I say. "And I wasn't ready to tell anyone it happened. Fuck, I'm not even ready now."

"Okay first of all, you have nothing to be ashamed of and second of all, you have nothing to feel guilty about," Dixie says firmly as she tucks up her legs, wraps her arms around them and rests her chin on her knees.

"Why did you finally end it?" Sadie says softly

"Dad told me to." I glance over and they're both staring at me. "In his letter."

"He flat-out said dump his ass?" Dixie questions and I laugh lightly.

"No. He knew I wasn't happy, and he urged me to go after my happiness," I say and swallow the lump in my throat. "He said it was now or never, and he's right. I mean, Holden is an example of that. Dad wanted to renovate the cottage forever and never did, and now he's not going to get to see it."

"Dad's right." Sadie nods, staring out at the ocean. "Life is now or never. I'm trying to remember that and not put things off and enjoy everything I'm doing, every moment with Griffin and even every good day at work but...I still miss him so much."

"Me too," I sniff. "How is Mom doing?"

"Better than I thought she would be," Sadie says. "She has her bad moments, but she's going to a grief counselor and she's coping."

I nod and guilt fills my heart. I haven't kept in contact as much as I should. "I will call her."

"She'd like that." Dixie reaches for my hand and squeezes it gently. "But she's okay if you don't call too. She knows you better than anyone. She knows you have to handle this your own way. Like a weirdo."

I chuckle and squeeze her hand back. Sadie laughs too, and I suddenly feel lighter and stronger than I have in months.

"Since you brought Holden up...," Dixie says slowly. I look over at her and the curiosity in her eyes is undeniable.

"I didn't bring up Holden."

"Let's pretend you did. Because he's clearly the elephant in the room...or on the beach as location would have it." Dixie grins at her own ridiculousness. "Wanna enlighten us on whatever it is we saw when we got here this morning?"

"Honestly, no," I reply firmly. "Enough sharing for now. I'm starving. Let's go eat somewhere."

I stand up and they start to get up too. I know they aren't going to let this go and I'm going to have to say something about Holden and me soon, but I'm going to put it off as long as I can.

14

HOLDEN

As I drive back from hockey practice, my mind falls back to what I've been thinking about on and off all day long—Winnie. She and her sisters came back to the cottage after about an hour. They all looked like they'd been crying, but they clearly weren't fighting anymore. Probably talking about her dad and everything. Dixie and Winnie hauled their carry-on bags into the house and dumped them on the porch before turning around and leaving with Winnie. By the time I left for hockey practice, they hadn't come back yet.

I know I should just let her be with family, and I know she's mad at me and I'm the last person she wants around, but I'm aching to see her again. Last night wasn't just sex to me. It was the start of something real. It was—she *is*—what I've always wanted but never thought I deserved. I can't just walk away from that. So, she may need space, but she's not getting it.

I park the truck behind her sisters' rental and hop out. The lights are on in the cottage, so I pause and stare up at it, but I don't get out. I kind of want to go inside and see her, check on how they're doing, but I don't know if she'd want me to. I'm sure she's figured out I had no choice but to admit the truth to Jude, but that doesn't mean she's not still annoyed by it. I wonder if she's still thinking about the mind-blowing sex we had less than twenty-four hours ago and if she's hoping to get me naked again as much as I am dying to get her naked again.

Fuck it, I'm going in.

I take the stairs two at a time and knock twice on the screen door before letting myself in. "Winnie?"

"We're back here!" a voice calls, but it's not Winnie.

I walk through the living room, past the stripped-down bathroom and into the half-renovated kitchen-dining room area. Dixie and Winnie are sitting on a drop cloth on the floor with glasses of wine and a family-size bag of Humpty Dumpty dill pickle potato chips. I try not to wrinkle my nose, but I hate that flavor.

"Hey," I say and shove my hands in my pockets. "Just wanted to make sure everything is all right and you guys are managing around all the renos."

"We're managing," Sadie calls from the kitchen area where she is bent over, looking into the fridge. "But you sure as shit destroyed this place."

"That is part of the renovation process," I reply with a shrug. My gaze falls back down to the top of Winnie's head. I wish I could see her face, but I'm guessing she's avoiding eye contact on purpose.

"So will the power stay on tonight, or will all three of us have to snuggle up in your trailer?" Dixie asks me pointedly, and Winnie slaps her sister's arm. "Or is Winnie the only one you offer to keep warm at night?"

"She's the only one," I reply swiftly and that gets Winnie to finally look at me. When our eyes connect, I give her a soft smile. "The power will stay on now. We're done with the rewiring."

"Cool. Wine?" Sadie offers and holds up a bottle from the fridge.

I shake my head. "Thanks, but I should get back to the trailer and leave you guys alone."

"Bye," Winnie says with a cautious smile, but it's a smile and I take that as a good sign.

Dixie's smile is a little warmer, slightly less guarded as she waves good-bye.

I give Dixie and Sadie a nod and head back out of the cottage.

For the next few hours I try to keep my thoughts off her. I take a long, hot shower, I make some pasta and drink a couple beers. I try to watch some Netflix, but I can't stop thinking about Winnie. Even with the trailer windows closed, I can sometimes hear bursts of laughter or noises coming from the house. Eventually, that dies down too. I steal a glance out the window above the bed and it looks like all the lights are out now. They must have gone to bed. It's almost eleven but sleep doesn't even feel like a remote possibility for me. I'm riled up for some reason. I walk back over to the fridge, and stare at the contents debating another beer, when there is one hard, short knock on the door.

I turn to face it. "It's open."

The door opens and Winnie's standing there in nothing but a simple blue cotton nightie that falls just below her ass. I can't take my eyes off it and I know she knows what it's doing to me. "I'm sorry for barking at you about telling Jude."

"I didn't tell him," I remind her as my eyes keep sweeping up and down her perfect form. "He asked."

"I know and I'm sorry for being upset that you told him the truth," Winnie says and takes a step up into the trailer. I watch her long legs move gracefully, the hem of the nightgown lifting, precariously close to revealing much more than her toned thighs. My dick throbs. "I just didn't want to face my family yet."

"It seems like it's going okay, though," I say, my voice heavy with lust.

I think she nods, but my eyes are focused on how tightly this nightgown now wraps around her chest. The cold night air has caused her nipples to stand at attention under the thin cotton. I think about how perfect they'll feel in my mouth.

"Yeah. I think it's good I talked to them," Winnie says, and I finally lift my eyes to her face. The door is still swinging open behind her and I wonder if she's going to leave. "They want me to go home next month for an ALS fund-raiser that Jude is going to speak at, in memory of our dad."

"Oh." I can't find another word. And the fact that she called San Francisco home creates a tightness in my chest.

"Anyway, they're going home tomorrow," she says, her fingertips skimming the bottom of the nightie, drawing my eyes back to the tops of her thighs and my mind back to what's under it. "I'm going to pick up cinnamon buns in the morning if you want to come by and have one, say good-bye to them. Let them see you're no longer the jackass who used to terrorize the town, and us."

"I can do that tomorrow," I say and force my eyes to her beautiful face again. "But tonight, if you close that door, I can lift that tiny little nightgown and lick you until you come."

Her whole body tenses in shock. I take a step toward her. "Don't pretend you're surprised or I'm out of line because we both know you'd be wearing a hell of a lot more if you weren't looking to make my dick hard and my head fill with thoughts of tasting you."

She doesn't answer. She blinks and then reaches behind her for the door handle. As soon as the metal door clanks against the metal frame and the lock clicks, I'm on my knees, my palms skimming over her thighs, my fingers lifting the bottom of that cotton nightgown. As I press my lips to the inside of her thigh and she leans back against the door, I discover she's not wearing underwear. I groan and my heart starts to hammer. I lift my eyes to see her looking down at me, awash in desire. Her fingers graze my scalp. "You know you own me," I whisper.

"I wouldn't be here if you didn't own me too."

I close my eyes and lift my mouth to her core. She's wet and warm and I lick her and suck on her like it's giving me life, because it fucking is. She's darkness and light and softness and strength and everything I never thought I deserved. And she came to me, gave herself to me—and continues to—emotionally and physically and I will do everything to keep her. I worship her with my mouth and she shudders and whispers my name over and over as her legs quiver and it makes me feel like a god, especially when, moments later she comes so hard she collapses. Even as her body slides down the door and she lies in a crumpled heap on the floor, I don't take my mouth off her pussy, greedy for every single drop of desire and not willing to let the moment end. But she reaches down and tugs on my hair, pulling me up her body. I kiss my way across her stomach, pushing the nightgown up as I go and stop to worship her tits too because damn, they deserve it.

Finally, face-to-face she cups my cheek with her hand and I turn and kiss her palm, while I start to undo my pants. They're barely at my knees when she starts to wrap her legs round my waist. "Condom," I groan and try to get up. She tightens her grip with her legs.

"I have an IUD," she says.

I lean back down, balancing on my forearms, and nuzzle my face into her neck and kiss her earlobe. "Winona, I'm clean, but you don't fully trust me yet and I'm not letting you do something you'll regret."

I get back on my knees and dig around in my jeans pocket for my wallet, where I keep a condom. She sits up. "I'll never regret you, Holden."

I tear the purple package open but she reaches out and stills my hands. Our eyes meet. "I'm just making sure of that."

She crawls up on her knees too and as I roll the condom down my shaft with one hand I reach out and cup the back of her head with the other, my fingers tangling in her hair and my tongue slips past her lips. She crawls closer and then she's pushing me back, and climbing on top of me. She straddles my hips and guides my dick inside her and I lie back and let her take over. She rides me with abandon and I am just as turned on by the tilt of her neck, the bounce of her tits and the pink flush on her cheeks as I am by the warm tight feel of being inside her.

I play with her clit as she rides me in a steady rhythm and when I finally feel her pussy clench around me stars start to pepper my vision and I push up into her one final time, almost lifting completely off the floor, before I come. She collapses on top of me, her golden hair across my face as she nuzzles into the crook of my neck and I inhale the soothing scent of her lilac shampoo. We fall asleep like that and at some point, I wake up and carry her into my bed and cocoon us under the blankets.

The next morning, she's already gone when my alarm goes off at seven. I shower, put on my work clothes and I'm drinking a coffee when there's a knock at the door. I swing it open, assuming it's Winnie, but it's not. It's Kevin. And he's higher than a fucking kite.

"Dude, did you know there are like four trailers set up in driveways in this town," he mumbles and tries to step inside my house but I don't let him. Instead, I step down and join him on the driveway. My eyes jump up to the cottage but I don't see anyone on the porch, thankfully. "I almost got arrested for trying to get into some old dude's Minnie Winnie."

At the word "Winnie" my eyes dart up to the cottage again. Still no one standing there watching me with the town drug dealer, and that's a blessing. I cross my arms and stare at

Kevin and his giant pupils and doped-up smile. "What are you doing here? How do you even know where I live?"

"Kidd told me last night," Kevin explains. "He came over to party and he wasn't all that fucking stoked that you're digging up old issues."

Oh great. This is exactly what I need. I grit my teeth and take a deep breath before I speak. "I'm not involving him in this, and I wish you wouldn't have either. It's not anything to do with him. I just want to right a wrong that I consider my wrong, not his."

"Whatever dude, I honestly don't care, as long as you pay me."

"As long as you find it," I say.

"I found it," Kevin says, and I get excited. This whole thing, trying to find the pearl necklace that we took from Cat's house, was a shot in the dark to say the least. I mean it was decades ago and at first, I couldn't even remember what Kidd had done with it. "Thing is though, it's going to require heading to Boston and I'm gonna need half the money you promised to pay upfront to make the trip worth my while."

"I'll give you a quarter of it," I counter sharply, with no room for negotiation. "And you better have something for me by the weekend."

He nods and holds out his hand for money, but my wallet is in the trailer so I turn around and go get it. A second later I'm dropping fifty bucks in his hand. "By the weekend."

"I promise." He lazily gives me a thumbs-up and turns and walks away.

I run a hand through my hair and sigh. It'll all be worth it if I can get that damn necklace back. I grab my tool belt from the trailer and head into the cottage. I knock and someone yells "Come in," so I do. I find Sadie sitting on the couch in the living room, which is covered in a drop cloth. She's wearing pajama pants and a San Francisco Thunder sweatshirt and holding a mug of coffee. "There's more in the kitchen. Had to put the coffeepot on the floor but hey, it works."

"I had some in my trailer," I say as she tucks her legs up under her on the couch. "And I'm happy to report that the new countertops will be coming in later today so you can skip the floor brew tomorrow."

"I'll be gone anyway," Sadie says and pauses to sip her coffee. "I fly out this afternoon. I've got to work and I miss my boyfriend. And I'm confident now that Winnie is handling things in her own unique way."

"She is," I say with a nod. "And I don't think I've said it yet to you but I'm very sorry for your loss. Your dad was a great guy. He never made me feel unwanted, like most of the other parents in this town did when I hung out with their kids."

Sadie smiles. She looks a lot like Winnie when she does that. "Dad was a very easygoing, open guy who gave everyone a chance. He could forgive people anything... unless they hurt his wife or his kids."

She gives me a very pointed stare I couldn't miss if I tried. I chuff out a sheepish breath. "Winnie's pain right now isn't caused by me."

"I know that," Sadie replies and sits up a little straighter. "Judging by the fact that I saw her sneak into your trailer last night and stay there for four and a half hours, I'd say you're actually providing her pleasure, not her pain."

Am I bushing? I feel like I'm blushing. Fuck. Sadie lets out a breathless laugh. "But I know my sister and this...you...are out of character for her."

Ouch. That stings. But before I can figure out how to respond to what feels like one hell of a burn, she gives me an apologetic smile. "She's had one serious boyfriend in her entire life and the last time she saw you, she broke your nose, so you have to understand why this seems out of character."

"Grief changes you," I reply because I have my own experience to prove that.

"Grief makes you vulnerable." Sadie stands up from the couch, keeping her gaze level with mine.

I see where this is going. "I'm not taking advantage of Winnie. If anything, there's a chance she's taking advantage of me."

Sadie's blue eyes flare at my admission. I rub the back of my neck. I'm not great at dealing with my own vulnerability. "I just came here to renovate a damn house. I didn't expect to see Winnie again and I certainly didn't expect to develop feelings for her. But I did. Now whether this is just some crazy grief-induced fling for her, I have no idea. But it's not for me."

"Does she know that?" Sadie asks.

"She does," I say and any further conversation is interrupted by the sound of feet on the stairs.

"Sadie, why is Winnie still asleep?" Dixie says as she comes bounding into the living room already dressed for the day in leggings and an oversized sweater. She stops short at the sight of me. "Holden."

"Yeah, that's probably why," Sadie says under her breath with a smile. Louder though, so Dixie can actually hear, she says, "She probably didn't get much sleep. I'll go wake her up and change and we can go out and grab food."

Sadie disappears around the corner and I hear her climb the stairs. Dixie and I just stand there staring at each other awkwardly for a second. I clear my throat. "I'm going to head outside and wait for my buddy who's helping me paint this morning."

"That's not who was standing on the front lawn taking money from you this morning?" she asks and I stop breathing. Fuck, she saw me. Did Winnie see me?

"No," I say as she's stares at me with a single raised eyebrow. "That was a personal matter."

"Where you going to live after this job is done?' Dixie asks bluntly.

"I'll be getting an apartment and storing the trailer."

"Where?"

"Are you the one getting married here next summer?" I ask desperate to change the subject before I snap at her for being so damn nosy. My eyes land on the diamond ring on her finger. "A hockey player?"

She nods. "A goalie."

"So you like them crazy," I quip, and her hard, suspicious expression snaps as she laughs.

"Yeah, he's a little nuts, but so am I," Dixie says.

I hear more footsteps on the stairs and then Sadie and Winnie appear behind Dixie. My eyes go straight to Winnie. She's in jeans and a plain, clingy white T-shirt with her dad's gray cardigan. Her hair is in a messy bun and her cheeks pink slightly as she looks at me. I smile. "Morning, Winona."

Winnie smiles but quickly bites it back. "Hey. Sadie said the kitchen is almost finished."

I nod. "Painting this morning and cabinet installation later tonight. When I get back from my appointment this afternoon."

"Appointment?" Winnie echoes and her expression turns hard. I swear I can see her building a little wall around her heart right now, brick by brick, as we stare at each other. I could tell her where I'm going. I could validate it, but I'm so sick of her still searching for a reason to run from me, to distrust me and shut down her feelings for me. I'm sick of making amends and being the adult here.

I feel my shoulders tense. "Yup. An appointment."

The energy in the room gets tense fast. Both Sadie and Dixie's eyes are bouncing between Winnie and me like they're watching a tennis match. Winnie frowns and her eyes grow cold. I refuse to give in, snapping my mouth closed and folding my arms over my chest. Finally, without a word to me, she turns to her sisters. Dixie clears her throat. "You're all about the personal time," she says and Winnie looks at her quizzically. Fuck. I change the subject again.

"Don't worry, I'll have this place looking perfect long before your wedding to the crazy goalie," I say, hoping Winnie forgets her sister's last comment.

"Well that shouldn't be hard because we don't have a date set anyway," Dixie explains and both her sisters spin their blond heads to face her. "What?"

"I thought you were settling on Canada Day?" Sadie says,

confusion masking her features. "Mom was looking to book the church July first."

Dixie shrugs. I start to feel like a fly on a wall, eavesdropping on something I shoulder so I clear my throat. "I'm going to wait for Mike on the porch."

I head out of the room, but I can still hear them talking.

"Dix, did something happen? Are you and Eli okay?" Sadie asks.

"No! We're great. He's perfect. I love him more than ever," she announces and it's filled with passion and confidence. I feel a weird longing feeling start to fill my chest. God, I want Winnie to talk about her feelings for me with that type of conviction. "I just am not in any rush to get married."

"Really? Because it's all you could talk about for the first two months after Eli put that rock on your finger," Sadie says and I could hear the smile in her voice. "What changed?"

"Dad died," Winnie's voice is as clear and sharp as a glass shattering.

"It doesn't feel right doing it without him." Dixie's voice cracks on every single word.

I start to feel really bad about eavesdropping, but as I take a step toward the door, to go wait on the driveway, Winnie speaks again and stops me in my tracks.

"Because nothing is right without him. So don't do it. It's not like you're going to lose anything. You two live together. You're in love. Screw a big event that's just going to remind everyone Dad is gone."

"Winnie!" Sadie barks in protest, which is exactly what I want to do too. But it's definitely not my place. Still,

I'm disappointed in Winnie's attitude. Clearly any progress I thought she'd made in getting a handle on her grief didn't happen. She's still drowning in it and she's wants her sisters to drown with her. Fuck, Winnie. My heart breaks for her and at the same time, I want to shake her.

Before anyone can say anything else, there's a loud honk. My eyes dart to the road and find Mike's pickup pulled up to the curb. He's hopping out as he calls to me. "Get down here and help me unload supplies!"

I swing open the porch door and do what he asked mostly to avoid confronting Winnie about what she just did to her sister. The horn must have startled the girls out of their conversation too because before I can lift the first two paint cans out of the truck they're bounding down the stairs, one after another. None of them say anything to me but Sadie does give me a wave good-bye as they pile into her rental and drive away. Winnie refuses to make eye contact.

"There's three hot chicks living here now?" Mike asks with a grin and I just nod. "If all your jobs are like this, I'm available whenever you need help, buddy."

He chuckles as he carries a bunch of rollers and a bucket of paint toward the house. I glance back one last time toward their retreating car before following him.

15

WINNIE

Umm…lady, I don't want to get involved in some weird stalking thing between you and your boyfriend," my Lyft driver, Sterling, says in a nervous tone.

"He's my contractor, not my boyfriend," I explain, and I realize that doesn't make me look less crazy. "I will give you a twenty-dollar cash tip."

"I'm not supposed to take tips outside of the app," he informs me.

"Okay, Dudley Do-Right. Well, then I'll give you a twenty-dollar tip *in* the app," I counter. "Just keep following that white truck, but don't get too close."

I am officially off the deep end and I don't even need to see Sterling's judgey expression in the rearview mirror to confirm it. I'm sure if I hadn't just left Dixie and Sadie at the airport, they would be telling me the same thing. Still, knowing that doesn't stop me from doing what I'm doing—following Holden.

I had taken a Lyft from the Portland International Jetport, blurry-eyed from crying through my good-byes to my sisters, when I saw his truck heading in the opposite direction down Route 1. I glanced at the clock on the dashboard and realized it was three-thirty and he was going to his mysterious recurring appointment. So, I stopped sniffling and crying and told Sterling to turn his black Prius around because we needed to go the other way. When he did and asked for a new address to punch into his Waze app, I told him to just follow the white truck. And here we are—about three cars back from Holden's truck, going God knows where—and I'm sure Sterling will give me the worst passenger rating ever, but I'm still going to make him tail Holden. Even if it means I have to use Uber from now on.

Last night, as I lay in Holden's bed, curled up on his chest, I admitted to myself that I wanted him for more than just this moment in time. He is one of the few things that helps me get through the day. But I need to know how big a risk I've taken, and since he won't tell me where he goes every day, I'm going to force my Lyft driver into being my sidekick as I act like a private detective... or an unhinged girlfriend.

Holden follows Route 1 along to South Portland where he turns off on a familiar street and within seconds I realize where he's headed. The ice arena. I spent way more time at an ice rink in the summer than any normal kid vacationing in Maine. But normal kids don't have a hockey prodigy as an older brother. Jude played hockey twelve months a year, which meant when we were at the cottage, he played here. Holden used to play with him, but this was his year-round rink, since he lived here.

The long narrow road dead-ends at the arena, so as soon as Holden pulls into the large, pothole-filled parking lot and turns right, I demand that poor Sterling turn left and park in between a van and a Hummer.

"Listen, Winnie, I'm not, like, judging you, but this is not what Lyfts are supposed to be used for," Sterling lectures.

I ignore him and lean forward in my seat, peering at Holden through the windshield as he gets out of his truck, walks around to the back and opens his truck bed box and pulls out skates and a stick.

He's leaving work to play hockey? That doesn't make any sense. I wait until he's disappeared inside, count to ten and then get out. I turn back to Sterling and shoot him an apologetic smile. "I'm sorry. Thanks for indulging me. I will give you that tip."

"Okay," he says, looking leery. "Let me give you a tip. Don't stalk your boyfriend."

"He's my contractor!" I call, but Sterling has driven off already.

True to my word, I punch in a twenty-dollar tip in the app and a five-star rating, as I hurry across the parking lot. As I swing open the door and step inside the arena, I'm shocked and yet not shocked by the fact that everything is the same as it was when I was a teenager. Same chipped blue paint on the cinderblock walls, same green doors on the locker rooms, same rinky-dink concession stand tucked into the corner at the far end. I wonder for a fleeting second if Holden's coming here because he's going to be renovating it. Lord knows it could use it. But then the ice comes into view and I notice a bunch of pint-size hockey players. There's also a handful moms in the stands, most of them staring at their phones.

A whistle blows and three grown men skate across the ice to the center. One of them is Holden. They divide the kids into two groups and start calling out drills. Holden Hendricks is coaching hockey. I raise a hand to my chest and lay it over my heart as I sigh in relief. But why didn't he want to tell me this? He can't be embarrassed by this—it's heartwarming!

I watch him for about half an hour, sneaking my way into the stands and tucking myself behind a couple of moms so I don't stand out. The longer I watch him, the more I realize it's more the just warming my heart to see him out there gliding across the ice and laughing and smiling with the kids. It's warming other parts too. Because it's fucking hot. I've always thought of Holden as this tough, brooding, hard-ass type but here, with these young kids, he's lighter. He's smiling and joking and when one of them gets frustrated and smacks his stick against the boards after he flubs a drill, Holden skates him to a corner, pops off the kid's helmet, squats down and gives him what looks like a pep talk. The kid skates back to the group with a big smile on his face.

I know I should sneak back out and call another Lyft, if I haven't been banned from the service, but I can't take my eyes off Holden. It's an indulgence to see him like this and I've never been good with moderation when it comes to indulgences. I once ate an entire chocolate cream pie. For breakfast.

"Duke is developing quite the slap shot," one mom says to another, pointing to a boy wearing a number three on his jersey.

"He says Holden taught him a new way to grip his stick that's helping," the other mother says in a tight, tense tone. "He acts like Holden is a freaking messiah."

"Well, he is doing a great job as a coach," the first mom counters.

"If only he did the same bang-up job as a brother," the other woman bites back and as she glances at her friend, I catch a solid look at her profile. Is that...Bradie?

I didn't know Bradie at all when we were kids. I think I saw her maybe twice my entire childhood. She was a few years older than me and she didn't hang out with all the neighborhood kids like Holden did. She was a bookworm who spent the majority of her summers inside. She hated the beach and the ocean and hockey and all the stuff that we lived for back then.

"Anyway, it doesn't matter," she says. "Duke is failing classes and the rule is if he doesn't get good grades, he doesn't get to play. Which is fine because the longer he hangs around his uncle, the bigger his disappointment will be when Holden gets tired of being a good, reliable guy."

She must feel the weight of my stare because she glances over her shoulder and I immediately avert my eyes, but it's too late. She does a double take, tucks her long flat brown hair behind her ear to get a better look and speaks. "I know you."

Inwardly I'm groaning as I slowly bring my eyes back to hers. "Yeah. I'm Winnie Braddock."

"Shit! Right!" Bradie smiles. "Your brother used to play with my brother, and now he plays hockey professionally, right?"

I nod. "Yeah. Jude plays for the San Francisco Thunder."

"Right." Bradie's brow furrows. "What are you doing here?"

"I-I," I stutter and swallow. "I was in the area, so I just wandered in. Walk down memory lane and everything. I spent a lot of time here as a kid because of Jude."

I shift uncomfortably on the hard concrete bench and change the subject. "Your brother is actually renovating our cottage."

"Yeah?" Bradie's eyebrows shoot up. "How's that going?"

"Fantastic," I say. "He's doing an incredible job. We're really pleased. He's professional and the quality of work is top-notch."

I feel like I'm passionately reciting a Yelp review, but I don't care. Something inside me feels the deep need to defend Holden. Bradie is silent for a second as she absorbs what I said and then she nods. "I'm pleasantly surprised to hear that." She pauses and her eyes narrow. "Aren't you the girl who punched him?"

A whistle blows on the ice and we all turn to see what's going on. The older guy calls the end of practice and my blood runs cold. I have to get out of here before Holden sees me. Although I'm sure his sister will probably mention I was here. Shit. I definitely didn't think this through. Bradie and her mom friend both stand and start down the stands. I sit there, frozen by a complete lack of any idea of what to do, and of course Holden glances up from center ice where he's talking to his nephew and of course his eyes land right on me. *Of course.*

He looks completely stunned. His nephew skates to the

boards, where Bradie is now standing. Holden stays put, staring at me. I bite my bottom lip and give him a little guilty shrug as if to say *Yeah I know I'm as surprised as you are that I'm here.* He shakes his head. His nephew calls him and as he skates to the boards, I decide it's time to bolt. I scurry down the concrete risers and am about to disappear down the hall to the front door when he calls my name.

"Winona!" His tone isn't angry. It's actually maybe slightly amused.

I turn slowly, like a Scooby-Doo criminal being caught by those dastardly kids. Holden is waving me over as Bradie and Duke look on. I slink my way toward them and smile at Bradie. "Hi again." And then I turn to Duke. "You must be Duke. Hi, I'm Winnie."

"Hi, Winnie." He waves at me, his hand engulfed in a giant hockey glove. "You know my uncle?"

I nod. "He's working on my cottage, but I've known him since he was just a little bit older than you."

"Remember I told you I used to play with Jude Braddock from the San Francisco Thunder?" Holden says to Duke and he nods. "This is one of his sisters."

Duke's brown eyes are the size of hockey pucks and he turns back to me. "Your brother is the coolest hockey player ever. He's the best in the league. I try to model my game after him. You're so lucky."

Behind him, Holden's face burst into a goofy grin as I try not to laugh out loud at the cute kid. I am so proud of Jude and I know he deserves to be idolized for his skills and abilities but at the same time, he's my brother and I used to watch him stick Legos up his nose. "You know next time Jude is in town I can get him to come here and skate with your guys. He can teach you some moves himself if you want."

"Hell, yes!"

"Duke!" Bradie chastises.

"Sorry, but seriously that would make my life," Duke declares.

"Go get changed. We need to get you home to start on your schoolwork," Bradie says sternly and Duke nods, despite being visibly disappointed. He skates off to the other corner of the ice where the tunnel to the changing rooms is located. She then turns to me and smiles. "I appreciate your offer and we may take you up on it one day if you're serious."

"Deadly serious," I reply and cross my heart. "Jude is all about encouraging young players."

"Well, Duke probably won't be playing at that point. At least not on a team," Bradie says, and I remember what she was telling her mom friend. "He just tanked another test."

"So you're pulling him out? For sure?" Holden asks and the dread is dripping off his voice. It occurs to me suddenly that his nephew is why he's coaching. And right now as Bradie says yes he looks like someone just sucked the life out of him. My heart clenches.

"What subject is he struggling with?" I ask.

"Math mostly. Although his social studies grade isn't great either."

"I could tutor him," I say without even thinking about it. Bradie and Holden both let their jaws drop. "I'm a certified teacher in Canada and I spent the last year and half tutoring grade school kids at an acclaimed after-school program in San Francisco. You can call them for references."

Bradie's expression goes from stunned to cold. "I'm sure you're more than qualified, but honestly, I can barely keep a roof over our head. No matter what you charge, I can't afford you."

"I'll pay," Holden volunteers but I shake my head.

"I'm not charging," I say firmly. Bradie opens her mouth to object but I raise my hand to stop her. "Look, I just lost my dad after watching him suffer through a brutal illness. I'm just trying to take baby steps back into the real world. If you let me tutor Duke, it will be doing me a favor too, so I don't just sit at home watching Holden work and wallowing. It will make me feel good to help him. He seems like a good kid."

Bradie's face instantly softens and she reaches out and touches my arm gently. "I'm so sorry for your loss."

"Thank you." I manage a weak smile. "So let me tutor Duke. I can do it twice a week for an hour. We'll work around hockey practices. It can't hurt."

"No, it definitely can't," Bradie agrees and smiles. "Thank you."

"My pleasure." I give her my email so she can send me his current curriculum. She hugs me as Duke appears with some other boys walking toward us on the outside of the rink, hauling their giant equipment bags. "I'll see you later."

I turn to leave, but Holden reaches over the boards and touches my shoulder. I turn to look at him and he's got this really intense expression I have never seen before. "I'm driving you home."

It's old Holden, all demanding and gruff, and I feel heat build between my legs. "I can take an Uber."

"I'm driving you."

I nod.

Bradie and Duke are halfway to the front door, walking with her friend from earlier and her son, when she turns back. "Wait a minute…you didn't answer me earlier. Are you the one who punched Holden when you were teenagers?"

Holden groans.

"Yup!" I smile guiltily.

"What?" her mom friend gasps.

"Trust me, he probably deserved it," Bradie tells her friend.

"I did," Holden mumbles, but I don't think they can hear him.

"Holden was a completely different person then," I tell her.

The mom friend still looks kind of horrified, but she nods and leaves, Bradie and Duke following along with her. I turn back to Holden. That weird intense look on his face has deepened. "I'll be two minutes. Don't move."

I watch him shoot across the ice and head off down the tunnel toward the locker rooms. I wander to the entrance doors and stare out at the emptying parking lot. By the time I hear footsteps behind me, there are only two trucks left in the darkening parking lot—his and the rink manager's I assume. I glance over my shoulder to find Holden right behind me. He reaches up, cups both my shoulders and turns me around. The feel of his hands on me makes that warmth inside me grow hotter.

And then, without a word, he covers my mouth with his

in a hungry kiss. I wrap my hands around his waist, my finger curling around the fabric of the back of his shirt, and he tangles his hands in my hair as his tongue slips into my mouth. I welcome him with a whimper. He presses his whole body against me, and the glass door rattles as my back hits it and he rolls his hips, grinding his hardness against my belly. I tug harder on his shirt, struggling to overcome the urge to just pull it off his body right here. The need to feel his skin against mine is blinding.

"Take me home. Please," I beg against his lips. He grunts a yes and, holding my hand firmly in his, pulls me through the front doors and to his car.

The ride home is excruciating. All I want to do is strip him naked, run my lips and tongue over every part of him and then ride him into oblivion, but I have to wait. He's staring straight ahead the whole ride and pushing the speed limit, clearly as eager as I am to get home. I move my hand to his thigh and let it ride up, skimming over his strong, hard muscles until I land on his rock-hard cock. I press my palm gently into it and rub him through his jeans. His jaw flexes under his scruffy beard and his knuckles turn white on the steering wheel.

"Winnie…" He hisses my name as a warning. A warning of what? That if I don't stop he'll pull over and take me on the side of the road? Like that's something I don't want? I squeeze him again.

We're on the long, narrow main road that leads into our town. It's lined on both sides with century-old pines, which is where Ocean Pines got half its name. The area is technically parkland, but other than a few bird-watching tourists and kids looking for a place to drink in the summer, it's always empty. When I rub him slowly for a third time he yanks the wheel to the left, cutting across the double line and pulling the truck into the edge of the trees, off the street. He jams it in park, unclips his seat belt and lunges across the cab to kiss me again.

"You push every damn button, good or bad, that I've ever had," he growls against my throat, his beard scratching my skin and sending prickles of pleasure through my body.

"I'm just returning the favor," I say and dip my head to join our lips.

If our last kiss was hungry, this one is starving. He reaches around me and unclips my seat belt and then, yanks me closer. I do one better and climb right into his lap, never breaking the kiss.

We're tugging and yanking at each other's clothes like desperate, wild animals. I manage to get his shirt off and he gets mine up enough that he can pull down my bra and wrap those perfect lips around my nipples. But then as I fumble with the belt on his jeans and bang a knee against the console next to me, I realize that anything more in the confines of this front seat is impossible. Holden is a big boy—in every way—and I'm too tall for this too.

He must have the same thoughts as he tugs on the back of my leggings and accidentally punches the horn. He pulls his mouth from my breasts and tips his head back to look at me. His silver-blue eyes are wild. "Fuck this."

He reaches for the door handle and pushes open the door with one hand wrapping the other around my back. He starts to turn, getting out of the car with me still sitting on him so I wrap my legs around his back. He places his free hand on top of my head pushing it down a little. "Watch your head."

He swings his legs out, stands up and starts walking. The setting sun isn't penetrating the thick overhang of pines much and so everything around us is dark and the air cool. The pine needles crunch underneath his work boots and I close my eyes and kiss my way up the side of his neck, his jugular pumping wildly beneath my lips. Then suddenly the sound under his feet grows solid. I look down. He's on the small, covered footbridge that runs over a tiny ravine about fifty feet into the forest.

It's even darker in here and it smells like wet wood planks and damp pine needles. His lips glance over my jaw. "I'm going to fuck you right here."

He lowers us to his knees. I unhook my legs from his waist and kneel in front of him as he quickly unfastens his belt and jeans. I push my leggings down my thighs along with my thong. "No," I tell him kissing his collarbone lightly before nipping it. "I'm going to fuck *you* right here."

I grab his shoulders and push him back. He falls back onto his bare ass as I get one leg out of my leggings and climb into his lap again. His wide, strong hands spread out across my back just below my bra and he bites a nipple through the thin cotton fabric. It causes me to arch my back and push my bare pussy into his bare shaft. If lightning clapped across the sky right now it would be less electric than the current that runs through me from that intimate touch.

I grab his head in my hands and join our lips again, my tongue sweeping into his mouth, colliding with his. I pull my hips up and lower myself onto him. He tenses as soon as my entrance finds his tip. But I refuse to break the kiss and let him warn me. I know what I'm doing. I hold his head in place, keeping my lips to his and lower myself completely over him. But he grabs my hips before I can start to ride him.

His light eyes are clouded with lust but serious just the same. "Winnie. Protection."

"IUD," I whisper and run my hand gently across the side of his face, letting the beard tickle my palm. I lean forward and kiss the side of his jaw just below his earlobe. "And I don't need protection from you."

His grip on my hips relaxes, and I start to move. God, he feels incredible. This is incredible. His hands and lips roam my body as I roll my hips and move up and down, finding the perfect rhythm. As our releases build, he starts whispering to me, his lips against the crook of my neck.

"You're dangerous. This is dangerous...," he confesses and I start to slow my pace, worried he's still concerned about the lack of a condom. But he grabs my hips again and keeps moving me, hard and fast. Our eyes meet. "The way you feel around my dick...the way you make me feel when I just look at you. Fuck, you're beautiful, Winona."

My thighs quiver as my orgasm rips through me. He holds me closer with one hand, pressing our torsos together, and uses the other to balance as he continues to push into me until, moments later, I feel his whole body tighten and he lets out a guttural groan. He collapses back onto the wood floor of the bridge and I go with him. After a few seconds of catching our breath he rolls us over so we're on our sides facing each other. He gently runs a hand across the side of my face and into my hair. I can barely make out his beautiful face because the sun has set and it's almost pitch black now in the bridge. And it's freezing. I shiver. He starts to sit up and pulls me up too.

"Let's get you home." He stands, pulls up his pants and reaches for me.

I quickly wiggle back into my leggings. He pulls me to my feet and we leave the bridge, hand in hand, and make our way back to the truck. I pause before climbing in and brush the pine needles off his back. He turns to face me, shirtless, a sexy, satiated look on his rugged features and the moonlight glinting off his hard, bare upper body. I let my fingertip trace the lines of his arm tattoo. "You kind of look like some kind of hot country singer out here in the woods in your faded jeans, work boots and nothing else."

"You're a country music fan?"

I shake my head. "No, but Sadie is. You, sweetheart, would sell a hundred albums looking like this. Maybe you should take it up as a side gig."

"First of all, I'm definitely a rock-and-roll boy." He smirks, which makes my panties wet—again. "And secondly I sound like a dying cat when I sing."

I burst out laughing. He leans forward and kisses me with a dominance that does nothing to help my panty situation. "Well, I think I might buy you a cowboy hat and maybe some chaps anyway. You know, for future role play."

His eyebrows raise and the smirk deepens. "I'm going to ignore almost everything in that sentence and just concentrate on the word 'future.' Because I like that you're thinking of a future with me. Actually I fucking love it, Larry."

"Ugh!" I give him a shove, but I'm laughing—until I feel something lick my ankle. Then the laughter turns into a shriek of horror.

Holden pushes me against the side of the truck and stands in front of me ready to fight whatever vicious wildlife assault me. His head dips down and he chuckles, standing up with a black and tan Dachshund in his arms wearing a plaid bow tie. I recognize him instantly, because she keeps pictures of them behind the checkout counter. And then her familiar voice fills the air.

"Garth!" comes the frustrated voice. "I said HEEL!"

I rock up on my toes and peek over Holden's shoulder to see Cat charging toward us through the darkened woods from the road, another Dachshund, this one brown is running along behind her, trying to keep up. She's holding a flashlight, the beam bobbing around wildly as she runs. It lands on Holden and freezes, because she does.

"Hey, Cat," Holden says casually, like we haven't just been caught with our pants down...well, almost anyway. Wayne, the other little dog, wearing a bow tie that matches his brother's, trots ahead of Cat and stops at Holden's feet. He bends to pet him, and reunite him with his brother, and leaves me exposed. Cat's flashlight is now on me. I move my hands, crossing my arms over my bare midriff. Not like it matters. I'm very clearly in nothing but a bra and leggings. Cat went to Yale. She's a smart cookie.

"Please say you're fucking kidding me, Winnie. Him?"

"Yes. Him," I confirm and drop my hands and stand taller because I'm not ashamed.

Cat walks over to Holden and scoops Wayne and Garth in her arms and without another word marches out of the forest. Holden sighs and turns to me. "I hope she doesn't hold me against you."

He walks back over to me and opens the passenger door so I can climb in. I look up at him and give him a small smile. "If she does, that's on her. I'll be okay with it. I know you've changed because I've let you show me." I pause and my smile turns sheepish. "And I'm sorry I followed you to the rink like a stalker."

"I should have just told you what I was doing in the afternoons." Holden returns my sheepish smile. "I was annoyed and sick of explaining myself."

"Well, that's true. And I mean, of course that was totally your fault," I say, my sheepish grin turning devious. "I wasn't acting like an annoying brat at all."

He laughs. "Get your ass in the car before I go for round two."

His grin is much more loving than lustful. He's falling for me as much as I'm falling for him and knowing that fills me with joy. The emotion is startling because it's been so damn long since I felt pure happiness. I pull my shirt on as he starts the truck and my first instinct in my blissful haze is to call my dad and tell him about this. That I'm happy. That things are starting to not just go well but be great. And I can't. He'll never know.

And just like that, my mood plummets.

16

HOLDEN

Winnie got really quiet on the way back to her place. And it isn't a contented, post-orgasm quiet. It's also not a *Shit, my friend just caught me sleeping with the enemy* quiet either. It's something deeper. Sadder. I want to talk to her about it, but I still have work to do on the kitchen tonight if I am going to meet the deadlines I promised Jude. And honestly, she doesn't look like she wants to talk about it.

"I'm going to take a shower," she says as we climb the stairs to the porch.

"Call me if you need someone to scrub your back," I say and wink. She smiles, but her eyes remain filled with sadness.

She's all I can think about as I head into the kitchen and start placing the cabinets against the now dry, freshly painted walls. I have to wait until Mike and Dave are back tomorrow to drill the top ones to the wall, but I get all the bottom ones in. As I'm adhering the last one, she wanders into the kitchen, hair wet, wearing pajama bottoms and a T-shirt. She's breathtaking.

She glances at my work. "I love the Shaker style."

I smile. "I thought it would match the character of the house."

"It does." She nods and walks toward the fridge. "Thank God you didn't let Jude pick them. We'd have some weird modern cabinets made out of recycled hockey pucks or something and they'd end up melting in the Maine humidity."

I laugh, but she doesn't. Something is very up. But what? I watch her as she peers inside the fridge. "Well, these are made out of salvaged wood. Your brother is very environmentally conscious."

"Yeah, he always cared more about saving the world than saving himself," she mutters the profound statement almost absently. "Thank God Zoey came back into his life and made him want to improve more than just the world around him."

She pulls a half-empty bottle of white from the fridge and turns toward where the cupboards should be. "Right, the glasses are in the dining room now."

She starts to walk past me, but I step into her path. "The fact that your brother married Zoey Quinlin is amazing. He had such a crush on her when we were kids it was painful to watch. He must feel like he won the lottery."

Winnie nods. "He did. She's way out of his league."

I'm blown away. "He threatened to murder me once when I flirted with her."

"And that stopped you?" Winnie says, shocked. "You were pretty much into anything that would have wrecked shit back then. I'm surprised you didn't sleep with her after a threat like that."

"I knew your brother was serious," I reply with a shrug. "I was a menace to myself, but I wasn't suicidal. Besides your brother was the only person who put up with my shit. I mean aside from Kidd and a couple others who used my bad attitude to their advantage."

"How'd they do that?" she asks and I follow her into the dining room where she sets the wine bottle down on the counter as she reaches for a glass.

"They were bad eggs. I was acting like one. They cheered that on instead of talking me out of it, like your brother constantly tried to do," I explain, but I'm more focused on watching her pour a giant ass glass of wine and take a huge gulp. "We should probably eat something. When was the last time you ate? I've got a really good frozen lasagna I was going to cook. More than enough for two."

"I'm not hungry," she mumbles and gulps down more wine. "I'm going to go sit on the porch. Have you seen my sweater?"

"You mean your dad's sweater?" As soon as the words leave my mouth a lightbulb goes on. This is about her dad. This mood. The sadness.

She nods curtly. "It's probably upstairs."

She turns abruptly on her heel and stomps upstairs. Fuck. I get this now...I just don't know how to fix it. I head back into the kitchen to finish up my work and ponder possible ways to lift Winnie out of her funk. When I'm done about an hour later, she's finished the bottle of wine. I offer again to make us lasagna but she declines. So I leave her, wrapped up in her dad's sweater and a blanket in a rocking chair on her porch and head to my Airstream. I pop the lasagna in the oven and take a shower. I change into some clean clothes and throw together a salad.

When everything is done, I make two plates filled with salad and lasagna, and kick open the trailer door and carry them up to her porch. It's really getting chilly, but she doesn't seem to notice. There's a new bottle of wine beside her, but it looks untouched. I balance the plates on one arm and open her door as she wipes away at tears she doesn't want me to see.

"I'm really not hungry, Holden," she says. "I'm just enjoying my time alone."

"No, you're not," I reply and hold out a plate to her. "You're enjoying being miserable and like I said from the beginning, when you hated me, that's really not a path you want to fall down. Enjoying the pain."

"I'm not fucking enjoying it," she snaps and when she won't take the plate I walk over and put it down on the small table next to her. "But I can't just jump ahead with my life like everything is fucking peachy."

"No one is asking you to, Win," I say firmly. "But everything is pretty fucking peachy. You got yourself out of a shitty relationship. You're in your favorite place on the planet and you're falling for a really fantastic guy who treats you the way you deserve and gives you some pretty fucking spectacular orgasms. The world is definitely looking up for you. Letting yourself enjoy that isn't dishonoring your dad's memory."

"I don't want to talk with you about this," she says with acid in her voice.

"Okay, then let's talk about Dixie."

Her hazel eyes blink. "Why?"

"Because I accidentally overheard you this morning and you totally cock-blocked her wedding," I say and drop down onto the rocker next to hers. I cut my fork through the gooey, cheesy lasagna.

"First of all, mind your own business," she says and sits up indignantly in the rocker. "And second of all, I didn't cock-block it. She thinks it will be too sad without Dad, and it will be. For everyone."

"Is that what your dad said to you in that letter you carry around with you?" I ask and brace for impact because she's going to explode when I'm done confronting her with the truth. "Did he say, 'Don't bother doing anything meaningful or pursuing dreams and goals now that I'm gone. It'll suck, so just give up'?"

"Of course he fucking didn't." The anger in her voice borders on yelling. She slams down the empty wineglass on the table as her bottom lip wobbles. "But it's too fucking hard. He never got to walk any of us down the aisle. We never got to share that with him. He... it just wouldn't be the same."

Tears are falling freely down her high cheekbones now and my heart is cracking down the middle for her. I put my plate in my lap and lean forward to wipe her cheeks with my thumb, but she swats my hand away. I sigh.

"My mom was the first one who told me I was good enough to be a professional hockey player. She wasn't just blowing smoke up my ass either. She believed it, so I believed it. And every time I had dreams of it happening, of skating out there in an NHL jersey, she was in the stands." I feel a lump start to grow in the back of my throat and try to swallow it down.

"My dad was never into sports and never came to a game, let alone encouraged me to play. Bradie didn't give two shits either. So, when my mom died, I let myself believe that even if I made it to the NHL, it wouldn't be the same. It wouldn't feel worth it anymore. So I stopped practicing as hard. I stopped playing as hard. I goofed off at practice. I mouthed off to coaches. I started fights on and off the ice with players. I tanked my own dream."

She's listening and she's stopped crying, which I take as a small victory. "And it wouldn't have been the same, to play in the big leagues without her watching. But it still would have been great and worth it. I fucked it up all on my own. Dixie will regret not marrying her crazy-ass goalie boyfriend. She'll regret it more than her dad not being there to see it. So don't play into that. You will regret encouraging it."

She doesn't look angry anymore, but she still looks like a wounded animal. I grab my fork and scoop up another bite of lasagna. "And you'll regret not eating this. Especially if you're going to drink another bottle of wine."

I hold the fork out to her. She doesn't take it, but she also doesn't slap it out of my hand so it's not a total fail. Her eyes are glued to mine. "Do you regret not making the NHL?"

"Every goddamn day of my life." I rock forward on the chair, fork still poised in front of her mouth. "Eat. Please."

She opens her mouth and I feed her. She heaves a heavy breath as she chews and tears pool in her pretty eyes again. "I shouldn't have given into my grief like that. I'll call Dixie tomorrow. I don't know how I will get through it. I don't know how she will. Just thinking about such a big life moment happening without him makes me feel like my soul is being crushed, but you're right. I will call her. And it will happen. And I will survive."

"Yes, you will," I promise her. I lean forward with another forkful of food and she takes it while wiping the tears from her eyes with the back of her hand. I kiss her forehead. "You'll do more than survive, gorgeous. You're one of the strongest women I've even known and I'm not just talking about your right hook."

She gives me a wobbly smile and then takes my plate out of my lap, stealing my fork next. "This is really good."

I chuckle under my breath and grab the second plate off the table. We eat in silence but it's comfortable. She looks tired. Exhausted, really. But even I'm not stupid enough to think that's something you tell a woman, so I keep my trap shut and eat.

When we're done, I force myself to yawn. "Been one hell of a long day."

She nods, lifting a hand to stifle her own yawn and then she reaches for my empty plate. I cover her hand with mine, stopping her. "Leave them. We can do them in the morning. It's late," I remind her, standing up and pulling her to her feet in front of me. "Come to bed with me."

"Your mattress *is* really comfortable," she murmurs.

"I'm surprised you noticed," I laugh. "Every time I wake up there's more of you on top of me than the mattress."

"You're comfortable too," she says with a pink tint growing on her cheeks. "Is that a complaint?"

"Hell no." I brush my lips softly against hers again. "I'll be your human pillow any day of the week, Larry."

"If you don't stop with that nickname you will be my human punching bag," she warns, but I can feel her smile against my chest as I pull her into a hug.

We head down to my trailer, and inside we get ready for bed. She's still a little tipsy from all the wine she consumed and it's making her frisky. As we crawl into bed her hands are everywhere. I don't mind at all, but I'm not having sex with her right now. She's too vulnerable and too tipsy. So I take her hands and pull them up and out from under the blankets. I kiss both her palms before moving them on my chest.

"Are you turning down sex?" she gasps in an overly dramatic, drunk fashion.

"I'm not turning it down. I'm postponing it," I explain and she sighs in defeat and nuzzles closer to me, dropping her head onto my chest and draping a leg over my midsection and my rock-hard erection.

"I don't think that gorgeous dick of yours got the memo," she mutters and I laugh.

"He's usually the last to know," I reply and run a hand through that long, silky magical hair of hers, which isn't going to help that erection die anytime soon, but I can't help it. "And I don't think he's ever been called gorgeous before."

"You have a history of being underappreciated," she says sleepily. "We're going to change that."

"We are, are we?" I can only assume this is the alcohol and exhaustion causing this conversation so I'm trying really hard not to take it to heart even though, damn, she's drunkenly saying everything I wanted to hear for a very long time.

"Mmm...," Winnie coos, definitely on the brink of sleep.

"You're a good man now, Holden Hendricks. I think maybe you always were. People will see it. I'll make sure of it."

"Winona Skye Braddock, my own personal superhero," I joke and tenderly press my lips to the top of her head.

"You know my middle name?" she whispers. "Stalker."

I chuckle but don't bother to explain I saw it on that letter I almost accidentally threw out. The one she won't tell me about. I close my eyes and concentrate on the soothing tickle of her breath against my chest. And then, when I think she's already asleep she lets out a long sigh and says, "Your mom would be proud of who you've become."

Fuck, this girl is everything. I am never letting her go.

17

WINNIE

I take a big breath and swing open the door to Cannon's Corner Grocery. The bells jingle above my head, and Cat looks up from where she's sitting on a stool behind the counter, reading the *Portland Herald*. Her expression remains passive, which I realize is a very bad sign. I've known her since I was four years old and she's never been anything but bold, bright and expressive.

"Cinnamon buns are fresh. Coffee is too. Just brewed a new pot," she says in a monotone voice and looks back down at the paper.

I walk over and lean on the counter, peering up at her desperately. "Come on, Cat. Let me have it."

She sighs and closes the sports section. Her blue eyes are filled with confusion. "I don't get it. You hated him most of all when we were kids. Up until he robbed me, I was actually the one trying to convince you he wasn't so bad. But you were right. He was bad. He *is* bad."

I shake my head. "No, he isn't. Not anymore. Now he's just a guy trying to turn his life around, and he's succeeding."

Cat's bold red lips curve downward. "He's always been great at pretending to be what you want him to be. I know you're going through a lot, Win, but I thought you'd see through that."

"I would if he was playing me, but he's not," I argue. I stand up again and sigh. "Look, Cat, I can't and won't sell you on him. I know who he is, and I trust him and I like him. A lot. He doesn't have to prove anything to me anymore."

She stands up and walks over to the counter, her arms crossed tightly over her chest. "Sorry, Win, but I don't think he can prove anything to me. I'm not buying what he's selling. But I adore you and I don't want this to impact our friendship."

"Good. Neither do I," I agree and reach over the counter and grab her arms, forcing her to uncross them and hold my hands. "So please, can we agree to disagree right now? Eventually though, I will try to make you see what I see. I'm hoping I don't even have to try and you just see it yourself."

Her face twists for a second like I just told her something that was equal parts unbelievable and distasteful. Great. I clearly have a long way to go with her. However her face slips back into a friendly smile and she squeezes both my hands. "For the record, I hope I'm not right. Because you deserve the best guy ever. And if, sadly, I am right, I will be there to pick up all your pieces. I promise."

"You won't have to. I promise," I reach across the counter and hug her.

"Cinnamon bun?"

"Three, please."

Her eyes grow steely. "I am fighting the urge to tell you we have a one bun per customer maximum."

"Fight hard, Cannon. I want three," I reply and she groans, but walks over to the warmer where she keeps the buns.

I woke up this morning feeling mildly hungover but yet still better than I have in months. Holden was about to get in the shower, but I reminded him he had postponed sex. That's all it took for him to delay his shower and make good on that rain check.

Before yesterday I knew I was done fighting the attraction I had to him. I'd made that decision the night my sisters were here and I snuck out of the cottage to be with him. But it was only yesterday, watching him coach those kids and then later enduring his sister's skepticism, that I decided I was done fighting against the bond that we were so clearly forming.

I walk over to the coffee station and pour myself some dark roast and add hazelnut creamer. Back at the counter, Cat puts the buns in a box and rings up the total. "No discounts when I know my glorious masterpiece is headed for the belly of the enemy."

"And his coworker," I add with a happy smile and hand her the cash. She bites back her own grin and hands me my change.

I give her a wink, grab my goodies and head toward the door. The bells chime again as I swing it open, but I pause and turn back to her. "I promise to drop it, but let me just go out on this. I was just as skeptical and dismissive of Holden as you were. But I decided, just yesterday in fact, to believe him when he said he changed because I couldn't deny the way he made me feel anymore."

"You mean he's good at sex?" Cat says. "You can't deny the orgasms."

"No," I reply firmly. "I'm talking how he started making me feel pre-orgasms. Happy, safe, loved. He isn't the same mean-spirited, dangerous asshole, because I wouldn't be in love with him if he was. I'm a good judge of character. I like you, after all."

Cat laughs. "Go back to your hoodlum and eat your cinnamon buns. Leave me to chew on your words of wisdom."

"Bye!" I step out onto the sidewalk and hum as I make my way back to the cottage.

The early fall cold snap has broken and the weather is balmy and the sun is shining. Life is fucking excellent.

"You would love it here today, Dad," I whisper to myself…and to him. The tears are ready to well up, but I don't let them. Things are good, and that's what he would have wanted. No tears required.

Dave and Holden are overjoyed to get the buns, and it takes away from the stress of Mike being too sick to make it today. I offer my services, since I have little else to do, but Holden declines. "You're client adjacent, and I don't let clients help in their own renos."

I ask him if I can hang out in his trailer and he says yes, so I head in there and answer emails on my phone. Sadie emailed me to say she's back and Mom was doing well. She wanted to talk about what I said to Dixie. Apparently, Dixie told Eli they should postpone the wedding, and he was not thrilled. I sigh. Right. I still have to handle that.

I call Dixie. She answers on the fourth ring. She doesn't sound like herself when she says hello. She sounds depressed. "Listen, I was wrong," I say immediately. "Don't postpone the wedding."

"Who is that?" I hear Eli ask in the background.

"It's Winnie, and now she's agreeing with you," Dixie tells him and she sounds exasperated.

"Good! Now I don't have to fly to Maine and scream at her," Eli says loud enough that it's perfectly clear through the phone.

"It doesn't matter. I still think she was right," Dixie argues and he swears.

"Dixie, you don't," I say. "You're just hurting, which is logical, but postponing the wedding isn't. Dad wouldn't want us putting our lives on hold, especially the good parts."

She doesn't respond at first and through the silence I hear her sniff. My eyes instantly start to water and unlike earlier, I can't stop them. "Dixie, I'm a mess too right now. That's why I said something so stupid. But Dad got to give his blessing on your wedding, so you should do it. The cottage is going to look beautiful and he always hoped we'd get married here, so do it. Please. You won't regret it. It'll have moments of pain, but it won't be painful. Please. Listen to me for once."

A sob-laugh escapes her. "I always listen to you. And Sadie and even Jude, but don't tell him."

"And are any of them telling you not to do this?"

"No. It was just you."

"I was wrong," I say and wipe the tears from my eyes.

"Okay," she sniffs again but she sounds better. "July first, Canada Day weekend it is."

"Yes!" I hear Eli cheer and then Dixie squeals. I bet my life he either picked her up or tackled her. Those two are more like WWE partners than lovers sometimes. "Thanks for fixing this, Win!"

"You're welcome!" I call into the phone, hoping he hears me.

"Get off me. I need to talk to Winnie about her man situation," Dixie says to her fiancé. A second later her voice grows serious. "Sadie told me on the plane ride home you spent the night in Holden's trailer."

"I did. I do. It's like an ongoing thing now."

"I'm…well…I'm shocked," Dixie says. "Is this some crazy rebound thing? I mean, I know it's been a while since you've been single and you've never had a fling. You've been dating Ty since you were old enough to date, and Holden's hot. Douchey but hot."

"He's not a douche," I tell her and my eyes land on a pile of papers on the edge of the kitchenette table. On top is his business license paperwork. It's all filled out except the business name. "He's different than when he was kid. And it's not a fling. It's something…more."

"Oh." She sounds more worried than stunned now and that makes me upset. Why can't anyone just be happy for me?

"Dixie, I need support right now," I say tersely. "We all do, and he's the only one giving it to me."

"Wait a minute. If you'd just come home, we'd be giving

you support," Dixie says angrily. "I want to be there for you. We all do. You're the one who ran away."

"I know that. And I don't know why I couldn't go back to San Francisco after I dumped Ty," I say and reach for Holden's paperwork. "I used to think I was running too, but now I'm beginning to think it was *to* something, not from something. I needed to be here. I needed to find this new, improved Holden and he needed me."

"Winnie, I want you to be happy and I would trust that if you think he's changed his ways, he has," Dixie replies quickly and her anger has turned to sympathy, which I like even less. "But while we were there, I saw a creepy dude who was totally tweaked out come by his trailer early in the morning. And Holden gave him cash."

"What?" My heart plummets.

"Yeah. I mean I thought it was totally sketchy but typical Holden," Dixie explains. "But you're saying that's not him anymore so...I just thought you should ask him about that then."

"I'm sure it's nothing, but I'll ask him." I swallow but my mouth and throat are dry. "What did this guy look like?"

Dixie gives me a description and even though it's vague, I know it's that guy Cat and I saw him talking to in the alley the other night. The one Cat claims is the town drug dealer. My heart sinks further until it feels like it's in the bottom of my stomach.

I walk over to the fridge and grab a bottle of water from it. "Okay. I'll talk to him about it. In the meantime, start planning your wedding and let me know when you're going dress shopping. You know I'm not missing that."

We say good-bye and I hang up. I look around the trailer as I sip the water that for some reason, doesn't keep my mouth from staying dry. I could snoop right now. I could dig around in his drawers and look for something that proves my fears—and everyone's insinuations—are valid. But that would be wrong. Easy, but wrong. I could march over to the cottage and demand the truth. That would be easy too, but it would hurt him. I know this. Especially after last night, it would look like I hadn't made up my mind about him. Like I was still looking for reasons to derail this thing between us, and I'm really not. I don't want to actively look for reasons anymore. And I didn't seek this out.

"Fuck, Holden," I whisper to myself. "Do not let me down."

I decide I'll wait until tonight, after he's coached hockey and I've tutored Duke. Maybe casually over dinner. He's stressed right now with Mike being sick.

Ugh. It's going to be a long day.

Five hours later, I'm in the same spot, at the dinette in the trailer, sitting across from Duke as he bites his bottom lip and stares at one of the cookies I baked earlier for this purpose. First, I had him cut it into fractions and now I'm giving him fraction sizes and he has to make that size using the smaller pieces. If he gets it right, he can eat it.

"Half...," he mutters to himself. He grabs to pieces. "Two quarters make a half."

"Exactly!" I say and he grins. "Eat your fractions."

He grins and pops a quarter into his mouth as his mother opens the trailer door and peeks in. "Ready to go, Duke?" Bradie asks as he chows down. She looks confused by the cookie consumption.

"I was teaching him fractions using cookies," I explain. "I find visuals help."

"Cookies make everything better," Bradie says with a smile.

I scoot out of the booth after Duke, who is gathering his stuff off the table. He turns to his mom and holds up his homework. "Done. Whole thing! And I, like, understood how Winnie explained it."

"Good!" Bradie says and there's definitely relief in her tone. She inhales deeply. "What smells so delicious?"

"I'm cooking dinner. It's my secret meatloaf recipe," I say.

"For Holden?" Bradie could not sound more shocked if she tried.

"Well, for both of us," I say and suddenly feel a little sheepish. I didn't actually tell him I was making dinner. I went to the store to buy the ingredients for the cookies, for Duke's tutoring, and the idea struck me there. I love cooking. I haven't done it since my dad died and I didn't do it much in the years he was sick either. And to be honest, the impulse to do it now wasn't so much some kind of romantic gesture for Holden—like Bradie clearly thinks it is judging by her expression—it was more a way of keeping my mind off what Dixie told me.

Holden walks up behind Bradie. Standing there together I can really see the family resemblance. They both have the same light brown hair color and the same full mouth. They both seem to have the same acute sense of smell too because he leans toward the open door and sniffs. "What smells fantastic?"

"I'm making dinner," I say and turn back to Bradie.

"There's enough for four if you guys want to stay. I mean, you're already here and it'll be ready in a minute."

She looks uncomfortable, like I just asked her an overly personal question or something.

Girlfriend, I just asked you to have dinner with your brother, not give me a kidney. She looks so weirded out by the possibility I'm about to rescind the offer, but then Duke pipes up, "Ma, you wouldn't have to cook. You hate cooking."

Bradie looks horrified by her son's candidness. "I don't hate it," she says sternly. "I just am exhausted by the time I get home and so it feels like a chore."

"It smells so good!" Duke says in one of those longing, singsong voices that only kids can do. Bradie, in no way seems like the type of mom that will give in to that tone, but to my surprise, she relents.

"Fine," she says and Duke looks as surprised as I am. Bradie turns her blue eyes on me. "It does smell better than the chicken fingers and steamed broccoli I was going to make."

A look of happiness flickers across Holden's face, but he turns away before I can completely enjoy it. It was a beautiful thing. "It's going to be a tight squeeze in here."

"I was thinking, since it's such a nice night, we could eat out on the back deck. There's a big picnic table out there," I say and no one objects, but Holden does look sheepish.

"I don't know if I have enough dishes for everyone," he admits.

"Do you have like one fork, one knife and one plate?" Bradie asks.

"Two of each," he replies and Bradie laughs.

"You're hopeless," she says but she's smiling, which is awesome. She turns to me. "Are there more plates in the house?"

"Yep. Everything is conveniently piled up on the dining room table until the kitchen is complete," I say and walk over to the oven to turn it off. Everything should be ready to be plated now.

"I'll go get them and set the table," she offers.

"Front door is open," Holden tells her. "I'm going to wash up real quick."

Bradie nods and grabs Duke. "Put your backpack down and help me, buddy."

Duke does what he's told and the two head out of the Airstream. I grab Holden's oven mitts and open the oven door. As I place the bubbling meatloaf tin on the stovetop, I realize he's still standing there staring at me. I look up at him. "What?"

In one wide stride, he's bridged the space between us and he's kissing me—hard. I don't know if it's the way he's so confident or the pure passion in the kiss itself but all my worry and fears about what Dixie told me start to feel ridiculous. And all I can think about is how stupid I was to invite Bradie and Duke to dinner because right now I would much rather let the meal grow cold and just have made hot sex with Holden. He pulls away and the look on his ruggedly gorgeous face is intense and it catches me off-guard.

"There's a fine line between fishing and standing on the shore looking like an idiot," Holden explains, his already low voice has dropped an octave and has a rough, gravelly quality to it suddenly. "My mom used to say it all the time."

I want to grin at that because the double entendre of it is smart, but his expression is still so intense—almost dark—that I can't. Is there something here I'm not getting? He cups the side of my face and kisses me softly, quickly. "I really hope we're fishing, Win, and I don't end up looking like an idiot."

Before I can figure out what that means, he leaves me and disappears into the bathroom. I want to chase him into the bathroom but I still have to get the Brussels sprouts and roasted potatoes out of the oven and make the Braddocks' special meatloaf gravy to go with the meal. So, I don't follow and instead let his words echo in my head. I would never make him look like an idiot. He's the one who might be making me look like one.

18

HOLDEN

The woman of my dreams. That's what she is. I mean, I was pretty sure of that fact before Winnie volunteered to tutor my nephew so he could stay on the hockey team and spend time with me. And before she invited my sister to stay for dinner and hang out with me, which Bradie actually seems to be enjoying. But any last inkling of uncertainty was erased when I ate this meal. Winnie is an incredible cook. I shamelessly had two helpings of the meatloaf with the decadent gravy and the roast garlic potatoes and bacon-roasted Brussels sprouts. So did Duke and he went so far as to lick his plate.

"Duke!" Bradie chastises.

"Are you kidding? It's the ultimate compliment." Winnie laughs and ruffles his hair.

Bradie stands as Winnie does to help her clear the dishes. I start to join them, but Winnie shoos me away. "Sit. Relax. We've got this."

I lean over the table and kiss her cheek. There is no way to ignore Bradie's pointed stare or Duke, who moans, "Gross."

"You'll change your tune," I tell him.

"Don't give him any ideas," Bradie warns as she follows Winnie off the porch and around the house to the trailer.

Duke and I talk about hockey and pile up the remaining dishes. As Bradie walks back to grab some more, Winnie's phone starts to wail. She left it on the picnic table. The ringer is on really loud and so we all look at it. The lit up screen flashes with a name. Well, not so much a name as a title.

Boyfriend.

My eyes move from the screen to Bradie. She's looking down at it with a hard expression, which doesn't get softer as she raises her gaze to look at me. I try not to look too shocked. After all, I am fairly certain that it's just an oversight that her ex is still programmed in her phone that way. I mean, I still fucking hate it, but we haven't even defined what we are doing so I can't exactly pitch a fit.

"I assume you aren't pocket dialing her," Bradie says and doesn't wait for my confirmation. "So what are you doing with her if she has a boyfriend?"

"She doesn't," I say. "It's complicated."

"Which is probably the last thing you need," Bradie remarks and before she can say anything else, Winnie rounds the side of the house.

"I don't have anything for dessert," she announces apologetically. "But I think there's ice cream in the freezer in the house and there's coffee or tea if anybody wants that."

Bradie reaches over to Duke and gives his sleeve a tug.

He stands up. "Actually, this has been great. The food was fantastic and it was nice to hang out but we have to get home. I'm sorry to eat and run."

"It's okay," Winnie says easily. "I'm just glad you stayed. Duke, I'll see you in two days for another session but remember, you can always call or text me if you are having trouble with your homework."

Duke nods, but he isn't wearing his usual smile. Fuck. Did one ring of her cell phone ruin this night for him too? I grab his shoulder and give it a squeeze. "Have a good night, bud. See you at practice in a couple days."

We watch Bradie and Duke walk around to the front of the house and hear her car drive off. Winnie turns back to grab the remaining dishes off the table, but I've already scooped them up. She gives me a beautiful, grateful smile. "Please say you're going to help me do dishes too. I forgot the dishwasher isn't installed yet in the cottage and the Airstream doesn't have one."

"I will help you do dishes," I say walking around the table to lay another kiss on her cheek. "And later I will help you have an orgasm."

She blushes and it's really becoming my new favorite thing. I want to bring up the call—and I'm about to—when her phone starts screaming again. She jumps and grabs it so quickly that I can't see the full name before she turns it away from me, but I do see "Boy" so I know it's him again. She turns off the ringer and looks up at me. This is where she says something to make me feel better about her ex—still listed as "boyfriend"—in her phone—calling her late at night, repeatedly.

"I have to take this, but it will just be a second," is all she says as she walks across the deck to the other side, opens the screen door and slips inside the cottage.

I don't know what I needed to hear, but that wasn't it.

I carry the dishes into the trailer and start to wash them, my least favorite chore in the world. I've gotten all the pots and pans washed and am moving onto the plates when there's a knock at the trailer door. Is Winnie knocking before entering now? That's ridiculous. I turn off the water and grab a dishtowel. Wiping my hands I reach for the door handle and twist. "Since when do you knock—"

It's not Winnie. It's Kevin. My mood flips so quick it scares even me, but I told him to stay the fuck away from here. It's not my place and he's not allowed to just show up here. "What the fuck are you doing here?"

He looks astonished by my reaction. He fucking shouldn't be. I warned him last time to stay the fuck away from here. I glance up at the cottage. Winnie is nowhere in sight. I step out of the Airstream, forcing him to back up. I glance around. No car so he walked. Fuck.

"You don't want me here? Fine, I'll leave with my information," he says and starts backing away.

"What information?" I bark but keep my voice low so Winnie doesn't hear me from inside.

"I found her!"

"You told me that last time," I say through gritted teeth. "Do you have something I can actually use? Like does she still have the fucking necklace?"

"Yeah, actually she does," Kevin says, annoyed. "I drove

down to Boston like I said I would and turns out not only does she still have that stupid thing, she's willing to sell it back to you."

"Sell it?" I scoff. "She never paid for it. Kidd gave it to her as a gift."

"Well, now she wants money to part with it," Kevin shrugs. "Is that an issue?"

"Yeah, it's a fucking issue, but not a deal breaker," I grumble because I am so sick of giving these scumbags money. But if I can give Cat her grandma's necklace back then I'm sure she'll forgive me. And I need her to because if I'm going to keep Winnie in my life—and in Maine—then Cat will be in my life too. I need her to tolerate me, at the very least.

"How much?" I ask and I glance at the cottage again. Still no Winnie, thank God.

"She won't tell me. Says she'll only meet with you," Bruce explains. "She's staying at the Driftwood Motel until Monday."

"Just a second."

I dart back into the trailer, grab my wallet and keys and when I come back outside I grab his arm and start to walk us both over to my truck. "We're going now?"

"Yes," I say and open the passenger door and shove him toward it. He gets the point and climbs inside as I jog around to the driver's side. "I need to get this over with."

As we drive away, I call Winnie. It goes straight to voicemail probably because she's still on the phone with her ex. That makes my dark mood darker but I try not to show it when I leave a message. "Hey, Win. Listen, I had an emergency.

Nothing serious, just a thing I have to take care of. I'll explain when I get back."

This is not how I wanted tonight to go. Fuck, this isn't how I want any night to go. But I'll fix it. I just need to get that damn necklace and see Winnie and I can fix it.

19

WINNIE

I miss you."

It's the fifth time in twenty minutes he's said it, and I feel the same thing I've felt every other time—nothing. The Winnie who was with Ty, who put up with so much for so long, kind of doesn't exist anymore.

"You don't miss me," I say back and try not to sigh. "You miss the familiarity. The comfort, but you don't miss me."

"How can you say that?'

"Well, first of all because you and I fought like cats and dogs in the last couple of years," I remind him and keep pacing the dining room, careful not to trip on any of the boxes of kitchen stuff piled up everywhere. "And you cheated on me so, like, if you thought you were going to miss me, you probably shouldn't have done that."

"It was a mistake," he says and now that lonely, sad tone of his voice is getting harder and angrier. Good. He has been drinking; I can tell by the slight slur to his words. "You said you forgave me. You stole years of my life by lying about that."

"I've told you, I wasn't lying on purpose." I know that still sounds lame but it's the truth. "I tried to forgive you."

"All you tried to do was be there for your family," he snaps back. "You didn't care that it took you away from me. You didn't care that I was going to be lonely or what it would do to our relationship."

"I cared about the fact that my dad was dying," I say, pain and anger bubbling over. "And if you loved me the way I deserved, you'd have cared about that too instead of cheating on me."

"Well thanks for making me remember why we're done," he says. "I can't believe I wasted a fucking decade on you."

Before I can answer, he hangs up. Good. I don't care who gets the last word as long as it's the last. I don't want to talk to him again. God, was he ever really in love with me? Was I ever in love with him? The way I felt about him was different than how I feel about Holden now. With Ty, I always felt like I was trying to win him or woo him. I never felt secure about his feelings for me. I was an insecure nineteen-year-old when we met, and I was just so grateful someone I thought was charming and cute seemed to think the same about me.

With Holden, I don't feel like I'm chasing him or that I have to work hard to keep him interested. He's interested, whether I like it or not. I smile at that thought and start through the cottage toward the porch and front door. Holden has seen me at my absolute worst and he's been there, as a friend and then when I was ready, a lover. I feel like we are more solid in a few weeks than Ty and I ever were at any point during our ten years together. Which is why I am going out there and I'm going to ask him about the guy Dixie saw him with. Because the Winnie who is falling in love with Holden is different from the one who dated Ty. I confront problems now, I don't try to ignore them into oblivion.

I step out onto the porch and see the lights on in the trailer. I open the screen door and head down the stairs toward the trailer but when I swing open the door, there's no one inside.

"Holden?" I call out his name as I walk to the tiny bedroom and then over to glance in the bathroom. Nothing. He's not here. I walk back over to the kitchen area and stare at the half-washed dishes. As I lean against the counter and lift my phone to text him, I see I have a voicemail. Right. Someone called when I was talking to Ty, but I ignored it assuming it was one of my sisters or something. But the number it's showing is Holden's so I quickly retrieve the message.

I stand there in the middle of his empty trailer listening to it three times in a row. Emergency? What the fuck is going on? Why does he sound annoyed and cold? My brain starts to spin out of control with possible situations that would have him leave without actually talking to me. I decide to call him but it goes straight to voicemail.

Was it Bradie and Duke? Did their car breakdown again or something? I check the time. It's only nine thirty. Not too late to call Bradie, so I do. When she answers, I ask her if Holden is with her.

"No. I left him with you at the house."

She sounds oddly cold too. "Oh. Okay, well I was in the cottage on the phone and when I came out, he was gone. He left a voicemail about an emergency or something so I thought maybe—"

"Were you on the phone with your boyfriend?" Bradie cuts in. "The guy who called you when you were clearing dishes?"

"What? I...he's my ex. How did you—"

"The number that popped up on your phone when you were in the trailer said 'Boyfriend,'" Bradie explains. "Which you should probably fix if you're dating my brother. Are you dating my brother?"

"I don't know," I admit because I don't. "I mean we're involved, and I really like him."

"Okay, so then maybe change your ex's name in your phone," Bradie says, still as cold as ice. "And I have a feeling Holden's absence tonight might have to do with that. I know everyone says my brother has changed and honestly, I'm beginning to believe maybe he has, in some ways. But I can tell you one way I don't think he'll ever change. If he thinks he's going to get hurt, he will shut down and shut you out so quick it'll make your head spin. And he won't let you back in. Ever. I know because I'm the same way."

"Solid advice," I say quietly. "And I swear, I am not going to hurt him."

"You don't have to convince me. You have to convince him," Bradie says. "Night, Winnie."

After I hang up with Bradie, I feel even more confused and worried than I did before. Is he really upset I was talking to

Ty? The idea that he is, that it caused him to leave, makes me feel like such a screwup. Ugh. I am all about the fails today clearly. Giving people I care about labels that aren't their names in my phone started as a safety thing for Jude after I caught a girl in college going through my phone when I left a lecture to go to the bathroom. She was trying to find my superstar brother's number. So, I changed everyone's names who meant anything to me. My parents are listed under "Couple Goals," my sisters under "Blond and Blonder" and Jude is "Putz." I changed Ty's to "Boyfriend," just for fun, around the same time.

I try to call Holden again and he doesn't answer again. Damn. Ocean Pines is a small town that is more than half empty this time of year. I could walk the streets and probably find him, if he stayed local. But he took his truck, so he could have driven into Portland or Ogunquit or anywhere. Fuck. My. Life. Now I just have to sit here and let my brain wander to all the horrible things that he could be doing or, worse, thinking about me—and us.

I finish the dishes and put them all away and when he still hasn't called or texted, I decide to go out—not to look for him but just to keep from going crazy sitting here waiting. I head to the beach first and sit there for about half an hour on a bench by the dunes watching the tide roll in under the moonlight. It doesn't do anything to stop the tornado of bad feelings swirling in me, which is rare. The ocean always makes me feel better.

I walk down Main Street, the same street that, if you walk far enough, will take you to the bus station. How does it feel like a lifetime ago that I was walking it in the other direction, home from the bus station, trying not to be noticed by Holden?

The streets are just as deserted tonight as they were that night. All the tiny motels that pepper the street between closed sundry shops and empty restaurants have flickering vacancy signs. I look up at the sign for the Driftwood, which has been the same since I was little. It's a white neon clamshell with the name in pink neon script across the middle. The building is the same, squat two-story structure it's always been, the white and teal paint peeling now, unlike when I was a kid. Normally, I wouldn't look twice at it, as it's so familiar I could sketch it with my eyes closed, but tonight it has more vehicles in the parking lot than the other motels. And one of those vehicles is Holden's truck.

My steps falter and stop completely. I stand there, on the sidewalk across the street, unmoving and staring at the building for what feels like eternity. I don't know what else to do except wait while I let my brain and my heart fight a battle. My brain says it's sketchy as hell that he's at some motel and that he must be up to his old no-good ways again. My heart says he isn't. It's something else... but what?

Finally, the door to a room on the bottom floor opens, second from the end. Holden steps out. He turns back to the open door and he's saying something to someone, but I can't see who it is. He looks... different. And yet familiar. His shoulders are tense, his hands in fists at his side. His jaw is so tight I can see the tautness of the tendons in the side of his neck from here. The scowl on his face as he turns away from the motel room brings me back to my youth—all the painful parts. Because he wore that expression permanently when he was young. It was always on his face and I stared it down while I died inside when he teased me mercilessly.

Suddenly someone else comes out of the room, as Holden is reaching for the driver's door on his truck. A woman. Skinny, not slim, in a pair of cutoffs so short I can see her ass cheeks hanging out from here as she reaches for his shoulder, holding him in place and pressing the front of her body up against the back of his.

My emotions are spiraling, pulling my heart with them into a dark vortex.

She says something, her chin resting on his shoulder, her lips near the shell of his ear. Holden turns and gently moves her back, off him and then proceeds to get in his truck. I can't move. I'm just standing there, rigid, stuck in this strange *Twilight Zone* where everything I've clung to—like the belief that he's changed, that I'm a stronger person and wouldn't see a cheater like Ty again—is disintegrating before my eyes.

He starts the truck and pulls out of the parking spot. As soon as he reaches the exit, his headlights shine directly on me. Despite the fact the road he's about to turn onto is wide open he doesn't pull out. Instead, his window goes down. "Winnie?"

I don't respond. I can't.

He gets out of his truck, leaving it running, in park in the middle of the motel driveway. He jogs across the street and as soon as he's in front of me, I'm released from the trance I was in. I shrug off his touch when he reaches for my shoulder, which causes a wounded look on his face. "What are you doing in a motel with...whoever that is?"

"Were you following me?" he accuses, his tone hard.

"How can I follow you?" I ask angrily. "You took off without even telling me and you weren't answering your phone. I was just on a walk and saw your truck. I'm not some psycho stalker."

"Well, I would have told you, but you were busy talking to your ex-boyfriend," Holden says icily.

Bradie was right. He's hurt. So what? He runs to a motel with this girl?

"The key word in that sentence is 'ex,'" I say my voice as hard and cold as his even though I feel like crying. "And just because I talk to my ex means you get to run off to a motel room with some woman?"

"Who are you to tell me what I can and can't do?" he says.

"I guess I'm no one," I reply and start down the sidewalk away from him, back toward the cottage. He follows.

"Wait! Winnie!" he calls. My sad little heart is yelling at my feet to keep moving but I slow to a stop. And then he's standing in front of me again.

"I don't know what we're doing. I don't know if this is something to you, like it is to me but I do know this," he pauses, "I wouldn't run off and fuck someone else just because I'm upset about something. That's not who I am anymore and the real problem is the fact that, no matter what, you don't get that."

"I just don't know what to think, Holden," I reply, wishing, praying, crying inside for this to be easier. For this to be simple. But it's not.

"Hendricks! Are you going to drive this thing or what?" I look over Holden's shoulder, back to the motel driveway where the drug dealer guy is standing beside Holden's truck. "And can I hitch a ride? I have some deliveries to make and my car won't start."

Holden doesn't acknowledge him. His silvery eyes stay laser focused on me so there's no way he misses the look of disappointment on my face. Our eyes lock. "I'm so fucking sick of trying."

He starts to stalk away.

"Holden, wait! Talk to me!"

He stops and turns back to face me. "No. Coming back to this place was a mistake. I'm done. I'm finishing your cottage and I'm moving back to Boston. Or somewhere else. Somewhere people don't know about my past so I don't have to fucking waste my time trying to convince people I've changed."

I watch him stalk across the street, get into his truck and drive away, the tires peeling, going in the opposite direction of the cottage until my tears blur my vision.

20

HOLDEN

I am my own worst enemy. Always have been and apparently always will be. I could have just told her everything—where I was going, why I was going, who I was seeing—all of it. But I didn't and when she seemed suspicious, I got angry instead of honest. It's just the easier response to me. Anger is like an old comfortable sweater that only later on I realize is made of barbed wire and leaves me with more scars than I can heal. Deep metaphor I can take no credit for. Some therapist I was mandated to see once a week when I was in juvie spewed that line out once and, as much as I hate to admit it, it stuck with me all these years.

And that anger fueled more bad decisions than just pushing Winnie away. After I left her I went to the Brunswick and drank until they cut me off and then, unable to drive, I started the stumble home. Somehow, I wandered into the twenty-four-hour 7-Eleven and bought a six-pack and took it to the beach and now here I am—facedown in the beach dunes with the boot of a police office nudging me awake.

I roll over and stare up at him. I'm freezing cold, my skin and clothes are damp and I have one behemoth of a hangover in full effect. "Get the fuck up, you hobo."

I can't. I just can't go to jail. I've had a perfect record my entire adult life and I've blown it. Maybe Winnie, Bradie, and everyone else are right and I haven't changed at all. Fuck.

"Officer, I am so sorry," I start but he doesn't want to hear it.

"Stand up, slowly, hands behind your head."

I do as I'm told, the pounding in my head getting worse with every second. I close my eyes while he pats me down for weapons. He pulls my wallet out of my back pocket and the necklace out of my front pocket. "You know it's illegal to sleep on the beach and it's illegal to drink alcohol on the beach? And since I bet you don't wear a pearl necklace while you get drunk on the beach should I even ask if this is stolen property or should I just assume it is?"

"No sir, it's not stolen. I mean it was, but it's not now." He opens his mouth to say something more, but I keep rambling as his hand is moving toward his handcuffs. "I am so very sorry. I have no excuse for the drinking and passing out except that I had a really horrendous night. I've had a really horrendous life actually if I want to feel sorry for myself, but I don't. It's not an excuse. I fucked...I messed up, but that necklace is being returned to the owner. That's why I have it. I wasn't stealing it. I never stole it to begin with I just—"

"Holden? Hendricks?" the officer says and his tone is no longer authoritative. Now it's surprised. "Shit. Is that actually you?"

"Yes, sir."

He smiles. "Joel Moore. I played hockey with you. Went to school with you too until you were arrested."

"Right! Joel!" I remember him now. He was two inches shorter and twenty pounds lighter and had way more hair when I knew him, but I remember him. I think we were actually friends. I mean, I don't think I ever punched him. "How are you?"

"Better than you, I guess," he jokes. Now he's joking, which even with my pounding headache and the shivers I have from my dew-soaked clothes, I realize is a good sign. Still, I keep my hands behind my head until he holds out his to me. "Relax. Shake my hand, buddy."

I do and smile back at him. "I really am sorry, and I swear I didn't steal that necklace." I pause, scrambling to figure out how to word this without lying. "I found it and I know who it belongs to and I was going to return it."

Not a total lie but an easier explanation for a police officer—friend or not—than saying it was the necklace my buddy stole, which I was blamed for when we were kids. I tracked it down from a stripper with the help of a drug dealer so I could return it and finally make the owner forgive me so her friend will let herself love me. Jesus, that sounds crazy.

"Listen, buddy, I won't arrest you," he says and glances around to make sure the beach is deserted. "But you can't do shit like this anymore. I mean when kids do it, we give them a warning, but adults…usually that's at least one night in jail."

I nod gratefully. "Yeah, I know. It's just…girl trouble. But I won't let it happen again. I promise. Thanks, Joel."

"Girl trouble," he rolls his eyes. "Twice divorced, so I feel you."

I nod again, poor bastard. He claps a hand on my shoulder. "So what are you up to these days? Hopefully more than this."

He hands me back the necklace and my wallet and I put them in my pockets and bend and collect the empty beer cans at our feet. "Things are going okay actually. I have my own renovations business. Working on the Braddock cottage right now."

"Really? That's great," Joel says as I walk toward the garbage can by the boardwalk and he follows. "I'm thinking about redoing my apartment. Make it more of a bachelor pad since the last wife moved out and I'm never marrying again. Maybe you can swing by and give me a quote for it."

"Sure. Would love to," I say because at this point, if he's not going to arrest me or even give me a ticket, I would do his renos for free.

"Do you have a business card or a website or something?" he asks as we both make our way down the boardwalk.

"Not yet. Working on that." Instead, I offer him my phone number, which he punches into his cell and says he'll give me a call.

"No more of this shit okay?" Joel cautions.

"Yeah, no worries there," I reply, and he nods and heads back to his cruiser just a few yards away. I watch him drive off and tip my head to the sky and thank whatever is looking out for me. Then I make my way back to the cottage.

I don't know how to fix this thing with Winnie, but I know I have to, because despite what I said, I'm not leaving Maine and I don't want this thing between us to end. Life without her wouldn't be easier or better. Life with her is what I want and I deserve to get what I want.

The street is eerily quiet and the trailer and cottage unsettlingly still as I approach. I stare up at the cottage for a long time, but I decide I need to be more presentable before I go in there and try to save this. And maybe I can dig up some Advil for this damn hangover. I open the door to the trailer and stop in my tracks. Winnie is asleep, curled up in the middle of my bed. And instead of wearing one of her dad's sweaters, she's wearing a hoodie of mine. She must have been waiting for me all night. I walk to the foot of the bed. She's dead asleep, snoring lightly, which makes me smile. She's on top of all the blankets and her bare legs are covered in gooseflesh. I notice there's no wineglass or open wine bottle in the trailer. She didn't try to drink her way out of the pain of our fight. That makes me very happy—and relieved. I walk to the small cabinet where I keep extra blankets and grab a throw. As I get ready to place it over her, I notice the paper with the crisp handwriting on it.

I can't help but read the first line. It says *My sweet Winona Skye* and I know it's the letter her dad wrote her before he died. I reach for it, so I can move it out of the way and make sure it doesn't get crumpled. As I place it on the small night table, she wakes up.

"You're home," she whispers and starts to sit up.

"Keep sleeping," I say softly and cover her with the blanket. "I have to shower anyway."

"We should talk."

"We should," I agree and tuck the blanket around her. "And we will. I promise."

She yawns and her eyes flutter closed but not before she sighs, "I don't want you to go away."

"I'm not going anywhere." I promise her and I mean it. I slip into the bathroom and clean up. In the shower, I realize I don't just have a pounding headache, I have a scratchy throat too. That's never been part of a hangover before. This aging thing sucks. I'm having a hard time accepting the fact that I can't just curl up beside her and sleep this off, but I can't. The house still needs work and if I skip a day I'm likely to miss my deadline. Jude might not mind if it takes me a little extra time, but I'll mind. That's not how I want the first job of my new company to go. Plus, I have a roofing job lined up after this and it has to be completed before the first frost.

When I step out of the bathroom, wrapped in only a towel, she wakes up again. She silently watches me as I dress, sleepy-eyed, still curled up on my bed. As I'm pulling my T-shirt over my head she sits up. I walk over to the bed and sit on the edge. "Were you waiting in here for me all night?"

She nods. "I wasn't going to let it end like that." Winnie sits up a little straighter. "I wasn't going to let things end at all."

I reach for her. We hold each other for a long time. Finally I say, "I was trying to find Cat's grandmother's necklace. The one I was accused of stealing back when we were kids."

She pulls her head off my shoulder to look in my eyes. "What?"

"Cat hates me because I stole her grandmother's necklace, and a bunch of other shit, when she had that party at her house when we were sixteen," I say and stand up to retrieve the necklace. "Only I didn't steal anything. Kidd did. I knew he did and didn't do shit about it and I was caught with him when he was trying to sell some of the stuff so I was still guilty. But I took the complete fall because Kidd had spent the summer before in juvie and he was scared he'd be tried as an adult or get a harsher sentence. Also, his father had already caught him stealing from one of the plumbing jobs they'd done and nearly beat him within an inch of his life. And honestly, I just didn't give a fuck what happened to me."

"Jesus, Holden." Winnie winces at my words. "You went to juvie for him? It ruined your chance at a hockey career?"

"Yeah." I try not to let the dark, cold regret fill my chest like it usually does when I think about that. "I would have found another way to fuck it up, trust me. I was hell-bent on ruining my life. So in a way, it's probably a blessing I did it because it straightened me out."

I pause and pull the necklace from the jeans I left on the floor before my shower and carry it over to her. I lay it on the bed between us as I sit back down. "I remembered that this necklace wasn't one of the ones we tried to sell at the pawnshop. This one Kidd gave to some girl he was dating. Kevin's cousin's friend. So I had Kevin track her down and that's who you saw me meeting last night."

"She still had it?"

"Yeah. I guess it was sentimental or something and she made me pay her a hundred bucks for it." I roll my eyes. "But she gave it back. And then she chased me out to the parking lot and propositioned me. But that was it. Nothing more."

"I know. I believe you," she says and takes the necklace and runs her fingers along the pearls. "I can't believe you went through all this and it wasn't even your fault that it was stolen."

"Cat's opinion of me matters because she matters to you," I say quietly. "And you, Winona Skye Braddock, matter so much to me it's kind of fucking terrifying."

She looks at me from under those thick ash-blond lashes and gives me the sweetest smile before leaning forward and giving me a gentle kiss. "You matter to me too. But honestly, I'm still a mess."

"Your dad's death is going to be hard on you for a long time," I say as I take her hand in mine. "And honestly, it never fully leaves you. It's always there, in the back of your chest with the door open, waiting for you to fall back into it. But you'll be okay and that's not going to scare me off."

"It's not just my dad...," she admits and there's an embarrassed look on her face. "I've been with one guy my entire adult life and he cheated on me. I can't help thinking I did something to deserve it. Like I wasn't enough. And Holden, if I'm not enough for you too..."

"I'm in love with you," I blurt out and I know it's early and she may think I'm crazy but it's also a goddamn fact and if she's doubting herself at all she needs to know.

"I'm in love with you too, which is why you terrify me too," she confesses. I wasn't expecting those words, and it's like being surprised with a winning lottery ticket or a new car or something you didn't deserve and were too scared to even hope for.

I grab her face in my hands and kiss her. She crawls right up on me and when the kiss breaks she hugs me and for the first time in longer than I can remember, I feel pure happiness.

And then my phone rings. I glance over at it and see Dave's number. "I have to get that."

"Of course," she says and I stand up and grab my phone.

"Hey Dave," I say, but I'm not sure he can hear me over his own coughing. Oh fuck. When he finishes coughing he proceeds to tell me he's too sick to come to the job today. I believe him too. He sounds like shit. But after I tell him to take it easy and feel better and hang up, I see I have a text from Mike who is still sick and won't be coming in. I start to swear a blue streak.

"What's wrong?" Winnie asks.

I stand up and run a hand through my still damp hair and then scratch my beard. "My crew is sick. Both of them. So I'm on my own today."

"I can help," she volunteers.

I smile. "It's okay. I'll be fine. It's just going to be a long day."

"Holden…"

I cough. I still have a headache too. And I need coffee and something greasy to help absorb this vicious hangover but I don't have time. Not now that I'm flying solo. I walk back over to the bed, lean down and kiss her. "I have to get started. Your brother is coming this weekend."

"He is?" She looks dumbfounded.

"Yeah. He hasn't told you?"

She shakes her head. "I have to call him."

"When was the last time you talked to him?" I ask.

Her expression grows sheepish. "The day I was supposed to get on the plane back to Toronto."

I'm stunned. "You didn't call him when I told you he knew you were here?"

She shakes her head no. "He tried calling me but that's what voicemail is for."

"Call him. I'll see you in a few." I kiss her again and try to ignore the stress and concentrate on the fact that this beautiful, amazing woman loves me.

21

WINNIE

As soon as Holden leaves, I dig my phone out of the pocket of his hoodie that I'm wearing. I find Jude's number in my phone, under "Putz" and hit dial as I crawl out of bed and move to the kitchen. I open the fridge and try to figure out what I can throw together for Holden for breakfast.

"Hi, Win."

"Hi yourself. Were you going to tell me you're coming to visit?"

"Were you going to tell me your banging my contractor?"

"No. It's none of your business," I say firmly, trying not to sound shocked that he knows. I'm going to have to murder Sadie or Dixie later, whichever one told him. Maybe killing them both would be easiest. "Why are you coming?"

"Why are you banging the contractor?"

I grit my teeth. He's in one of those snarky moods that he's been perfecting since he was a preteen. Back then he used to parrot back everything I said on our twelve-hour drives to

Maine from Toronto and it would get me so mad I would scream. If he wants to play, I'll play to win. "Well, where can I start...he's built like a tank and hung like a horse."

"Winnie!"

"Not to mention that scruffy beard and the way it feels between my—"

"Why are you turning into Sadie?" he yells in anguish. "Goddamn it. You used to be so..."

"Boring? Lame? Timid?"

"I was going to say dependable, calm, uncomplicated," Jude says.

"Like a dog you adopt from the ASPCA." I roll my eyes and pull some eggs from the fridge.

Jude chuckles self-consciously. "Okay, I'm not great with words. You're the articulate one, not me. But seriously, Win, talk to me. What happened with Ty?"

"It wasn't working out. I know you know that." I'm not going to tell him all the dirty details because even though Jude likes to act like his sisters are the bane of his existence, he would make it his life's mission to destroy anyone who hurt us, or, say, cheated on us. "It should have ended a long time ago and then Dad died and I realized I couldn't fake it anymore."

He doesn't say anything for so long that I say "Hello?' to make sure our connection didn't crap out.

"And Holden takes the pain away?" he finally asks, his voice sounds funny—thicker. "Is he a distraction?"

"He's not a distraction," I say. "He isn't taking away the pain. He's helping me cope with it. Jude, you like him. You wouldn't have hired him if you didn't."

"I do like him. I always have and you always haven't." I can hear the smirk in his voice. Jerk.

"People change."

"Dixie's not sure he has," Jude replies. Now I know which sister to kill.

"Is that why you're coming?" I turn back to the counter, open a cupboard and pull out a frying pan. "Because don't. I promise you, he's changed. I've changed too. We're good."

"I'm coming because Zoey wants to show Declan the leaves changing colors. He doesn't exactly get a fall here and hockey starts in a week so it's our last chance to do it," Jude explains. After a pause, he bursts out, "And Mom is worried about you and is making me check on you in person and possibly kidnap you and drag you back here. Okay, see you soon, bye!"

He hangs up before I can respond.

I sigh. My poor mom. I haven't told her anything that's going on, but clearly she knows. I start to chop up the leftover potatoes from last night and toss them in a pan to fry, and then I make an omelet with cheese and chives, and contemplate calling my mom. Finally, I decide I have to. She picks up almost right away and answers with, "Jude just texted me that you'd be calling. It's about time."

Of course, he knew I'd call her.

"Sorry, Mom," I say. "I haven't been purposely shutting you out."

"Yes, you have," she says back but without any anger. "You've shut us all out and that's exactly what I expected. You did it to protect us from you because you thought you were taking it harder than the rest of us. And you probably were."

"No. This has to be hardest on you and I know that," I reply, fighting tears as I beat the eggs in a bowl before pouring them into another pan on the stove. "But I knew I wasn't going to be able to handle all the additional questions or concerns about breaking up with Ty and everything, so I hid. Honestly, Mom, it was nice to be here in Maine because it feels so much more a part of Dad than San Francisco or even Toronto."

"I know, sweetie. I'm actually glad you're there instead of Toronto. And I'm glad you broke up with Ty." That last statement shocks me. I always thought she liked Ty. "You two had grown apart and I wasn't seeing the happiness you once had. In fact, I wasn't seeing any happiness at all, and I knew it wasn't just because of Dad being sick."

"No, it wasn't." I cradle the phone as I slide the second omelet from the pan to the plate I pulled out of the cupboard. "I wanted that one great, romantic love of my life the way you and Dad had. The day you met Ty, after we'd been dating a few months, you said the way we were with each other reminded you of how you and Dad were when you first met, and I was so thrilled by that. When it started to fall apart, I was too ashamed to admit it. I'm sorry I didn't confide in you."

"You've never been a sharer," she says. "Even when you were little you kept things bottled up and ignored your feelings. You're just like your dad in that way, which is why when he did share feelings, you had to take it seriously."

"Like the letters he wrote," I say and a lump starts to form in his throat.

"Like the letters," she agrees and then sighs. It's not as heavy as it used to be and that's a good thing.

"I took what he said to heart. This path I'm on..." I pause and bite my lip. "Whatever this is...being here and everything...it's what I need to do."

"I hear the everything part is Holden Hendricks," my mom says, never one to dance around an elephant in a room. "I won't bother you with a bunch of questions—even though I have a bunch of questions. I just want you to talk to me when you're ready."

"I will, Mom. I love you."

"Love you too, sweetie."

We say good-bye and I tuck my phone back into the hoodie and make some coffee. When it's done I carry two plates with potatoes and eggs and two steaming mugs of joe into the cottage. Holden is in the bathroom, struggling to install the new vanity. I put the food down on the dining room table and walk into the bathroom and promptly pick up one end of the heavy gray wood cabinet.

He gives me a look like he's going to complain, but I just smile at him. "Teamwork makes the dream work!"

He laughs and lets me help him get it into place. He's sweating pretty hard, which makes me think he was struggling with it for a while before I got there. He wipes his brow with his forearm as he bends and grabs a drill to secure it. "Can you take a quick break and eat this amazing breakfast I made for you?"

He glances into the dining room and I swear I hear his stomach rumble. "I shouldn't, but I will. Hopefully, food will help with this headache."

As we eat, he makes his usual hot-as-fuck groaning noises,

which means he loves my cooking. But I can't help noticing he still looks a little overheated. I reach out and touch his forehead. "Holden, you're burning up!"

"Just been overexerting myself. It's fine."

Something tells me it's not at all fine.

"Jude told me on the phone he's not worried about the progress on the house," I say as I watch him chew a forkful of eggs. "So if you're a little behind, he won't be upset. I mean Dixie's wedding isn't even until the summer, so it's not like we're in a rush."

"I am," he admits. "I took a roof job after this one because it would be quick and easy, but it needs to be done before the weather turns. I'm supposed to start there the Monday after this job is complete."

He coughs. It sounds deep and congested, making me cringe. I feel his forehead again and I swear he's hotter than before. "Holden. You're sick."

"I can't be," Holden replies, then takes a big gulp of coffee and stands up. "I have to get back at it."

"What's left to do?" I ask, giving up on talking him into taking some time off because I know he won't. I pop the last potato into my mouth and follow him into the bathroom.

"I have to get all the new fixtures installed, paint this room and the kitchen, install the new trim in both rooms, tile the kitchen floor and hook up the new appliances when they arrive tomorrow. And deal with whatever else comes up." He sighs and rubs the back of his neck. "Because something always comes up."

"I can help you with a lot of that," I offer. "In fact, I

insist. If you're worried about some weird client-contractor rule you're breaking, keep in mind I didn't hire you. I didn't want you here at all."

His lip quirks up in the corner. "But now you love me."

I smile back at him. "I'm pretty sure fucking your client is a bigger broken rule than just having them do manual labor for you."

He laughs guiltily at that but doesn't have a rebuttal so I continue my argument. I put my hands on my hips and try to look stern. "You're not paying Mike or Dave, so pay me instead. I'm a replacement worker. I could use the cash. I haven't worked since I got here."

He gives me a look that says he thinks the need-the-cash argument is bullshit, which it is, but I can also tell I've worn him down. He sighs and nods. "Okay fine, you can help a little."

"Cool!" I clap my hands. "Tell me what to do, boss!"

"I might like this after all." Holden chuckles and gives me a wink. I step closer and lean up to kiss him, but he stops me and takes a step back. "I don't want you to catch whatever this is."

He admitted he's sick, which means it must be even worse than it looks. I promise myself to do as much as possible as quickly as possible so we can get him to bed early. Hopefully he can sleep this off.

But even with my help, we don't get as much done as either of us would like. He's moving slow and his strength is down because of what I'm convinced now is the flu. And then we discover the new kitchen sink is leaking and we can't figure out why, so at barely two o'clock I demand that he call it a day and go take a nap. He doesn't argue—much—a sure sign something is definitely wrong.

After another shower, he collapses onto his bed and I tell him I'm running out for supplies. I head to the market and grab chicken, fresh ginger, lemons and a bunch of other stuff I need to make the soup my mom used to make for us when we were sick. As I drive home I think of my dad was when he used to get sick. Like Holden, he never wanted to admit something was wrong, and my mom stopped trying to make him. She'd simply make this soup for dinner. My dad would smile gratefully and look around the table. "Which one of you rug rats is sick?" he would say through sniffles or coughs.

I smile now at the memory. I loved his stubbornness, even when it drove me crazy.

Back at the trailer, Holden hasn't moved. He's still flat on his back in a dead sleep in nothing but his underwear. I grab the blanket he gave me earlier and cover him with it before starting the soup. Then I call Bradie.

"Hey, Bradie," I say when she answers. "It's Winnie Braddock."

"Hey, Winnie," Bradie says. "How did things go with Holden?"

"We're great. We worked it out." I skip the details that he stayed out all night because I feel like she sometimes looks for a reason to think badly of him and that information might give it to her. "But he's got the flu. It's actually pretty bad, so he won't be at hockey practice. I just wanted you and Duke to know so you didn't think he was just blowing it off."

"Oh." Bradie pauses. "Yeah, I would have thought that," she continues with a tone full of guilt.

"I know. But I swear he's sick." I start adding chicken broth to the big pot I've placed on the stove. "Can you do me a favor and tell the head coach? I don't have his number, and Holden's asleep. I don't want to wake him to get it."

"Of course. No problem," Bradie replies. "Is there anything I can do to help? He's not the best patient. He used to hate being sick when he was a kid."

"I've got it covered, but thanks for asking."

"Thanks for letting me know," Bradie says. "And please tell him Duke and I are sending him get-well-soon vibes. Hope to see him at practice again soon."

"I'll tell him." I smile as I hang up, confident now that Bradie might be a hard-ass but deep down she wants Holden back in her life—and Duke's—as much as he wants it.

When Holden wakes up a couple of hours later, he looks even worse. "Hey. Something smells good. If I had any appetite at all I would be devouring whatever that is."

"It's a special Braddock family soup," I explain, sliding out from the bench by the table and walking over to him. I place a hand on his forehead again. He is on fire. I try not to panic and walk over to the stove. I'm no nurse like Sadie, but I do know someone with a fever has to stay hydrated. I pull a bowl from the cabinet and ladle some soup into it. "This stuff is specifically designed to ease the symptoms of man flu."

"Man flu?" He rolls his eyes. "It's just a little cold."

"Yeah, that kind of man flu," I say, ignoring his lie. "There are two kinds of man flu: the one where the guy acts like a helpless toddler as soon as he gets the sniffles and the one where he acts like it's no big deal as his internal organs liquefy and his brain melts from fever. You've got the latter, just like my dad used to get, and this soup is for that."

He laughs, but it morphs into a thick cough. I try not to cringe and hand him the bowl as soon as he stops. He sits up and takes the bowl but seems skeptical. "I'm not hungry."

"I know, but you have to eat it," I reply. "It will help."

He takes a sip. "I'm surprised I can even taste it, I'm so congested, but it's good."

"It's fabulous," I correct him with a grin but inwardly, I'm really nervous about how sick he is. I'm worried I should call Dr. Whittaker. Holden, though, is worried about something else.

"I have to get some more bodies in here tomorrow," he says between spoonfuls of soup. "Even with your help, it's not going to be enough."

"I agree. Especially because if you are even half as sick as you are right now, I'm not letting you out of this bed," I say firmly and he looks instantly frustrated. "You getting so sick you can't do the roof job after this is going to defeat the purpose."

"I'm going to have to find other guys then," he murmurs and puts the soup bowl on the night table. He finished a little more than half, so that's better than nothing. He reaches for his phone, which I plugged in and left on the other night table. His frown gets deeper and deeper as I watch him scroll through his contacts. "Mike and Dave were working for a discounted rate, because I promised they'd be permanent hires once my company got going. I don't know many other people who would be willing to do that. And the ones I do know..."

"What?" I prompt gently when he doesn't finish his sentence. He looks up at me, his eyes clouded.

"Kidd has the experience and he'd do it for any cash, no matter how discounted," Holden says and my face twists with disgust before I can stop it. "I know. He's the worst possible option. Forget I said anything."

He goes back to scrolling through his contacts. I clean up the kitchen and pour him a glass of water as he calls two guys. Turns out both have other jobs right now. I walk back over and pick up his soup bowl. "Call Kidd," I say and start praying I don't regret it.

"I know you hate him. I'm not a fan either. I'll find something else."

I shake my head and tuck a chunk of hair behind my ear when it comes loose of my low ponytail. "We're out of options. Just call him. It'll be fine. It's just a day or two and I've still got my left hook if I need it."

Holden smiles in amusement and relief. "I'll punch him myself if he acts like an ass."

Kidd agrees to come work on the house starting tomorrow morning. Holden wants to get up and continue working now, but I don't let him. He argues but I win. As he drifts off to sleep, I tiptoe outside to call Dr. Whittaker. My eyes land on Cat's grandmother's necklace, resting on the shelf by the front door.

Holden may take responsibility for how things played out when he was a kid, but I blame Kidd one hundred percent. And I get to spend most of the next forty-eight hours with him. Oh joy.

22

HOLDEN

I sneak into the cottage as quietly as I can to take a look at how things are going. If Winnie catches me, she's going to pitch a fit. Dr. Whittaker came to the house last night, thanks to Winnie calling him, and he said I have severe influenza B. He gave me Tamiflu and told me I was on bed rest for at least forty-eight hours. I thought that was overkill, but now that I'm up and walking around, I realize it wasn't. Every single muscle in my body aches. My joints are stiff and I'm still feverish. But I can't stop myself from checking on the guys.

Kidd showed up, remarkably on time at seven in the morning and to my surprise Dave was back. He said he wasn't a hundred percent, but his fever and aches were gone and he wanted to help out for at least a few hours. I was beginning to think that this job might end on time, but I still wasn't relaxed about it. I hated that I wasn't there working with them.

I quietly walk up the porch stairs and slowly open the screen door, hoping it won't squeak. I can hear them talking.

Dave is telling Winnie about his kids. "They just started Thornton Academy. Can you believe I have kids in high school? I can't."

"That's awesome. Do you like Thornton? Is it a good school?"

"They love it. Pam and I like it too. All the teachers are great," Dave explains. "They're a little short staffed though. I think they're looking for more math teachers and a biology teacher. Are you interested?"

"I don't know...," Winnie says vaguely and it hits me...we haven't talked about whether she's going to stay in Maine. We never got that far, but if she's not interested in a job...maybe she's thinking of heading back to Toronto. Or San Francisco to be with the rest of her family. Maybe she thinks we can do this long distance. The idea makes me feel sicker than the flu. I don't want long distance, but I also don't want to leave Maine. Does she expect me to if this continues?

"What are you doing up?"

Her voice startles me out of my thoughts, and I blink and realize I was standing frozen on the porch. Like a tool. She is holding a paintbrush as she walks over to me in a pair of jean overalls her hair in pigtails. "Do you need something? Are you feeling worse?"

Oh my God, she's fucking adorable. I smile but shake my head. "No, I'm feeling a little better, so I wanted to check in."

"Hey, Hendricks," Kidd calls and pops his head out from the kitchen. "Don't come too close, dude. I don't want to catch your disease."

"Yeah, yeah, how's the sink coming?" I call back. He grins and I wonder if he's been to a dentist once in his adult life.

"Fixed. It was nothing for a pro like me," he says. "I'm working on helping Dave with the appliances now."

"Cool. Let me take a—"

"Nope!" Winnie blocks my path. "Pretend it's a design show on HGTV and you don't get to see it until the final reveal now."

"But I'm not the client. You're the client," I remind her.

She winks at me with a sassy little smile on her face. "Role-play. You've got a wild side, Holden. Aren't you into role-play? I'm your naughty little contractor and you're my sexy...sick client."

I laugh, but it just makes my muscles start to ache again. "You wait until I'm healthy, Winona, and then we'll see how you feel about role-play."

"You aren't going to get healthy if you keep disobeying doctor's orders," she says in her favorite snarky tone and points her paintbrush at me. "Back to bed. I will be in at lunch with an update. I ordered and Cat's delivering."

I'm instantly sad at the thought of missing out on lobster rolls. "Fine, fine," I grumble and leave the cottage.

Almost two hours later at a little before one in the after-noon, I'm dozing on the bed when there's a knock at the trailer. Winnie's pretty face appears in the open door. "Hi you. How you doing?"

"Not great but better than yesterday," I reply and pull myself up to a sitting position.

She walks up and into the trailer but doesn't close the door behind her and then I see someone else—Cat. She's frowning but holding a brown paper bag. "Winnie, my ex lifelong friend, ordered lunch for the crew and included a lobster roll and lobster bisque for you."

"Which you wouldn't have made if you knew it was for me," I say and she nods.

As soon as Cat is fully in the trailer Winnie takes a subtle step back toward the door. I get off the bed and grab the necklace out of the night table. "Well, how about you give me the soup and sandwich and I give you this."

I hold out my hand and let the pearls dangle. Cat stares at it, eyes narrowed in suspicion. Behind her Winnie slips out of the trailer. Cat doesn't notice as she puts the paper bag down on the kitchen counter and reaches out for the necklace. "You bought me a new pearl necklace?"

"No. I found your grandmother's," I reply, and she looks absolutely baffled. "It wasn't fenced. It was given to someone. I just had to track that person down, and luckily they still had it and were willing to give it back."

"It can't be the same..." She lifts it up to examine it in the light streaming in through the windows. She fiddles with the clasp. "Holy shit! It has her initials engraved on it. It's actually hers!"

Her face lights up and tears swim in her eyes as she looks at me. "I can't believe you found it!"

"I meant it when I told you I would change things if I could," I say and shrug. "So I found a way to change things."

The next thing I know she's hugging me. "Thank you."

"Cat, I have the flu. You might want to stay away," I warn.

"I got a flu shot," Cat explains and squeezes me harder. "I'm not a dummy like you."

I laugh as Winnie appears in the doorway again, sees the hug and smiles. "Everything okay in here? Is he getting his soup and roll or do I need to share mine?"

"He gets whatever he wants," Cat declares and lets go of me to turn to Winnie and hug her. "You were right about him."

My heart swells and I feel a wave of relief.

We all eat lunch together on the porch, and by the time it's over, I'm feeling wiped out again. God, this sucks. I have no choice but to go back to the trailer and sleep. When I wake up again the sun is setting and the trailer is almost dark. I feel better, but I know I'm not one hundred percent. I'm, like, fifty, tops.

I hear Winnie talking and then Kidd's voice. Neither sound angry, although I can't make out what they're saying. I start to sit up just as an engine roars to life. Winnie opens the door and steps inside. She walks right over to the bed and flops down on it face first. "I'm so exhausted," she mumbles into the pillow.

I rub her back. "How'd it go? Was Kidd a jerk at all because if he was…"

"No," she murmurs and slowly rolls over. She looks exactly the way she says she feels—exhausted. She has flecks of paint in her hair and on her cheeks. "He was…decent. He worked pretty hard actually, and guess what? It's all done."

"All of it?"

She nods and her eyes start to droop as she yawns. "Well, except putting everything back like the dishes and artwork and crap. I wanted you to approve things first. You are the boss."

"I like when you call me the boss," I say.

"Don't get used to it." She yawns again. "This is a partnership."

"It is, huh? Like a girlfriend-boyfriend partnership."

Her eyes open again. "No like a brother-sister partnership."

"I don't know what you and Jude—"

"Oh gross!" she bellows dramatically and reaches out and swats me. "Don't even joke about that."

"Sorry, but you started it." I kiss her cheek, still too scared to kiss her on the mouth and give her this death flu. "I feel like I should go over there and take a look. What time does Jude get here tomorrow?"

"I think around noon." Her voice is growing fainter and her words are slurred with fatigue. Poor beautiful girl. "I can't remember. Right now I can't remember my own name."

"Winona Skye," I tell her softly and kiss her cheek again, but I swear she's asleep before my lips leave her skin.

I watch her for a little while and have plans of getting up and checking on the cottage and then making her dinner, but I'm still so sick all I manage to do is drift off beside her.

23

WINNIE

I wake up achy with a grumbling stomach because I slept right through dinner last night. And now something in this house smells absolutely delicious. I sniff and my eyes flutter open. Holden is sitting on the edge of the bed beside me, waving half a breakfast burrito in front of my face. It's filled with gooey melted sharp cheddar and crispy bacon and fluffy eggs. I reach for it.

Holden laughs. "You're like a zombie on *Walking Dead* trying to catch a live one."

"Hrpmf." I think I'm trying to agree but who knows. "Need food."

He lets me poach it from his grip and I take a big, glorious bite. He watches me in amusement. I swallow. "Did you make this?"

"I did," he says proudly. "And now I could sleep for a week."

"Still not better?"

"I'm about seventy-five percent," he explains. "No fever, still tired and a little achy but only bit of a cough left."

"Well, I'm not letting you overdo it today," I tell him.

"I won't have to, thanks to you busting your sweet little ass yesterday," he says with a smile.

I eat the burrito—both halves—in bed as he brings me a coffee. "I could get used to this."

"I hope you do," he replies and smiles. "Then maybe you'll stick around."

I pause mid-bite. "What?"

"We just haven't really talked about how long you're staying," Holden says and his voice sounds a little tense. I think he's worried I won't stay.

"There's nowhere else I have to be," I reply between bites of burrito.

He looks at me, expressionless, for a long moment and then he smiles, but it seems guarded. My phone beeps from the bedside table, and I lean over and read the message that flashes across the screen. "Jude's plane landed! I have to shower."

I scramble off the bed.

"I'll head inside and make sure everything looks great," Holden says and I can see he's nervous. He doesn't want to disappoint Jude, but I know he won't. Even without Kidd and me jumping in yesterday, the place was together enough that Jude wouldn't regret his decision to hire Holden.

I rush through my shower and head into the cottage in my towel, because most of my clothes are still in there. I pause and admire the place as Holden walks around trying to put back all the knickknacks and paintings that we had to take down. "It looks amazing in here."

I head upstairs and change into a pair of jeans and a

Henley, throw on some mascara and lip gloss and run my fingers through my damp hair. I remember what I was like when I first started dating Ty. I would stress over my hair and makeup and clothes, but that was never the case with Holden. He has seen me at my worst and loved me anyway.

I bounce down the stairs feeling confident and content, two things that I haven't felt in a very long time.

Twenty minutes later, Jude's rental is pulling to a stop in front of the house. I jump out of the rocking chair and rush out the door. Zoey is closest, so I hug her first and as I hug Jude, Zoey opens the back door to get Declan out of his car seat.

Jude holds me in the hug for a very long moment and when he pulls back he opens his mouth to say something, but I hold up my hand to silence him. I smile. "Don't start with your Dr. Phil psycho therapy before I get to hug my nephew."

I turn, bend and extend my arms to Declan. "Deck!"

"Auntie Winnie!" Declan squeals and runs toward me on his chubby almost three-year-old legs. I scoop him up and swing him around as he giggles.

Dropping him onto my hip, I look up and see Holden in the doorway of the cottage. He's smiling. I glance at Zoey and Jude. "Come on. You guys aren't going to believe how great this place looks."

They follow me up the stairs. Jude and Holden do that bro-hug, hand-clasp thing that guys do, and then Zoey hugs him. "I haven't seen you in what feels like a century," Holden says.

"I know," Zoey says with a friendly smile. "But it's great to see you back here."

"It's great to be back," Holden replies.

"Show me your work," Jude urges. "Let's see if I have to run you out of town."

Holden laughs. "Come on."

We spend the next forty minutes going through the first floor because Holden is giving every possible detail about every single change. You'd think it might be boring, but the way he talks about his work is so animated and passionate, it's keeping Jude and Zoey intrigued and impressed.

"Everything is beyond perfect," Jude says happily. "I can't thank you enough."

Holden grins and it's filled with pride. "I'm really happy you think so."

Declan squirms on my hip. "Potty!"

Zoey and Jude both jump but Zoey reaches him first. "I got you, little man. Let's do this!"

She lifts him off my hip and rushes to the bathroom, kicking the door closed with her foot. "We just started potty training," Jude explains. "No accidents so far, but we live in constant fear. Constant."

Holden laughs. I pat my brother's shoulder. He looks around the renovated first floor again. "Dad would have fucking loved this."

I nod and my eyes water, but I don't cry. "He would have. I can see him sitting at the new peninsula in the kitchen, checking the hockey scores in the paper and ranting about some stupid penalty you took the night before."

Jude laughs, but it's heavy, choked. "You have to picture that? Him pissed at me."

"They're some of my favorite memories of him," I say back and laugh as Jude gives me a little push.

Jude looks up at Holden. "We need a family minute."

Holden nods and starts toward the porch.

"We don't," I argue before Holden can leave. He freezes, his gaze bouncing between me and Jude, wondering who he should listen to. I turn back to Jude. "You guys are staying for the weekend. We can have some annoying brother-sister moment later. Just enjoy it."

Jude sighs but lets me win.

Zoey opens the bathroom door and Declan comes running out. "I peepeed in the bowl so I get a weeward."

"A weeward?" I repeat.

"He has trouble with Rs," Zoey explains with a laugh. "But if you think about it, 'weeward' kinda works perfectly."

"How about as a weeward we go to the beach," Jude says to his son. "There might be surfers."

Declan claps his hands.

"He loves surfers. We watch them on the beach in San Francisco every weekend," Zoey tells us. "I can't get him to watch two seconds of a hockey game. Even when I tell him Daddy is on the ice."

"So we raise a surfer not a hockey player," Jude says with a shrug. "As Dad would say, 'As long as they're happy, we're happy.'"

As we all head to the beach, minus Holden because I make him take a nap so he his flu doesn't get worse, I'm struck by how much like Dad Jude is. I never realized it before. Yes, he and Dixie look the most like him, physically, but I never really stopped to notice the other ways they were like him. Jude, right now, with Declan, is Dad reincarnated. And it doesn't make me cry. It fills me with joy.

So much joy, I'm almost drunk on it and I reach over and hug my brother while we watch Declan play chicken with waves as they roll up toward him. Jude hugs me back and lets out a shocked laugh. "What the hell is that for?"

"For being a good dad," I reply. "And a decent brother. But trust me, you won't hear that again so enjoy it."

"You're a good sister too," Jude replies, and I act like I'm flabbergasted, gasping loudly and smacking my chest with my hand. "Even if you run away from home and hook up with my employees."

I push my hair back from my face as the wind picks up. "I hooked up with my teenage nemesis. That's even worse."

"Yeah, it would be if he was still old Holden," Jude says. "But he clearly isn't."

"You knew that."

"Nah, I didn't. I took a bit of a risk when I hired him." Jude shoves his hands in the pockets of his jeans. "But if you fell in love with him, then I know he's a good guy, just like I thought. You've always been an incredible judge of character."

I smile proudly at that. Jude and I aren't usually the type to have moments like this, and I suddenly find myself hoping that changes. This should be the first of many. He leaves my side and begins chasing Declan around the beach. Zoey comes over and gives me a side hug. "You're good?"

"I'm getting there."

"So is Jude. But he worries about you," Zoey says as the wind twist and twirls her auburn hair off her shoulders.

"I don't worry about him because he has you," I say as Declan claps when a surfer glides across the water on a white tipped wave. "And he doesn't have to worry about me because I have Holden now."

"I need to hear more about this," Zoey says, smiling. "He used to scare the shit out of me and I didn't scare easy. But the guy I met today, he is definitely different."

I nod. "I was thinking we could have a barbecue tonight and maybe invite his sister and her son. I have to tutor him this afternoon, so they'll already be here."

"I don't see why not," Zoey replies.

Everything is perfect for the rest of the day. Zoey, Jude and Declan take a nap after lunch. Holden rests most of the day, but I can see him getting stronger every time I check on him. This flu is definitely on its way out.

After their nap, Jude takes Declan on a nature walk through the woods while Zoey and I do a grocery run for barbecue supplies. At the store, Zoey asks me if I want red or white wine with dinner and it makes me realize it's been days since I had a drink. That's normal. Before my dad died I didn't drink a lot—definitely not a bottle a night. I'm back to normal...but yet I'm different.

When Bradie and Duke show up, I invite them for dinner and Bradie accepts. She hangs out in the cottage with Holden and everyone else while I tutor Duke in the trailer. When he's done with his homework and aced the fractions flash cards I've been doing with him, I decide to let the cat out of the bag.

"You know who is inside my cottage right now?" I ask him.

"Holden," he replies innocently.

"Holden and my brother, Jude."

Duke looks stunned. "What? Really? Jude Braddock?"

"Yep."

"Can I meet him? Please?" He is bouncing in his seat and it makes me laugh.

"Of course," I say and stand up so he can slide out of the bench behind the table to stand too. "In fact, you and your mom are going to stay and have dinner with him, and us."

"This is the best day of my life!" Duke proclaims and then he hugs me, so hard and fierce that he almost knocks me backward.

"Come on." I open the trailer door and he jumps out and scrambles up the steps to the cottage as fast as his legs will take him.

Jude is thrilled to meet Duke. "Come help me with the grill," Jude suggests, and Duke nods vigorously.

I head out on the back deck to set the table and grin to myself as I listen to their conversation. "So you played hockey in Maine too?"

"With your uncle, yes, but only in the summers," Jude explains. "I played in Canada the rest of the year."

"Do you think you'll ever skate here again? Like practice or whatever, when you aren't in San Francisco?" Duke says and his voice dips with disappointment. "It only costs five dollars to go to the free skates on Sunday afternoons. I bet they even let you skate for free."

"I think I'd love to do that. Or maybe even your uncle

Holden will let me come to help coach one of your practices," Jude replies easily and pats his shoulder with one hand while he flips a chicken breast with tongs with his other hand.

"You'd want to do that? For real?"

"Of course. Maybe tomorrow."

"My team is going to be so psyched!"

"Duke, go wash your hands before dinner," Bradie calls from the doorway.

Duke bites his bottom lip, like he's trying to keep himself from arguing and looks up at Jude. Jude smiles. "I'll be here when you get back, buddy."

Duke darts back into the cottage, and Jude gives me a giant grin. "That kid is great for my ego."

"Don't make me regret this," I warn but smile at him.

"You know, I could hire you to run my fan club, since you're so good at finding people who see me for the true athletic superstar that I am," Jude says, his grin even deeper.

"Yeah, I can do that," I reply casually. "But every kid I bring to you from now on will be painted up in full clown makeup. Sound good?"

Jude's grin slips and his eyes widen fearfully. "That's not funny. You know as well as I do clowns are terrifying. And child-size clowns?"

Jude actually shivers. I laugh. "You are going to hate the Halloween costume I bought Declan."

I walk away, leaving him horrified, as Duke comes bouncing back onto the deck and runs to Jude's side again.

An hour later, we're all sitting around the dining room table, full from our meal, laughing and having a great time until Jude takes Declan to the bathroom after he shouts "Potty!" Because when he emerges, he says something that turns everything on its ass.

"I'm glad to see you finally stopped putting my Stanley Cup ring over the toilet."

"What?" I ask, confused at what he's talking about. Last I saw it, that ring was there.

"The ring isn't in the bathroom," Jude pauses. His face starts to fill with worry. "It's in the bedroom, right? On his night table?"

My heart slowly slides into my flip-flops. "I don't…" I pause. It has to be. It does. I stand up from the table. "Yeah, it must be."

We both walk to the bedroom, but it's not there.

24

HOLDEN

I'm on the back deck turning off the grill and making sure everything is cleaned up when I hear Winnie's voice—it's angry. I turn and look through the windows of the dining room. She's standing there, facing her brother, and they both look tense as hell. I head back inside. Every step feels ominous for some reason.

"I know what you're thinking and it's not true!" Winnie says as I open the back door and step inside.

"Then where is it?" Jude wants to know.

"We should go," Bradie says cautiously as she stands and motions for Duke.

"What's going on?" I ask and everyone turns and looks at me. Each person has a different expression but none of them is good. Bradie looks uncomfortable. Duke looks confused. Jude looks disillusioned and Zoey looks worried. Winnie's face is filled with anger.

Bradie clears her throat, but her voice is still clogged with skepticism, like she can't believe the words she's saying... or at least doesn't want to. "Jude is missing his Stanley Cup ring."

Her support seems foreign to me too. I can't remember ever having it before. Winnie raises her hand and points at me. "See! He looks baffled because he *is* baffled."

"Look, I'm not saying—"

"But you are!" Winnie interrupts him. "You think he stole your ring. And Bradie clearly does too."

"I don't want to think that!" Bradie says defensively.

"And I don't know what to think," Jude argues.

"Is there any place else it could be?" Zoey asks, looking around the room like it's going to magically appear under the table or something.

"Yeah, like maybe it got put in a drawer or moved into another room?" Bradie adds, and I realize she's fighting for me too, just like Winnie.

"Holden wouldn't do that," Winnie says, her eyes on Jude. "You said at the beach I was a great judge of character and I am. I wouldn't be with him if I didn't think he would guard me, this house and everything else I love with his life. He's trustworthy. I would bet my life that he didn't steal that ring, Jude."

Everyone looks at me again. I'm still reeling but this time from her words. She's standing up for me. She's got no more doubt, no more fear. She's no longer looking for excuses. She's mine as much as I am hers—finally.

"I didn't steal your ring," I confirm. "And I have to say, that if I thought you believed that I ever would, I wouldn't have taken the job."

Jude moves his eyes from his sister's anguished face to mine.

He's expression is pure contrition mixed with anguish. "I'm sorry. I don't mean to be an accusatory ass. It's just...that ring means a lot to me, because of what it meant to my dad. He loved that I gave it to him and...I'm not thinking straight. I have to find it. But I'm wrong to jump to conclusions, and Winnie is right. I trust her opinion and I need to rely on my gut, which has always said you're a good guy."

"I want to believe in you too," Bradie says, looking at me with sadness in her eyes. "But where is it?"

"Kidd," I say and Winnie jumps.

"Oh God, you're right," she exclaims. "Stephen Kidd helped us the other day when Holden was out with the flu."

"We don't know a hundred percent that it was him," I find myself saying because...I don't know why. Force of habit. "But he's stolen before. Granted it was when we were kids and I thought he'd changed or I never would have let him on the job site."

"We were desperate and I told you to call him," Winnie says and sighs. "Let's find him."

"No," I argue and grab my phone out of my pocket. "Let's let the police figure it out. If he did do this, he needs to face the consequences. I am done giving that guy a free pass."

I scroll through my contacts until I find Joel's number. I figured if he was willing to help me out in the dunes, he'd still be friendly now. I explain the situation to him, and he says he'll look into it.

"Kidd," Winnie repeats his name and shakes her head I can tell she wants to say much more but there is a child in the room.

"I'm sorry," Jude says to me and I can tell he means it.

"Don't be sorry. This is all my fault," I say and I feel worse now than the fucking flu ever made me feel. "At the end of the day, if he did take it, that's on me for hiring him. I was sick, but I should have known better than to rely on Kidd."

"I gave him the chance too," Winnie pipes up. "And I was the client by association. You said it yourself. I approved it, so I'm to blame."

"No one is to blame but Kidd, if he did this," Bradie says. "Let's keep looking around. Maybe it got put somewhere else by mistake, or it's under a piece of furniture or something."

Jude nods. "Good idea."

"Duke, you go take Declan in the other room and play okay?" Bradie suggests.

Duke pushes back from the table and Declan says to him. "I have Legos!"

"Cool!"

They head into the living room while the rest of us start hunting around the house, looking under the furniture in the sunroom and dining room. Winnie turns to me. "The boxes we used to store stuff are in the recycling bin on the back deck. I'm going to make sure Jude's ring didn't get stuck in one of them."

She walks out the back door and I follow her. I lift the lid on their recycling bin and watch her start to pull out boxes.

"Thank you," I say.

Winnie looks up at me, distracted. "For what?"

"For defending me."

She sees the box in her hand is empty and drops it at her

feet. "You're welcome. Damn. This is the only box that isn't broken down. I think you would have seen it fall out when you tore apart the other boxes, right?"

I cup the back of her head. "Thank you. No one has ever given me the benefit of the doubt before, let alone someone I love."

She smiles softly, her skin glowing in the moonlight. "I've been thinking about your silly fishing analogy from the other night. You were talking about how invisible fishing wire is, right? And how you can hold a pole on the beach and no one knows if you're actually fishing because you can't see the line from afar. We're fishing. There's a strong line. I'm in. All in. And that means defending you because I trust you and know you and believe you when you say you wouldn't do this."

"I love you."

"I love you too." She rocks up on her toes and kisses me chastely.

The back door swings open, and Bradie leans out onto the deck. "Zoey found it!"

Winnie and I follow Bradie through the house to the front porch. Zoey is in the dining room holding the small Plexiglas box with the shiny white gold and diamond ring inside. "Floor vent!" she says triumphantly. "You had the covers off them at one point didn't you?"

I nod, too dumbfounded and grateful to speak. "It must have tumbled in or been knocked in my mistake. I always check the vents. Well, ever since Declan shoved a slice of cheese through the one in our living room. You'd be amazed how quickly cheese starts to stink," Jude says and makes a face. He looks over at me as he takes the ring from Zoey. "I can't begin to tell you how sorry I am."

"Apology accepted," I say and dig my phone out of my back pocket. "But I just did the same thing to Kidd, so if you'll excuse me, I have to call Joel and try to catch him before he gets to Kidd's."

I step back onto the porch as I hear Jude call to Duke. "Hey, Duke! Wanna try on a Stanley Cup ring?"

"Are you kidding me? Yeah!"

I smile but it's short-lived because I feel like shit. I've spent the last few months here in Maine being judged for my past and I just did the same to Kidd. Luckily, Joel answers the phone right away and he hasn't been to see Kidd yet.

"No need to bother him. I was completely wrong. We found the ring. I'm so sorry to bother you, Joel," I tell him.

"No problem. It's my job," Joel replies easily. "Now speaking of jobs, can you come by this weekend and give me a quote on some renos to my condo?"

"Definitely." When we hang up, I decide I'm going to ask Kidd to help me on the roofing job I'm starting next. Maybe he just needs the same thing I did: a second chance.

When I walk back in the house, Duke's got Jude's Stanley Cup ring on his finger. It's way too big, but the beaming smile on his face says he doesn't care at all. "Can I get a picture with you and the ring?" Duke asks.

"Totally!" Jude replies, and Bradie pulls out her phone. She's smiling, which makes her look younger. It's the first time since we reunited that she doesn't look skeptical or stressed. She snaps the photo and hands the phone to Duke to approve it, and then looks up at me. "You better teach him all your tricks because he's definitely not going to give up on his NHL dreams now."

I grin. "I'll do my damn best to make his dreams come true."

"I'm going to hold you to that," she says quietly. "You wanted in. You're in."

"Good." I reach over and give her a small side hug and she wraps an arm around my waist and hugs me back.

Winnie calls from the kitchen. "Boston cream pie is being served!"

When dessert is over, Zoey picks up a sticky Declan and excuses herself to get him into the bath. "I'm so glad we have a tub now. That stand-up metal shower stall was a nightmare."

"Seriously, dude, you did a fabulous job, and I will write you a glowing recommendation if you need it," Jude offers.

"Thanks. I will take you up on that just as soon as I get my incorporation paperwork in and get a website up and running," I explain.

"The Hendricks Homes website will be up and running by Christmas," Winnie says. Our eyes meet. "I bought the domain name for you the other day."

"You..." I turn in my seat, cup her face and kiss her.

Jude groans. Duke joins him and Bradie laughs.

I turn to Jude. "Sorry. You're probably going to be seeing a lot of that. Your sister is completely in love with me."

Jude smiles at me. "You can do better."

"Shut up!" Winnie throws her napkin at her brother. Jude, having the reflexes of a cat, catches it easily. Then, his face grows serious.

"You make her happy," Jude says. "If that ever changes, I will destroy you."

"As expected," I reply.

He looks over at his sister. "Dad liked Holden. He'd be happy for you."

The sadness that ravaged her is still there, but not consuming her. "He would be happy. And in case you haven't figured it out, I'm staying in Maine. Indefinitely."

I release a breath and everything in me relaxes. It's like the last puzzle piece finally gets locked into place. I know it's going to create a bunch more groans but I don't care, I kiss her again.

Epilogue

WINNIE

Ten months later

I turn at the knock on the bedroom door. My mom is standing there in a beautiful rose-colored dress. It was my dad's favorite color on her. "Dad was right. That color brings out the pink in your cheeks."

She smiles. "I'm so glad Dixie wasn't serious when she kept saying she was going to make you and Sadie wear mustard taffeta and satin ball gowns as bridesmaids dresses."

"With giant matching bows for our hair," I add and then look down at my very classy, lacy blush-pink dress. "Thankfully she wasn't willing to ruin her own wedding photos for the sake of a joke."

"She's almost ready," Mom says about Dixie. "She's just getting her makeup retouched because she had a bit of a cry. We both did, but it was a good cry."

I cross the room and hug my mom. "Today is going to be full of good cries. It's the only cry he'd want us to have."

"He'd be blubbering worse than any of us," Mom laughs as

she lets go of me. "Not just for Dixie but for the joy he'd see in your face now too."

My heart swells. "You've noticed."

"Of course," Mom says, her eyes sparkling. "I miss not having you in San Francisco, but I can tell, in your voice when we talk on the phone and seeing you on FaceTime calls, that this is where you need to be. That he's who you need to be with."

I bite my bottom lip and hesitate but then decide to let her in on our secret. "We bought the house next door."

She blinks, her expression startled but not in a horrified way. "The two of you? Together? I didn't know the neighbors were selling."

"They asked Holden for a quote on renos and were so overwhelmed with the work that needed to be done they decided they were going to list it," I explain. "Holden and I decided to make an offer. They accepted."

She hugs me again, which is a clear sign she approves. "I'm so excited for you, Win! I love that you'll be right next door," she says. As she pulls back, her expression grows serious. "But renovating a house together can be stressful. Don't let it create too much stress."

"Are you kidding?" I say and wink. "We love living through renos together. If it weren't for renos, we wouldn't have found each other."

She laughs and then I hear Holden clear his throat from the door. My mom immediately starts out of the room. "Meet me downstairs in a few minutes and you can help us get Dixie into her dress." I nod and she turns to Holden with a friendly smile. "You look dashing."

"Thanks, Mrs. Braddock." He grins with pride and adjusts the bow tie on his tux. "You look lovely."

"I do," she agrees. "And it's Enid to you. You're family now."

My heart skips happily at that comment. From the expression on Holden's face I can tell his must have too. My mom disappears from view and as I hear her descend the stairs.

Holden walks into the bedroom we've been sharing for months and wraps his arms around my waist. "You're stunning."

I don't have my heels on yet so I rock up on my tiptoes and kiss him. God, we've lived together in the cottage for ten months, and I still cannot get enough of this man. I hope that never changes. When he breaks the kiss, I glance at the clock on the bedside table. Damn. No time for a quickie. I sigh and check my reflection in the mirror again to make sure my lipstick doesn't need a retouch.

"You told your mom about the place next door?" he asks.

"I did. She's thrilled," I say. "We can tell the others tomorrow. Today is all Dixie. I don't want to steal the bride's spotlight. She might beat me with her bouquet."

He chuckles at that but the grin he's wearing now is all about our new house. He's so excited we did this—together. I am too, but it feels incredibly surreal right now. Like I can't believe it. That will change next month when we get to move in. I hadn't expected to buy a place with him. When winter hit, I asked the family if Holden and I could stay in the cottage for the season. They agreed. No one asked us to pay rent, just utilities, so we both ended up saving a ton of cash.

With tons of word-of-mouth referrals, Holden's company was really taking off. In January, I became a substitute teacher at Thornton Academy, taking over a math class and science class for a teacher on maternity leave. I adore the school and they offered me a full-time, permanent position in the fall. I'm sure no one would mind if we stayed in the cottage indefinitely, but it's the family's house and we both were feeling the need to have a space just our own. We had decided to move his trailer back to the seasonal park he had it in last year and spend the summer there, but then the neighbor decided to sell. It was too perfect to ignore.

I turn away from the mirror, ready to go downstairs and help Dixie finish getting ready for her big day, when I notice Holden has opened his bedside table drawer and is pulling something out of it. It's wrapped in pretty paper covered in bluebirds. He gives me a tentative smile. "I did something for you. For our new place."

I smile and take the package from him. He looks kind of nervous. I tear the paper away and stare at my dad's letter, in a sleek, simple cherry wood frame. "I didn't read it or any-thing," he explains nervously. "I noticed that it was getting tattered just sitting on your bedside table."

I fight back tears. "This is the sweetest thing you could have done for me. I love it."

I drop down on the bed beside him and kiss him quickly before dropping my head onto his shoulder. I look at the letter, take a deep breath, and read it out loud for the first time ever.

My sweet Winona Skye,

My first daughter. When you were born, I was absolutely terrified. I grew up with brothers, and then I had a son, but you...with your big hazel eyes and your perfect dimpled chin, you were six delicate pounds that I didn't know what to do with. The first time I held you, you wailed like a banshee, your arms flailing. In panic, I tried to give you back to your mom, but you suddenly wrapped your little fingers around my pinkie and went completely silent. Our eyes locked and I swear you and I were making a promise—a pinkie swear—to always just be there. Just being there would be enough. If you're reading this letter, then I can no longer be there for you, and I'm sorry for that. I wanted it to be different.

But I'm so grateful for the time we did have. I watched you grow into a beautiful, bright, kind, strong woman...but I never got to see you realize it yourself. This is not a criticism, sweetheart. You were getting there, but my illness threw everything and everyone off track. But now...now I need you to do something for me, Win. I need you to get right back on track. Do not let my absence stop you.

Go after what you want, and know you deserve it. You deserve love and light and laughter, Winnie. You deserve joy. I haven't seen joy in your eyes for a very long time—even before I got sick. You tend to play it safe. You sometimes don't trust your gut. You wait. You hesitate. Stop that, and just go for it—whatever it is that

inspires you, that motivates you, that brings you joy. Go
for it. It's now or never, sweet pea.
   I love you. I believe in you.

Dad

When I look up, Holden's silver-blue eyes are swimming
in tears. I try to give him a stern stare. "Don't you dare!
I'll lose it!"

He sniffs and clears his throat, rising off the bed. "Your
dad knew what he was talking about."

"He did," I say, struggling not to let the tears fall.

"Win!" Sadie calls again.

I take a deep cleansing breath, put the frame on my bedside
table and take Holden's hand in mine. I look up at him as we
open the door to our room. Sometimes, like now, I'm in awe
of my life. Of this man, who loves me with his whole heart,
in a primal way I never even knew was possible.

He kisses my forehead. "Time to watch Dixie and her crazy
goalie get hitched."

I manage to keep it together as Sadie and I walk down the
aisle, one after the other, with our tiny bundles of lilacs and
forget me not's. I don't blubber when Jude walks Dixie down
the aisle, but he does—which I can't wait to tease him about
for the next ninety years. Dixie looks incredible in a form-
fitting antique lace dress as she glides toward Eli, who seems
like he's having a hard time not welling up as his brother,
Levi, grins proudly beside him.

I expect to cry when she and Eli light the candle in memory

of our dad, but I don't. I look up at the bright blue sky above us and listen to the waves crash just a few feet away. I curl my bare feet into the warm sand and smile. He would be prouder than a peacock today.

At the reception, we gather in tents in the backyard and celebrate until the wee hours. I know my dad would be the last person on that dance floor if he were here. At around two in the morning, Holden and I wander back up to the beach and drop down in the sand, exhausted. He holds me as I nestle between his legs and rest my head on his chest.

"Thank you," I say softly, not even sure he can hear me over the rolling tide, but he does.

"For what?"

"For letting me grieve but not letting me get stuck in it. For loving me, faults and all," I say quietly.

"Are you kidding me?" Holden says. "Thank you for giving me a second chance. You're my world, Winona."

"You're mine."

I kiss him until I'm breathless. This man showed me how to find my way...and now, miraculously, we're on this path together and I know, no matter what life throws at us, we'll be okay because we'll face it together.

ABOUT THE AUTHOR

Victoria Denault loves long walks on the beach, cinnamon dolce lattes and writing angst-filled romance. She lives in L.A. but grew up in Montreal, which is why she is fluent in English, French and hockey.

You can learn more at:
VictoriaDenault.com
Facebook.com/AuthorVictoriaDenault
Twitter @BooksbyVictoria

CPSIA information can be obtained
at www.ICGtesting.com
Printed in the USA
FFHW021705050119
50078508-54920FF

9 781538 763155